"How fast do you suppose we'll fit in the rest of the visits?"

"I'd say a week or two. It depends on how much time your schedule permits."

Cecilia tried to ignore the way her heart leaped at the thought of the time they would spend together. "Helping you make sure the children are all safe and happy is a priority."

With his eyes glued straight ahead, Simon pulled the reins to slow the horse. "Do I get the chance to take you home this time, or should we part ways here?"

"I hope you can forgive me for that, Simon. I overreacted and I'm sorry. I would appreciate it if you would drive me home."

He turned then, his eyes searching her face. As much as she should, Cecilia refused to break the intense stare. But she soon found herself falling into the pale blue depths, imagining that warm, even romantic feelings were hidden in them. She had to look away. Her fickle heart was running wild without reason. And that would lead only to pain.

After earning a degree in business and jumping from job to job, **Mollie Campbell** was more than a little surprised—and pleased—to find that writing was the perfect fit. A lifelong Midwestern girl, she currently lives in Indiana with her husband, two young kids and a rather energetic beagle. When she's not writing or reading, she loves watching superhero shows with her husband and collecting antiques.

Books by Mollie Campbell

Love Inspired Historical

Taking on Twins
Orphan Train Sweetheart

MOLLIE CAMPBELL

Orphan Train Sweetheart

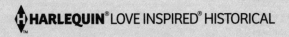

HARLEQUIN® LOVE INSPIRED® HISTORICAL

Recycling programs for this product may not exist in your area.

LOVE INSPIRED BOOKS

ISBN-13: 978-1-335-36972-7

Orphan Train Sweetheart

www.Harlequin.com

Printed in U.S.A.

The Lord is my strength and my shield;
my heart trusted in Him, and I am helped:
therefore my heart greatly rejoiceth;
and with my song will I praise Him.
—*Psalms* 28:7

To Mom and Dad,
with thanks for your endless support, constant faith,
unshakable love and all those hours
spent with the kids so I could write. I love you!

Chapter One

September 1860
Spring Hill, Nebraska Territory

"They aren't here yet?" Cecilia Holbrook turned from scanning the horizon at the sound of her sister's voice. She moved over so Cat could join her under the shelter of the hotel roof, both of them shivering when several errant drops of rain hit their heads. Cat dabbed her damp face with a handkerchief. "Those poor children will get soaked if they don't make it soon."

Cecilia's eyes swept the rolling hills past the edge of town again. "I expect them to arrive any minute."

Cat bounced on her toes as if it would bring their visitors faster. "Is everything ready? With all you had to do these last few weeks, I can't imagine any item could remain undone."

Stifling the urge to roll her eyes, Cecilia brushed a stray lock of hair from her face. "Yes, everything is ready. The hotel rooms are paid for and waiting.

The donated clothes are all clean and placed on their beds. The food Aunt Lily sent over for supper is in their rooms." Cecilia could have listed what felt like a hundred other details, all things the town expected her to handle. As the schoolteacher, they expected her to be in charge of everything that happened in town regarding children. Even if they were capable of doing it themselves.

Cecilia took a calming breath of cool, damp air. She had to remember that all this work hadn't been for the benefit of the old biddies in the Ladies' Aid Society. It was for the children who were set to arrive from the orphan train. Finding good families for each of them was worth being treated as a workhorse for a bit.

Smoothing her already perfect hair, Cat let out a sigh. "The excitement in town these last few days has been so invigorating. I'll be sad to see it end."

Raising her eyebrows at her sister, Cecilia waited for Cat to realize what she'd said. The woman never bothered to think before speaking. Sure enough, Cat gasped a second later. "Oh, that didn't sound right. Of course, I want all the children to find good homes. But it's thrilling that we would get children from the orphan train coming to Spring Hill, with no railroads in the territory. It feels like a surprise party for the whole town."

Glancing down the street again, Cecilia nodded. "I know what you mean. People have been quite excited about our little guests. It's hard to believe they made all those stops and there are still children who haven't found homes."

Shifting from one foot to the other, Cat arched one eyebrow. "Well, I hope that doesn't mean even more work for you. You've been running around preparing for their arrival for days."

Cecilia was saved the trouble of coming up with a kind answer when the rumble of wagon wheels and thump of hooves on packed dirt drew the sisters' attention back to the street. There it was. Cecilia's first glimpse of the wagon showed two placing agents on the seat and a cluster of small heads peeking up in the back. Cecilia's heart pounded as she prepared herself to face the load of strangers. New situations always made her a little clumsy and she hoped that, this time, she wouldn't make a fool of herself.

A few more drops of rain splattered on the boardwalk as the vehicle drew to a stop in front of them and Cecilia's mind formed a quick prayer that the rain would hold. Next to her, Cat craned her neck as the male placing agent jumped down from the seat and went around the wagon to help the female agent climb out. His face remained obstructed by the brim of his hat, but the woman turned to look right at them. And her pinched expression didn't look pleasant at all.

Once the woman was steady on the ground, the male agent turned to greet them. Cecilia started to step forward when a gust of wind whipped around them and caught the brim of the man's hat, sending it hurtling toward her. She jumped in shock as the solid material hit her square in the face. Heat flooded her cheeks as she fumbled to grab the hat. Just as she'd feared, this was not an auspicious start.

Holding the hat out for the man to take, Cecilia found herself looking almost straight into the palest of blue eyes. They would have been beautiful if his expression had been less icy. He reached out one hand and yanked the hat from her grip. "Are you hurt?"

She almost missed his words while trying to determine if his dark hair was brown or black. "What? Oh, no, I'm fine. It was only a hat."

His face hardened and she couldn't believe she'd already managed to get on his bad side. Standing in front of her with a serious expression as he settled the hat back on his head, he didn't look like a man who smiled often, but she thought he might look even more handsome if he did.

Turning to the female placing agent, Cecilia offered a smile that went unreturned. The woman was older than Cecilia had expected, for someone who spent her time trekking across the prairie with groups of children. Her cold eyes swept the main street of Spring Hill with obvious disapproval. Her graying hair was pulled back into a bun so tight it made Cecilia's head ache just looking at it. Those poor orphans must have had a joyless trip with these two in charge.

Stepping forward, Cecilia extended her hand to the man. "I'm Cecilia Holbrook, Spring Hill's schoolteacher. It's a pleasure to have you here."

He took her hand in his large, rough one. "Simon McKay. Nice to meet you, Miss Holbrook."

"Please, call me Cecilia. Some things tend to be rather informal out here on the frontier."

Turning to the woman and trying to smile again, Cecilia wasn't at all surprised by the look of disdain on the agent's face as they shook hands. "And I'm Effie Wright. Miss Wright, if you please."

All too aware of Cat's muttered grumbles behind her about Miss Wright's aloofness, Cecilia pulled her sister forward. "This is my sister, Cat. We're very glad you made it before the rain started."

Simon greeted Cat in much the same way he had her, but Cecilia couldn't miss the way his eyes lingered on her sister. She had come to expect that response. Cat was stunning and vivacious. Men were always drawn straight to her, as Cecilia had learned the hard way. Fighting to unclench her jaw, Cecilia gestured toward the door. "Let's get you all inside before we get soaked."

Miss Wright sniffed in displeasure, as if Cecilia was somehow responsible for the weather, then started herding children out of the wagon.

The four adults made quick work of getting them all inside the building. The Thomas House was a quiet, clean establishment and Cecilia had made certain to get their special guests the best rooms available. Just as the ladies of the town had instructed.

Inside the lobby, Cecilia retrieved keys from the young man at the desk. She handed two to Simon, who then took the four boys in the group and led them to their reserved rooms. Cecilia took the other two keys and led Miss Wright and the six girls to their rooms.

It only took a few minutes before Miss Wright dismissed Cecilia with a haughty sniff. Heading back to the first floor, Cecilia paused halfway down when Simon called her name. He loped down the stairs to join her, his position one step above her putting him quite close. "Thank you for helping us get settled. Is everything ready for placing out the children tomorrow?"

Cecilia gripped the handrail. The pleasant, masculine scent that surrounded him caught her off guard. "Yes, I believe we'll have a fine turnout. The timing couldn't be better. This area took a hard hit with the financial crisis a few years ago. My own sister and brother-in-law adopted twins last year when no one else could take them. But we're recovering now and people are ready to reach out to the less fortunate. The town has responded with a great deal of excitement."

Simon held her gaze with those pale eyes. "That's good to hear. Part of the duties of a placing agent is to ensure that the children go to good homes where they will be well cared for. Were you informed that Miss Wright and I will be staying in town for several weeks to visit the families after their placements?"

Shaking her head, Cecilia bit her lower lip. "No, I wasn't aware of that. I'm sure your rooms can be reserved for that amount of time. And the Ladies' Aid Society will take care of any other needs you may have." Which meant more work for her. But it was for the children. It would be worthwhile.

"Thank you for that. We very much appreciate it. And…" He hesitated, a slight grimace coming over his face. "I'm sorry for Miss Wright's curt behavior. She's a little difficult to get to know, but she has boundless energy. That's vital with so many children to look after."

Cecilia felt some of the tension drain out of her shoulders. He could have apologized for his own demeanor, as well. But maybe his admission meant at least one of the placing agents would be easy to work with. Looking up from her spot one step below Simon, she thought she caught him sneaking an appraising glance at her. She mustered a teasing tone, hoping a little banter would lighten his mood even more. "We all have our burdens to bear, I suppose. I happen to have a sister I always have to apologize for. But please let me know if you need anything else."

Her heart fell when his lips turned down in another frown. She had offended him again. He started to turn away even as he spoke. "Yes, of course. I'll see you tomorrow."

She watched his retreating back for a moment before she rushed down the stairs, chest burning. As always, she had made a fool of herself in front of a handsome man. She chided herself for letting her imagination run away with her. What had made her think she could be lighthearted and playful with him? And she was a fool for imagining there could have been a spark of interest in his eyes. Simon was only in Spring Hill to do his job. And he didn't seem very happy about it.

* * *

Simon rose early the next day, feeling like he hadn't rested at all. He always slept poorly the night before placing out children. He couldn't help worrying about the orphans, about the people who would come to look them over and about his own feelings getting in the way. He wanted nothing more than for each child to find a happy, loving home, but that didn't always happen. And those instances haunted him.

Stepping into the hotel lobby, he was startled to see Miss Wright standing next to her travel bag, bonnet in hand. She met his gaze with a stubborn expression. "Mr. McKay, I'm sorry to inform you that I'm leaving. This trip is more than I can handle. I've made arrangements to leave on the stagecoach this morning."

It took several seconds before Simon could respond. "What do you mean you're leaving? We're placing out the children today. I need your help."

The woman's eyes shifted away. At least maybe she felt a hint of remorse for threatening to leave him shorthanded. "I simply can't stay. These frontier towns—with the dust and the rough people—are getting to be too much. I'm going back to Chicago to stay with my daughter."

Pressure built in Simon's chest, making his head throb. "Miss Wright, please. You know we're supposed to check in on the families in pairs. What am I supposed to do if you leave?"

Her face softened a minuscule amount but her voice was still firm. "You can find someone trustworthy here, I'm sure. Perhaps that young school-marm. She seems competent. I don't know, but it's no longer my concern."

It was clear that she wasn't going to change her mind and Simon refused to beg her to stay. The last thing he wanted to do was to ask the lovely teacher to spend hours riding out to rural homes by his side. But that was starting to look like his only option. "Fine, Miss Wright. I wish you the best and will pray you have safe travels."

He whipped around and went straight to the hotel desk. It took several minutes, but he managed to convince the young man there to keep an eye on the children during their breakfast. Then he left the hotel and walked to the small school, where they would gather the orphans and prospective parents later. If he waited a bit, maybe he could intercept Cecilia before anyone else arrived and he could ask for her help in private. But, to his surprise, the door was cracked open. He peeked in and saw that Cecilia was already there. Tension tightened his shoulders.

Their first meeting yesterday had not been his best moment. Her stormy blue eyes and tall, slender frame had caught his attention and that was something he couldn't have. Distraction led to mistakes. And he had too many young lives in his care to let mistakes happen. No, he had realized that his life traveling the rails would never mix well with women and marriage. So he had to keep his mind off them.

But it hadn't taken any time at all to see that Cecilia cared about the orphans and getting them placed in good homes. Now that he found himself in a situation where he needed help, she might be his best prospect in this town. He had to pull himself together and keep her on his side.

Pushing away from the door frame, Simon cleared his throat to make his presence known. Cecilia turned, eyes wide with surprise. "Oh, I didn't know you were here. I wanted to get an early start on clearing space so everything will be ready when the children arrive."

Simon joined her near the front of the room and took hold of the other end of the desk she was getting ready to move. "Let me help you. I appreciate the work you and the town are putting into this. There aren't many places that try this hard to make us feel welcome."

Cecilia's pretty smile distracted him for a moment and he almost smashed his toe on the leg of the desk. He tensed again. Another mistake due to distraction.

"We're pleased to have you all here and want to make sure we show it. The residents of Spring Hill are quite proud to be able to help a few of those unfortunate street children."

Swallowing a surge of irritation at her description of the children, Simon forced himself to remember that she meant well. Many people did, they just didn't understand the experiences these children had already been through in their short years. But Simon understood all too well and he hated the pity in the voices of those who claimed they cared.

With some effort, he let the comment pass and

helped her to carry the desk across the room. Cecilia had already shoved several up against the wall. He helped her move the rest of the desks and, in no time, the room was clear and ready for a crowd. Cecilia wiped her forehead with the back of one hand and stretched her shoulders. "Well, it looks like the hard part is done."

Walking to the front of the room, Simon wished it could be that easy. The hardest part for him was still to come. "We'll have the children line up here, where prospective parents can see them. Your approval committee will be present?"

She turned to point at the table they'd arranged in the back of the room. "Yes, and they've already selected a good number of families. We shouldn't have any trouble placing out all of the children."

Nervousness tightened Simon's chest. Although many towns were able to approve parents by a committee beforehand, there was always a chance that one of the children would be placed in a home where they wouldn't be treated well. He swallowed hard around the dry lump in his throat. He couldn't bear to see any of the children abused. *Like Michael.*

Shaking off the unpleasant memories, Simon turned back to Cecilia. "I guess everything is in place, then. I'll head back to get the children assembled and bring them over. But there's something I need to ask you first."

Her open expression and encouraging nod unnerved him. He wasn't used to people being so trusting. "I was hoping you might agree to help me with visiting the orphans with their new families after they're placed out. The Children's Aid Society tries to assure that there are two adults evaluating each home. Unfortunately, Miss Wright has decided to leave immediately and travel to Chicago, so I'm left without the second opinion I need to make complete reports."

She dropped her gaze and pursed her lips. "And all you need is for me to visit the children with you?"

Was helping him—and the children—so distasteful that she had to use that tone? Maybe she wasn't as caring and agreeable as he'd thought. He fought to keep his tone friendly. He needed her help, after all.

"Yes, that's it. I usually wait several weeks so they have time to adjust to each other. Then we would make a brief stop at each home to interview the children and the parents. You would need to record your impressions about the suitability of each placement. Nothing more."

She tapped slim fingers on her chin as she considered his request. Finally she met his eyes, lips turning up in a hint of a smile. "Certainly, I'd love to help the children in any way I can."

Simon nodded, his throat turning dry. One thing he hadn't considered until that moment was that he would have to be careful, spending so much time alone with Cecilia. The last thing he needed was a woman thinking he would put down roots and settle in a frontier town like this just for her. But he had Cecilia's agreement to help him complete his task. He would have to pray she would look out for the children's best interests and not hinder his work.

Cecilia offered to help him get the children, so together they left the building and walked back to the hotel.

The town was the epitome of frontier life with its uneven planked boardwalk, wide dirt streets and rough buildings covered with flimsy façades. Here and there, he caught a glimpse of buildings that were nicer, put together with more thought and effort, but a large part of the town seemed to have been thrown together in a hurry.

At least the hotel was a respectable place. The Thomas House, run by a kind older couple of the same name, had been a good choice for their stay. As he and Cecilia approached the front door, an older man came out and held it open for them.

Simon was surprised to see the children already lined up inside. Each one had on the new clothes the residents of Spring Hill had provided and carried a small bag with their meager belongings inside. The oldest girl, Ada, held baby Clara in one arm. They stood just the way Miss Wright had insisted on, with their chins held high like little soldiers.

Simon gestured for them all to come outside and line up in front of the building. Once they were in place, he walked in front of the row, examining each child. All ten faces—four boys and six girls—were scrubbed clean and their clothing was neat. But almost every set of eyes showed at least a hint of fear.

He stopped his pacing and tried to smile at each of them. "Well, children, it's time to go and meet your new families. I expect each of you to behave well.

Address adults as 'sir' and 'ma'am.' Say please and thank you. Speak when spoken to."

Simon swallowed the lump of emotion rising in his throat. *Oh, Lord, let them each find a good home.* Licking dry lips, he finished his talk before the waves of feelings got the best of him. "I know you'll make me proud today. Let's go."

He nodded to Ada, who spun on her heel and led the line of orphans down the street, chin still pointed in the air. Simon and Cecilia followed at the rear, behind Charles, one of the oldest boys. As they got closer to the school, Charles's steps slowed, almost imperceptibly, until Simon was walking next to him.

The boy looked nervous, fidgeting with the bottom button on his slightly too large donated jacket. "Mr. McKay, sir, what if they don't want one of us? You said this is the last stop. What if someone isn't picked?"

Charles's dark head hung low, nearly breaking Simon's heart. He rested a hand on the child's shoulder as they walked. "I assure you, Charles, no one will be overlooked today. There are more than enough families in Spring Hill who are excited to have a child join their home. Each of you is sure to find a good match today."

The boy nodded and sped up to keep pace with the others.

Feeling Cecilia's eyes on him, Simon turned to see the look of pity on her face. "The poor dear. I can't imagine the fear the children must feel. I do hope the day goes as well as we expect. For their sakes."

Simon couldn't bring himself to respond beyond a noncommittal nod. No, she couldn't imagine what the children were feeling at that moment. His own life experience had taught him how pivotal this day would be for the orphans. It could mean the difference between life and death.

He tried to brush aside the memories of childhood horror that started to rise but the surge of heartache must have showed on his face, anyway.

Pausing, Cecilia stopped him with one hand on his arm. "It looks like there's more on your mind than the children. I know we've only just met, but if you need to talk, I've been told I'm a good listener."

He couldn't help the pang of longing that hit him with her earnest words. As much as he would need help in this town for the weeks ahead, there was no way he was going to divulge his past or his feelings to her. No matter how pretty she looked, with that encouraging smile lifting her pink lips. Simon couldn't imagine that such a lovely young woman would commit to traveling the country with the orphan train rather than having a family of her own. And there was no way he was walking away from the one thing God had called him to do for a selfish reason like his own emotions.

"I'm anxious to get all the children placed out to good homes and return to New York. Nothing more." He winced at his gruff tone. So much for his determination to be nicer to her.

Drawing herself up straight, she trained her eyes

on the children as they entered the school. "You aren't fond of the frontier?"

Trying to sound more pleasant, he shook his head. "It's not that. There are always more children on the streets in New York. These trips take so long, it feels like I'm missing the chance to help someone. And I can't stand that."

Cecilia turned to see Simon's eyes scan the prairie behind the school. Her heart beat a little faster at the view of his strong profile and she chided herself. This was about the children, not about spending time with the handsome placing agent. He had just stated that he would return to New York as soon as he could. Was she going to be so silly as to put her heart in a position that would only lead to being hurt again? No, she couldn't let that happen.

Squaring her shoulders, she followed Simon up the stairs as he held the door to the school open. Entering the familiar room, she was pleased to see that all the children were standing in one very straight line in front of the large blackboard. The only sounds were the ticking of the clock on the wall and a slight shuffling of feet now and then. It appeared the children knew what was expected of them for the event. If they continued to behave this well, they would make an excellent impression on the potential parents.

Running her eyes down the line, Cecilia looked closer at the children, wishing she had time to get to know each one. She hoped their new families would send them to school for the fall term so she could continue to keep up with how they were doing. Grabbing paper and a pencil, she went to the end of the line, starting with the boys, who were lined up youngest to oldest.

The first boy was darling, with round cheeks and blond hair combed back. He looked up at her with wide blue eyes.

"What's your name, dear?"

"Edwin."

"And your last name?"

"Matthews."

Cecilia wrote his name at the top of her paper. "Edwin Matthews. Very good."

From behind her, a throat cleared and Simon corrected the child. "That's 'Edwin Matthews, ma'am.'"

The boy's face turned crimson. "Sorry, Mr. McKay. Edwin Matthews, ma'am."

Glancing behind her, it was all Cecilia could do to keep from rolling her eyes. But that was the kind of thing Cat would do and Cecilia had never been as forward and blunt as her younger sister. Still, she wished she could point out that Simon's gruff commands weren't necessary. These children behaved much better than the ones who attended classes with her.

Turning back to Edwin, she gave him her most encouraging smile. "And how old are you, Edwin?"

Thin shoulders shrugged. "The people at the home thought I might be around five. Ma'am."

Writing the number next to his name, Cecilia rested one hand on Edwin's head for a moment. How could he not even know how old he was? The things he must have experienced in his life on the streets were unimaginable to her. With effort, she resisted wrapping the child in a hug and moved on to the next boy. He was James Watson, age eight. As she went down the line, Cecilia also met Charles Wilkinson and Patrick Dalton, both age nine.

As she moved on to the girls, a heavy weight settled on Cecilia's heart. These children were so strong and brave. Each must have a story of such pain and loss. She had lost her father several years ago, as an adult, and that had been terribly painful. She couldn't imagine these little ones bearing such tragedy at their young ages.

She set her focus on filling out the paperwork as she met Helen Watson, age four and sister to James and Gertie, a lovely ten-year-old down the line. Then there was Sophia Butler, seven, and Jane Dalton, eight. Jane was very clearly Patrick's sister. They looked almost like twins, with matching dark hair and stormy gray eyes.

Finally she stood in front of the oldest girl, fifteen-year-old Ada Baker, who held six-month-old Clara Brown. Ada was a beautiful young woman, with a slim figure and wavy blond hair. Watching her bounce the baby with practiced ease, Cecilia fervently hoped the girl would find a wonderful home where she could experience a few years of childhood before marrying and having children of her own.

Standing back with the list still in her hand, Cecilia addressed the children, who stood at full attention thanks to Simon's prodding. "Thank you all for answering my questions so well. The people of Spring Hill are so pleased to welcome each of you. I know you'll all find parents who will love and care for you. And I hope each of you will attend school when the fall term begins since I'm the teacher and I would love to see you again."

She tried to meet as many of their eyes as possible with a broad smile as Simon took over from her, reminding the children of the process that would soon begin.

The weight of worry that had settled on her became a heavy knot in the pit of her stomach as Cecilia slipped outside to see people already gathering to look the children over. She prayed that they would be gentle and kind as they examined the orphans. She had heard stories of little ones being treated like livestock at auction at these events. She would hate to see any of those darlings handled that way.

The three men who formed the approval committee stepped forward to speak with her. Mr. Collins, the head of the school board and owner of Spring Hill's largest mercantile, greeted her first with a tip of his hat. "Miss Holbrook. A fine day for placing out some orphans and doing our Christian duty, eh?"

She nodded, trying to keep her irritation with the man at bay, as always. He had made it his mission for months to make sure she knew he didn't care for a woman teaching their school. Fortunately, the rest of the board hadn't voiced any disapproval with having a female teacher. Even if she didn't love teaching the school as much as she had expected to, Cecilia needed the job. It was vital to keeping her independence, and thus, worth the frustrations that came along with it.

The other two committee members greeted her with more sincerity than Mr. Collins. Then all three men filed into the school to meet Simon and the children.

Cecilia stood in the shadow of the building and watched the gathering crowd. She knew many of the faces, but Spring Hill was growing quickly and there were always new people settling in. She offered up another prayer on the children's behalf. There were so many unknowns about how this day would turn out. How could Simon stand the strain of doing this so often with so many children?

Finally, Simon stepped out of the school and came to stand at the base of the steps. "Hello, everyone. If I could get your attention for a moment, I'll give you the details of today's proceedings and then you can go in and meet the children."

He paused, looking around until the crowd had quieted and stood watching him. "Thank you all for coming today. We have brought ten children, four boys and six girls, ranging in age from six months to fifteen years. They are all healthy and strong. We have worked with them the entire trip, so they will be well-behaved. Feel free to talk to the children and look them over, but please, be kind."

Turning back up the steps, Simon opened the door and held it open as the crowd streamed into the school.

Cecilia watched from her position in the shadows,

examining each face that passed her, wondering if they were as nice as they looked. She tried to determine if that woman would be a gentle mother or if that man would take good care of a child not his own.

Shaking her head, she reminded herself that it didn't matter what she thought. Simon and the approval committee were the only ones who could deny a placement. After the last person walked through the door, she started up the steps. She tried to guess Simon's emotions as she approached him where he waited inside the door. His jaw was tight, arms crossed over his chest as he shifted on restless feet. Those intense eyes locked on hers as he spoke in a low voice. "Well, I guess it's time."

Pressing one hand against her stomach in an effort to calm the fluttering inside, Cecilia fixed a smile on her face. "It is. Let's go find good homes for your orphans."

Chapter Two

Simon's heart raced as he and Cecilia moved through the crowd toward the children, but no one paid any attention to them. The room buzzed with quiet voices. Many of the visitors stood around in clumps talking to each other and watching the proceedings. But one group of people had spread out in front of the line of children and were talking with them in low voices. Simon positioned himself at the boys' end, hoping to keep an eye on as many of the children as he could at one time.

A middle-aged couple stood in front of Edwin, their eyes appraising as they listened to him answer their question. Simon was pleased with the way the boy responded. He was respectful—

"No!" The loud shout broke through the hushed tone in the room, startling Simon. His heart froze and he tried to force air into his lungs. He looked past Edwin to see Charles fighting to pull his arm away from the grip of an older man. Rushing down the line of children, Simon just missed grabbing Charles's arm as the boy ran by him and escaped out the door. Simon was torn. He hated to leave the group, but he had to go after Charles.

When his eyes swung to Cecilia, she met his gaze and nodded even as she moved toward him. "The committee will take care of the other children. I'll help you find Charles."

He didn't want to think about how nice it felt when she fell into step with him as he hurried past gawking people and out the door. Instead he focused on praying that the boy hadn't gone far. But the schoolyard was empty, as was the street that led to the hotel where they had spent the previous night.

Turning to Cecilia, he tried not to let panic show, but he was certainly feeling it. He couldn't let one of the orphans down. Again. "You know this town. Where could a nine-year-old boy hide?"

She looked down the street, emotions playing across her face as she thought. Then it brightened and she pointed to the next street over. "Maybe the mercantile, around the corner, down Second Street. There are lots of shelves and displays to hide behind and enough people coming and going that he wouldn't be noticed."

Simon nodded in agreement and they took off in the direction she pointed. As they hurried down the dusty street, he tried to piece together what had happened. "Did you see anything? I only heard him shout and caught a glimpse of a man holding his arm, then he was running away before I could stop him."

"I saw Mr. Huntley talking with Patrick and Charles. Neither of them looked very happy. But then one of the girls started talking to me and I didn't see what happened to make Charles run."

Stomach clenching, Simon increased his pace. He had to find out what had happened before one of the other children went home with this Mr. Huntley. He and Cecilia entered the mercantile, several customers glancing their way as they barreled through the door. Simon scanned the room. Cecilia was right, this was a great place for a little boy to hide. He went straight to the counter near the front, where a woman in a richly trimmed dress covered by a tidy apron eyed them with derision.

"Excuse me, we're looking for a boy who ran from the orphan train placing out. About nine years old, with brown hair and brown eyes. Have you seen him?"

Raising her chin, the woman managed to look down her nose at him, despite her lack of height. "A ruffian fitting that description tried to come in here a few minutes ago, but I shooed him away. I won't have my customers' pockets picked while they shop."

Gritting his teeth, Simon managed to thank the woman and leave the store before he lost his temper. The nerve of her, calling Charles a pickpocket. She didn't know a single thing about these children. But he had been on the receiving end of that kind of quick judgment too many times to count. Lashing out at her wouldn't do the children any good. Pausing at the corner of the building, Simon sucked in a deep breath. He had to get hold of himself.

Cecilia's hand on his shoulder helped drive away the last tendrils of anger. "Simon? Are you all right? We'll find him, if that's what's bothering you."

Dropping his head, Simon shook it in response. "No, I'm sure we will. It was that woman's attitude toward Charles that upset me." Trying to rein in his irritation, he met her eyes. "I know the prejudice these children will face, even if they find respectable homes. There are too many people in this world that will judge them based only on how their lives started out."

He wanted to look away when the familiar heat of embarrassment spread through his chest. He didn't want to go on, to confess his own history and how close to home that sort of criticism hit. But, oddly enough, Cecilia's eyes held understanding. "I know how people can judge, too." Her voice was quiet and her eyes shifted away from his as she continued. "But that's one good thing about having the schoolteacher on your side. I'm in a great position to make sure these children aren't treated poorly. By anyone. Now, let's find Charles and see what happened."

An unexpected smile broke out on Simon's face before he realized what was happening. He hadn't known Cecilia for long, but he was finding that she was full of surprises. Turning back to the street, he glanced in both directions. "Where do we look now?"

Cecilia's head tilted as if she was listening to something he couldn't hear. She held up one finger, like one of the old schoolmarms from the orphan's home he'd spent a few months in as a child. Turning around, she took several confident steps into the dark shadows of the alley between the mercantile and the building next to it. "Charles? I know you're there, dear. Come on out and tell us what happened. We want to make sure you're all right."

Several moments passed but Cecilia never took her eyes off the shadowed space. Simon had decided that she must be a little crazy when he heard scuffling sounds and the slight sniffle of a runny nose. A few seconds later Charles's face appeared, tear-streaked and dirty even in the dimness of the alley. Simon's heart lifted in relief. They had found the boy, at least. But now to get him to tell them what had made him run.

When Charles stepped out of the shadows, Cecilia knelt and wrapped one arm around his thin shoulders. "Tell us what happened. Why did you run away?"

The boy scuffed his feet in some loose dirt at the edge of the boardwalk, head down. "That old man, he was looking me and Patrick all over. And not very nicely, either. But then he grabbed my face hard and started trying to look at my teeth. Yuck."

Cecilia spoke in a soothing tone but Simon didn't hear her words. Anger burned in his chest and he forced himself to relax, trying to calm it. It wouldn't do the children any good for him to lose his temper with some old farmer who didn't think before acting. Smoothing Charles's messy hair with one hand, he spoke with as much calm as he could muster. "You let us handle Mr. Hartley, Charles. Please come back with us. I know there's a good family in there waiting to take you home." At least, he prayed with all his heart that there was.

Heaving a deep sigh, the boy nodded. Cecilia kept one hand on his shoulder as they walked in front of Simon back to the school. Watching them, Simon's mind turned to his own childhood, as it did during every orphan train stop. How many young lives would have turned out better if there had been a good woman around who cared about them? Could some observant adult have stopped the tragedies that marred his memories?

Shaking his head to clear away thoughts of things that couldn't be changed, Simon reminded himself that he was that adult. He was doing everything in his power to make certain these children found caring homes. His only purpose in life was to place as many children as he could, in the best homes that could be found. No matter that he sometimes longed for his own family. God had placed Simon with the Children's Aid Society so that he could make up for his failings.

Back in the schoolroom, Cecilia walked Charles to the line. Simon looked around the room, noticing that three of the girls and two of the boys were gone. Striding over to the table where the approval committee sat with their paperwork, he said, "Gentlemen, could one of you tell me if Mr. Hartley left with a child?"

One of the men dug through a sheaf of papers and

pulled one out, handing it to Simon. "Yes, here's the form. He took Patrick Dalton."

Worry settled in Simon's heart. "Do you know this Mr. Hartley well? One of the children was frightened by his behavior. I can't let Patrick stay with him if the man isn't kind to him."

The committee head, Mr. Collins, raised his chin high, voice cold. "I can assure you that Mr. Hartley has been here for several years and I've never known him to be anything but a good fellow. This committee would never approve a placement that we know would be harmful to a child."

Tension started to creep up Simon's shoulders at Mr. Collins's offended tone. And the uncertain looks the other committee members shared didn't help any. "Of course, I know you wouldn't. I didn't get the opportunity to meet the man, that's all. I prefer to know who the children go with. But I'm sure the placement will turn out fine if you say so."

Turning away from the table before Mr. Collins could berate him again, Simon went to join the line of children. Charles was the only boy left. Simon was surprised to see that a young couple had gathered James and both of his sisters, Gertie and Helen. People rarely took more than one child. Would the siblings be able to stay together?

Fifteen-year-old Ada was the only girl left. She stood with her arms crossed and her face holding a deliberately disinterested expression that Simon knew all too well. As he watched, an older woman with a kind, wrinkled face hobbled up to the girl. He couldn't hear what they said, but it only took a moment before Ada's face relaxed and the girl threaded her arm through the woman's. He nodded to Ada in encouragement as the two went to the approval committee together. That might be the perfect companion for an independent, older girl.

Movement at his side caught Simon's attention. Cecilia, looking at him with shining eyes. Eyes that he could get lost in if he let himself. But he couldn't do that. His mission was to rescue children from the streets. Romantic thoughts about a pretty woman in some frontier town would only hinder his goals. No matter how much he might wish otherwise.

Cecilia watched Simon, wondering why she was so drawn to him. He was grumpy and often sharp. But when she'd looked over and noticed a sappy, approving grin on his face, something inside her had to know what had made him so happy. Until he looked at her and glared. Why did he glare so much?

Refusing to allow his attitude to affect hers, Cecilia nodded in the direction of the approval committee. "Did you see the sweet couple that was talking with Gertie, James and Helen? They're so kind and I think they might consider taking all three children."

She watched his gaze shift to the cluster of people at the table. Eleanor and Robert were new in town, but she had spoken to them several times and very much enjoyed their company. They had been married for a few years and Eleanor had confessed her disappointment that they didn't have children yet. She had been so excited about the orphan train stopping in Spring Hill.

But Simon's expression remained stoic. Didn't anything please this man? She tried again. "Isn't it wonderful? Three siblings staying together and going to a happy home. I doubt you could ask for a better placement."

Watching his face, Cecilia thought she saw his jaw relax and lips soften for a brief moment before his expression hardened again. "That would be nice. But I doubt that young couple can handle three older children. I'm afraid they'll change their minds in a few weeks. James can be quite a handful."

Cecilia couldn't help herself. His tone was so condescending. Resting her hands on her hips, she faced Simon head-on. "I'll have you know, that's a lovely couple and I have no doubt that they understand what they're getting into. They can handle three children."

Finally meeting her gaze, Simon raised one eyebrow with deliberate slowness. "I'm not saying they aren't good people with good intentions. But taking on three orphans is a lot of work that they might not be prepared for. I'm not going to intervene in the placement. I just don't think it will last."

"That's awfully cynical. I would have thought that someone who helps create families for orphans would have a little more faith in people."

His eyes slid away, focusing somewhere on the floor behind her. "Actually, it does the opposite. When it comes to orphans, most people aren't as kind and compassionate as you are. I know that from personal experience."

Trying to determine from his expression if that comment meant what she thought, Cecilia refused to let the moment pass without finding out a little more about him. "You're an orphan, too?"

His jaw tightened. "Yes. And no, I don't want to talk about it. Believe me when I say that I know what they'll face in life. And it isn't always nice, even if they do find a good home."

Cecilia glanced at the children again, her heart aching for them and for Simon, for the pain in their lives that she didn't understand. She couldn't imagine the kind of hurt the little ones had felt over and over as they'd continued on the orphan train, stop after stop, without being chosen. "Well, I still think that Eleanor and Robert will handle those three without a problem. You'll see. It will be one of the orphan train's most inspiring success stories."

Simon shrugged and crossed muscular arms over his broad chest. Cecilia squeezed her eyes shut as she turned away, chiding herself for noticing such things. She had a sure path before her and letting her heart hope for the love of a man who was leaving soon wouldn't serve her purpose well. She had to stay unemotional while she fulfilled her commitment to help with the visits. Even if Simon was terribly handsome. In a brooding, gruff sort of way.

Clearing her throat, Cecilia kept her eyes focused anywhere except on him as she moved the conversation to a safer topic. "What kind of help will you need from me for the next few days?"

"Tomorrow, I'd like to visit Mr. Hartley. I didn't get a chance to meet him and after what happened with Charles, I don't know if I trust him with Patrick. I'd like to go get a feel for the situation now, rather than wait for our official visit in several weeks."

Cecilia was about to answer when her sisters, Cat and Coralee, called to them from across the room. The two made a striking pair. Coralee always had a regal bearing and exuded complete confidence. And then there was Cat. Their youngest sister was small and delicate, with a perfect figure that would make any eastern socialite jealous. She had the most animated face Cecilia had ever seen and she was effortlessly delightful in public. Of course, her sisters had experienced her mood swings, but few other people saw anything but perfection from Cat. As much as she loved her sister, Cecilia had always thought it was rather sickening.

After her sisters greeted her with hugs, Cecilia nodded in Simon's direction. "This is Simon McKay, the placing agent. Simon, you met Cat yesterday. This is our other sister, Coralee Hadley."

Simon nodded in greeting to her sister, then stepped back as Coralee took one look around the room and started grinning. "Cecilia, this is wonderful. Have the children all found homes?" Since adopting twins Louisa and Phillip, Cecilia's older sister had a soft spot for adoptions. She had been as excited as anyone when they'd found out the orphans were coming to Spring Hill.

Glancing toward the front, Cecilia noticed for the first time that only Charles remained. His head hung low and no one seemed to be paying any attention to him. A wave of helplessness washed over Cecilia. He had been so worried about not being chosen and now his fears might become reality.

Turning to find Simon still behind her, Cecilia grabbed his arm. "Simon, Charles is all by himself up there. What if no one wants to take him?"

His eyes slid closed as a pained look crossed his face. Cecilia wondered if he had felt the hurt of being overlooked in favor of other children. She certainly knew what it felt like to live in someone else's shadow. Her spine straightened. She wasn't going to let that happen to such a sweet little boy. But as she took a step toward him, Coralee spoke up. "We can't have the little fellow left out. I'll go talk to him." Waving across the room, Coralee got the attention of her husband, Jake, and gestured for him to join her. Together, they went and spoke to Charles in low tones.

Simon's eyebrows rose. "Are they interested in adopting more children? I don't want him to get his hopes up if they're only being nice."

Resting her fingers on her chin, Cecilia tried to think back, to remember if Jake or Coralee had said anything about taking in another orphan. Beside her, Cat giggled. "Those two can't stand to see a child alone. I said days ago that they wouldn't be able to resist taking home another one."

Cecilia fought the urge to pinch her sister. Cat never seemed to think anything was noble or important. She rarely took anything more seriously than she took herself. Cecilia crossed her arms, eyes still glued to her older sister and the boy. "Well, I'm grateful that they care so much. Charles was so worried about not being chosen by anyone. But thanks to Jake and Coralee, he might find a loving home, after all."

Cat shrugged and wandered off to chat with their aunt Lily. Shaking her head, Cecilia turned her attention back to the scene unfolding across the room.

Simon's voice was close to her ear when he spoke. "Are they good parents? Will they treat him well?"

She turned to see him absently run one hand through his hair, displacing a few of the fashionably long strands. Her heart melted a tiny bit. He looked like one of the boys himself. Uncertain, hopeful and a little afraid. Offering a confident smile, she responded with a firm nod. "They're the best parents. Their twins are happy, healthy and well-loved."

He didn't respond as they watched Coralee wrap her arm around Charles's shoulders and follow Jake to the approval committee's table. Cecilia couldn't resist a happy sigh. "It looks like they've come to an agreement. I'm so pleased. The twins will love having a big brother."

The room was almost empty by the time Jake, Coralee and Charles finished their paperwork and left. The men from the approval committee approached Simon and Cecilia. Mr. Collins stuck out his hand to shake Simon's. "It seems we've had a successful day."

Simon's face was impassive. "That remains to be seen, Mr. Collins. Miss Holbrook has graciously agreed to help me with the home visits I'll be handling in the next several weeks since the other placing agent was called away as soon as we arrived. The placements will be successful if I find all the children are in happy situations."

Cecilia could see Mr. Collins clench his jaw at Simon's blunt response. But he and the other committee members tipped their hats and left the building without causing a scene. Noticing that everyone else had left, Cecilia went to the closet at the back of the room, grabbed a broom and started sweeping the floor. Without a word, Simon came along behind her and moved desks back into their places. They had the schoolroom put to rights soon enough.

By the time they finished and she locked the door behind them, Cecilia was feeling the effects of the emotional strain of the day. She was more than ready to get home. Simon gripped her elbow with one hand when she stumbled stepping off the last stair. "Thank you for all you've done, both today and before we arrived."

She mustered a smile through her embarrassment. "It was worth it to see those darling children find homes."

"Speaking of homes, I'll walk you back to yours. It's nearing dusk and I wouldn't feel right about leaving you to walk alone."

A hot flush started creeping across her cheeks and Cecilia was grateful for that dusk he spoke of, hoping it covered a bit of the pink tinge. After all the time she had spent trying to learn how to keep control over her emotions when it came to men, all it took to reduce her to a flushed mess was an offer to walk her home. Drawing her spine straighter, she pushed her chin in the air. "Thank you, but I can find my own way. I'll meet you outside the hotel tomorrow morning for our trip to Mr. Hartley's farm. Good night."

Without giving him the chance to insist and wear down her already weak defenses, Cecilia turned on her heel and walked away from the school and the distractingly handsome placing agent.

Simon stared after Cecilia until he realized he was standing in the middle of the street with his mouth open. Her refusal of his genuine offer stung more than he would have expected. Was it his company that made her walk away or had his thoughtfulness in some way offended her?

Making his way back to the hotel, Simon's mind retraced the events of the day. Had he done anything during those hours together that might have upset her? He gave up long before he arrived at the Thomas House. He hadn't had the best attitude that day. Or the night before. Any of his words in their short acquaintance could have hurt her feelings.

A stab of guilt hit his stomach at the realization. Cecilia had been kind and helpful. He could tell that she cared about the orphans. And he had treated her the same way he tended to treat most people when she deserved better. Deep down, Simon guessed his gruffness was a reaction to the judgment he usually faced when people found out about his childhood. But Cecilia hadn't responded with the contempt or suspicion he was used to. She had to think he was being mean on purpose. And, oddly enough, that bothered him. He hardly knew her, but he found that he cared about what she thought of him.

Forcing the guilt into a corner of his mind, Simon tried to go on with his evening. He started to write down some of his impressions of the placing out for his reports. But worry about how the children were getting along with their new families plagued him all night, which didn't improve his mood for the next day.

He ate breakfast in a hurry so he had a few minutes to sit and pray while he waited for Cecilia outside the hotel. But his time alone was cut short. Her brother-in-law, Jake, approached Simon's bench before he got far into his list of prayers for each child.

The man stuck out a hand with a wide smile. "I saw you yesterday, but we weren't introduced. Jake Hadley, Spring Hill's physician. I saw you sitting here and couldn't resist the chance to welcome you to Spring Hill."

There was no choice but to respond to the greeting in kind, no matter how much Simon wished for quiet. Simon shook the doctor's hand while examining his fine suit and expensive-looking leather case. "Simon McKay. Nice to meet you, Doctor."

"Oh, Jake is fine." Without waiting for an invitation, Jake dropped next to Simon on the bench.

So much for some quiet reflection to put himself in a better mood.

Wondering when the doctor would get to his purpose, Simon let his gaze roam over the landscape visible beyond the close-set buildings. The rolling hills covered in yellowing grass were peaceful in a way. Simon had been surprised by how comfortable he felt out here after spending his life in New York City.

After a few long moments of awkward silence, he decided that if the doctor wasn't going to move on and leave him alone, he might as well ask after Charles. "How was the first night with a new child under your roof?"

Jake snorted, catching Simon off guard. "Charles is a wily one, isn't he? I think he's a bit afraid to let us get close to him and I can understand that. We hope that once he realizes nothing he does will make us get rid of him, he'll settle down and open up."

Simon sagged back against the bench as the words brought a burst of admiration and relief. Jake seemed to have a good handle on what Charles was feeling and what he needed. Much more than Simon would have expected. Maybe Cecilia was right about this family being a good fit for the boy. "I'm pleased to hear you say that. And I…well, thank you. For taking Charles." Simon didn't know whether to go on or not as emotion thickened his throat.

But the doctor saved him the trouble. "You know, it took me a long time to come to terms with adopting our twins. When their parents died in a cholera outbreak, Coralee and I worked for months to find a family that would take them. We weren't married yet and I couldn't imagine how it would ever be possible for me to keep those children. But God arranged it all so everything fell right into place. The four of us are happier now than we could have dreamed."

Pushing up from the bench, Jake slapped Simon on the shoulder as he continued. "I believe God arranged for Charles to come to us, too, so I'm confident it will work out in the end. And I'm sure there's a reason you're here, too. Now, I'm glad I got a chance to talk to you, but I need to get to the clinic. I'll see you later."

Simon said goodbye and watched the doctor head down the street. What was it about Jake's confident faith that was so striking? Simon believed in God and he prayed for the children he worked with often. But Jake was so certain that God was in control of everything. Simon wasn't sure he had that much faith. He had seen too many cases where God could have stepped in and fixed a horrible situation, but He hadn't.

Cecilia's voice next to him startled Simon out of his deep thoughts. "Was that Jake I saw leaving?"

Turning to her, he was struck by her flawless skin and the way her eyes glowed in the bright morning light. With great effort, he forced the awareness of her away. He couldn't let himself get attached to a woman in some frontier town when he would head back to New York in a matter of weeks. In spite of his determination to be nicer to her, the conflicting feelings made his words come out sharper than he intended. "Yes, it was. He said things went well with Charles last night."

Her smile faded, sending another rush of guilt through him.

"That's wonderful to hear. I know you have doubts, but I'm sure the other placements will turn out well, too. The people of Spring Hill are good and caring, on the whole."

Praying she was right, Simon offered her his arm and led her to the street. "I guess we better be going. Here's the buggy I rented for our ride out to Mr. Hartley's farm. You know how to get there, right?"

Settling on the buggy seat, she nodded. "Yes, I do. I've never been to his farm, but one of my students lives nearby."

Simon went to the other side of the vehicle and climbed in. As they started out of town, he focused his eyes on the rutted path in front of them. "Did I mention I taught school back home for a time?"

She shook her head. "I don't think so. How long did you teach?"

"Two years. I enjoyed aspects of it, but I got restless too much of the time. I do much better when I can get out in the open now and then."

Cecilia's expression turned shuttered and her voice got quiet. "I can understand that. I'm not sure teaching is what I would have imagined doing when I was a girl. I love children, but being in the classroom all day, going over the same material every term, I feel… well, restless is a good word for it."

Simon let his eyes rest on his lovely companion for

a long moment. It was strange to think that a dislike for their teaching careers was what might connect them, but at that moment he felt a bond forming with her. Pulling his gaze away, Simon reminded himself that a feeling of connection was one thing. But letting his heart get involved in any way beyond that was not acceptable.

Clearing his throat, he pointed across the prairie. "Have you been any further west than Spring Hill? I've been watching with interest to see where the railroads expand. It would be exciting for the orphan trains to reach all the way to California one day."

Simon almost missed the way her face tightened. Had he somehow offended her again? Her reply was curt. "No, I haven't been anywhere since my family came here when I was very young."

Before he could stop it, the question that popped into his mind slipped out of his lips. "Would you like to travel, if you had the chance?"

His heart chilled when she turned away. That question had been a mistake. He had no right to pry into her hopes and dreams. If she hadn't wanted him to walk her home, she certainly wouldn't want him nosing around in her personal business. She spoke right before the moment turned awkward.

"I suppose not. I wouldn't have much reason to go far from home. Not to mention, as a single woman, traveling alone wouldn't be advisable."

Hoping to ease the tension that had risen with his thoughtless question, he tried to answer in a light tone. "Well, I can tell you, after all the time I've spent traveling on trains and stagecoaches with the children, the sights are hardly worth the difficulty of getting there."

Her lips pulled tight, drawing his attention to the pretty pink shade of them. What was the matter with him these days? He never had so much trouble keeping focused on his tasks. Maybe he had been away from home and familiar surroundings for too long. It would feel good to finish up in Spring Hill and head back to the east in a few weeks.

Silence settled over them as the horsed pulled the buggy up a small hill. At the top, Cecilia pointed to the left. "That's Mr. Hartley's farm. Looks like his house isn't too far from the road."

"House" was putting it nicely. Even from a distance, Simon could see that the dwelling was more of a haphazard shack than a house. His heart echoed with a prayer for Patrick, an innocent child who had been dragged into what seemed like a mess. If anything bad happened to the boy, it would be Simon's fault for letting him go with Mr. Hartley. And he knew from experience how that guilt would feel.

Before that fear got the better of him, Simon turned the buggy toward the shack and in a few minutes they pulled to a stop in the dirt nearby. There was no movement in the yard or around the dwelling. The place almost looked deserted and uneasiness settled like a rock in Simon's chest, making it hard to breathe. Something was wrong.

But by the time Cecilia's feet hit the dirt as he helped her down from the buggy, the door had creaked open on uneven hinges and Mr. Hartley stood in the entrance, scowling at them. "What do you want?"

His barking voice didn't do anything to calm Simon's fears. "I'm Simon McKay, the orphan train placing agent. I'm making visits to the children's new homes on the authority of the Children's Aid Society of New York City. I only need to speak to you and Patrick for a few minutes."

The annoyed scowl turned into a full-blown angry glare. "Now, I don't care who gave you authority, you've got no reason to go poking around in my business. I think it's about time you got off my property."

Before Simon could formulate a response that wouldn't make things worse, he heard a young voice shout from behind the shack. "Mr. McKay!" Patrick ran around the building at full-tilt, throwing himself into Simon's arms and nearly knocking them both off balance.

"Patrick, I'm glad to see you. But you don't have to hold on quite so tight." He loosened the boy's skinny arms from his waist, but rested one hand on his shoulder, feeling a need to keep the orphan close by his side while he was there. "How are you and Mr. Hartley getting along?"

Simon thought it was possible that his heart would explode with emotion when he saw tears welling in the boy's eyes. "Fine, sir." The words were mumbled and Simon wasn't sure if he could believe the statement or not. He had to talk to Patrick away from Hartley's earshot.

"Mr. Hartley, we can get off your property faster

if you'll show Miss Holbrook around your farm a bit while Patrick shows me the house. That's all we need to do today." Simon tried to sound as harmless as possible while praying desperately that the man would agree and not run them off his land.

Chapter Three

Cecilia didn't mind that Simon volunteered her to tour the property with Mr. Hartley. After all, she had agreed to help in whatever way she was needed and she got the impression that Simon wanted a few minutes alone with Patrick. But she wasn't at all happy that she had to handle the old farmer all by herself. The way that man looked at her made her skin crawl.

As soon as Mr. Hartley had offered a curt nod of agreement, Simon whisked Patrick into the ramshackle dwelling before she could blink. The old farmer cleared his throat before acknowledging her for the first time, his eyes raking her up and down. "Well, there's not so much to see, but come this way."

She followed him, stepping around muddy puddles that remained from the rain showers several days ago. She was watching her steps with such care that she didn't see Mr. Hartley stop and ran straight into his back. A smirk twisted his face. "You better watch where you're goin'. Hate to see you fall and ruin that nice dress."

The way his gaze lingered on her dress turned her stomach. Wrapping one arm around herself, she tried to take a discreet step back while forcing a tight smile. "Yes, thank you, Mr. Hartley."

The farmer motioned for her to go into the shed first. Cecilia's mind screamed that it was a bad idea. She didn't need to see inside the outbuildings. But she wasn't sure how else to occupy the man until Simon had a chance to talk with Patrick. There wasn't that much to see on the run-down property.

Stepping into the damp, dark interior of the shed, Cecilia stifled a shiver, almost tripping on the uneven dirt floor. She paused to let her eyes adjust to the dimness when she felt Mr. Hartley standing far too close behind her. Close enough that his dirty shirt brushed her back and the unwashed smell of him wafted around her. She wanted to retch.

Before she could step away, he grabbed her arm and pulled her around to face him. Again, he was too close, making her want to cough when his breath hit her face. "Seems we've got ourselves a minute alone, my dear. Why don't we have a little chat?"

Trying not to panic, Cecilia tugged her arm but couldn't pull away from him. "Actually, I'd like to get some fresh air. Please let me go."

He raised his free hand to run dirt-stained fingers down her cheek, making her flinch. A rumbling chuckle erupted from his throat. "Going to play hard to get, eh? Well, let me tell you what I have in mind.

Now that I've got that boy around, I need someone to care for the place for us. Why not the pretty little schoolteacher? You're getting past your prime. Can't be many other fellas lining up to claim you."

This time she couldn't stop the shudder that racked her body. The farmer laughed again and leaned closer still. Her eyes burned with tears that she refused to let fall. "Come on, what do you say? You get a roof over your head and the boy for company. And I get a clean house and warm meals. If you're smart, you'll take me up on the offer—"

With a sudden whoosh of air, Mr. Hartley was gone, leaving her arm aching but free from his grip. Cecilia wrapped her arms around herself in an effort to stop her hands from trembling. When she stepped outside, Simon had Mr. Hartley by the front of his shirt, lifting the farmer until he was on tiptoes. "What's the meaning of this? Are you threatening Miss Holbrook?"

The older man raised both hands, trying to shake his head. "We were having a little talk, that's all, McKay. Get your hands off me."

Simon shoved him up a fraction of an inch higher against the shed. "Next time you should think twice about putting your hands on a lady during a conversation."

Abruptly letting go, Simon stepped back while Mr. Hartley dropped to his knees and took a few deep breaths. "We've seen enough for today. Patrick has assured me that he's happy to be here. But, Hartley,

I'll have my eye on you. One misstep and I'll take Patrick back. We don't tolerate any sort of abuse."

Without another word to the farmer, Simon turned and wrapped one arm around Cecilia's shoulders, supporting her as they walked away. At the buggy, he helped her in then briefly spoke to Patrick, who stood by the house taking in every move with wide eyes. Their voices were too low for her to hear what they said, but it was only a moment before Simon jumped up into the buggy and they were finally leaving.

Her mind felt numb in the silence that hung between them until they drove over the first hill and out of sight of the Hartley farm. Simon stopped the buggy and turned to her, taking one of her hands in his. "Cecilia, please tell me you're all right. He didn't hurt you, did he?"

She shook her head. "He held my arm rather tight, but I'm fine. Just shaken up."

His jaw clenched and his eyes swung away from her. "I'm so sorry I left you with him. I never thought he would try to harm you."

Hoping her voice wasn't as shaky as the rest of her, Cecilia tried to act dismissive, like Cat would have. "It's fine, Simon. Really. He was awful, but I'm fine. Were you able to talk to Patrick?"

Releasing her hand, he rubbed the back of his neck hard enough that the skin turned bright pink. "A little, but I didn't get much out of him. He insisted Hartley treated him fine. But it's only been one night. Something about the man gives me a bad feeling."

Swallowing hard, she fought to keep her stomach from heaving. Poor Patrick, stuck out there with that terrible man. "Then there's nothing we can do?"

Simon shook his head. "Only if he actually hurts Patrick. My instructions are to let families get to know each other unless there's proof that the child is being neglected or abused. Sometimes it takes time for them to get settled into the arrangement. So for now, we'll have to watch and wait."

Cecilia dropped back against the buggy seat as Simon urged the horse into motion and they rumbled over the rough dirt path again. It was hard to accept that they had to wait and do nothing when Patrick was in the middle of such a mess. But Mr. Hartley hadn't hurt Patrick yet and Cecilia prayed that he wouldn't in the days ahead.

The return trip dragged on, giving her far too much time to relive Mr. Hartley's revolting proposal. What on earth made him think that manhandling her would convince her to marry him? If that was the kind of male attention she was going to attract as the years went by, maybe she was better off committing to remain unmarried, after all.

Thinking about living the rest of her years alone was painful, but Cecilia had come to realize that it must be God's purpose for her life. Yes, she got restless teaching. But God had placed her there and the opportunity to support herself independent of a husband was too important to throw away. After all, every man she'd been even a bit interested in had found Cat to be irresistible. Cecilia never got a second glance, unless it was from men old enough to be her father, like Mr. Hartley.

Simon's voice broke into her thoughts. "You look tense. Are you sure he didn't hurt you?"

Compassion flickered in the depths of his eyes. Flustered by his concern, Cecilia rubbed one temple with her fingertips, hoping the mild pain wouldn't turn into a full-blown headache. "Yes, I'm fine. I was just thinking." She tried to find something to say that would distract him from the episode with Mr. Hartley. She didn't want to think about it anymore. "I'd love to hear more about New York City."

To her surprise, Simon's face hardened at her mention of his home. "There's not much to say. It's a big city. Lots of buildings, lots of people."

Drawing back at his cold tone, she wondered why he didn't want to talk about his hometown. "There must be something you love about it. Or something that's vastly different from the frontier."

"Nothing worth mentioning. Life in a big city isn't as romantic as the papers make it seem."

Cecilia's head started pounding. Trying to draw him into conversation wasn't worth enduring that gruff tone. But a second later his softened voice reached her ears. "I'm sorry, I didn't mean to snap at you."

"You've mentioned how anxious you are to return to New York, so I thought you'd enjoy talking about it. But you don't have to if it makes you uncomfortable."

She glanced over in time to see his jaw clench. "It

doesn't make me uncomfortable, exactly. The city can be a rough place. And working with orphans, I often see more of the hardness than others might."

Sobering, Cecilia's heart constricted. "Is it terrible for the children, being on the streets there?"

His eyes fixed on a point in the distance. "It can be. Some of them come from wealthier families, left on the steps of a church or orphanage because the mother isn't married and doesn't want to shame her family. But many of them lose their parents in tragic ways and are left to fend for themselves. Sometimes there's still a parent around, but they aren't able to take care of the child, or they refuse to. No situation is good and there's sadness in all of them."

The pain in his expression made her throat tighten. Had he really seen that much horror in his time working with the orphans, or was there more to his story than he'd told her? "Don't organizations like the Children's Aid Society provide some help for them? It must make you feel good to know you can at least do something."

He shook his head. "Maybe for a bit, but it's never enough. As long as there are children wandering the streets, stealing and fighting for food or shelter, unloved and uncared for, it won't be enough."

She couldn't resist trying to offer a small amount of comfort by resting her hand on his arm. "But people like you are champions for them, giving of yourselves to help. It may not seem like it, but I'm certain that makes a world of difference to the children."

* * *

Simon didn't know how to respond. He wanted to believe her words, to feel her certainty that he was somehow helping the children. But knowing that he was bringing some of them all this way only to leave them in unhappy situations made him feel helpless and surly. He wanted to do more. He needed to do more.

When he didn't respond to her, Cecilia moved her hand from his arm, leaving behind a cold feeling. But he felt her eyes still on him and she sounded curious. "What drives you to push so hard? You're one man, doing all you can for the sake of street children many people would walk past without a glance. Why isn't that enough?"

The questions hammered at him like hail. As much as he hated talking about his past, maybe if she knew how much this meant to him, she would stop pushing to understand and accept that he knew what was best for the children. "It's not enough because I was one of them. I felt the hopelessness, the pain of knowing you aren't good enough for most people. And I won't sit by and watch innocent children go through that if there's even one tiny thing I can do to help them."

He refused to look over at her and see the pity in her eyes. It was always either revulsion, suspicion or pity when he talked about his childhood as an orphan. But her quiet words etched in his heart. "Simon, I'm sorry. I hate that you had to go through that. But I hope you see that those experiences have given you empathy far beyond what most people feel.

They formed you into a caring, dedicated man who is making a difference."

He didn't answer. Even if he wanted to, he couldn't. Her response was so different from any he'd experienced that he didn't know how to handle it.

They reached the outskirts of Spring Hill without speaking again. As they approached the bustling streets, he finally mustered the courage to glance at Cecilia. "Can I drive you home?"

He could see the hesitation in her face. What was it about him that made her want to keep him at arm's length? She'd agreed to spend the morning with him visiting Patrick, but she'd refused to let him take her home. Was she more put off by his past than she sounded? If he'd looked at her after divulging his past, he might have seen revulsion instead of understanding, after all.

Trying to find a hint of her feelings in her expression, he forced his tone to stay light. "I hate to leave a lady to walk home by herself. It's not polite."

But instead of disarming her, his words seemed to have the opposite effect. She drew herself up taller, jaw tight and chin in the air. "Really, it's fine. I'm quite capable of getting myself home without an escort. Please stop here and I'll walk."

Simon shook his head. This woman was either excessively independent or very uncomfortable spending one more minute with him. He reminded himself that it was none of his business either way. He needed her help for a few weeks and then he would be gone.

"Yes, ma'am. I'll stop assuming you'd welcome chivalrous behavior."

He pulled the buggy to an abrupt stop. For a moment it looked as if she wanted to say something. But then she clamped those rosy-pink lips tight and climbed out of the buggy before he could offer his assistance. Not that he thought she'd take it if he did.

"Thank you, Simon. The hotel staff can help you send word for me when you're ready to make more home visits. I hope your time in Spring Hill will be pleasant." And with that, she turned on her heel and started to walk away.

It was all Simon could do to keep his mouth from hanging open at her rude dismissal. Several minutes of deep breaths finally calmed the flash of heat that filled his chest. He couldn't decide if he should go after her and give her a piece of his mind or let her continue her haughty walk home. She disappeared around the corner at the end of the street and he decided it was best to let her go. He wouldn't force his presence on her any more than necessary since that's what she seemed to want. As he raised the reins to steer the horse back to the stable, a voice called his name. "Mr. McKay?"

An older woman approached the buggy with quick, efficient steps. Her dark hair was graying, but she had piercing eyes that looked like they wouldn't miss a thing. He climbed down and tipped his hat to her. "Yes, ma'am. I'm Simon McKay."

The woman stuck out a hand and gave him a firm

shake that would rival any man's. "I'm Lily Holbrook, Cecilia's aunt. It's sure nice to meet you."

Ah, the sisters' illustrious aunt. Simon couldn't help smiling. "It's my pleasure, ma'am."

She waved his formal greeting off with one hand. "It's Lily to everyone around here, son. No need for fancy niceties with an old woman like me. Now, I wanted to talk to you."

That caught his attention. He'd never even met this woman. Giving her his full attention, Simon watched her expressive face as she spoke. "It's about my other niece, Catrina. Have you met her?"

"Cat? Yes, I've spoken with her several times."

Lily continued with a brisk nod. "Then I'm sure you've noticed the way she has of flitting around from thing to thing. She doesn't seem to have much interest in settling down and getting married, which is fine for now. But I'm afraid if she doesn't fill her time with something beneficial, she'll get herself into trouble out of sheer boredom."

Simon tilted his head, trying to understand why Lily had stopped him to discuss Cat's flighty personality. "And what does that have to do with me?"

He immediately flinched at the way his words sounded. Why did he always have to act tough and cold? Thankfully, his tone didn't slow Lily down one bit.

"I hoped you'd consider finding a way to include her in some of your work. If she had a cause, something to care about, she might lose a little of that restlessness that could get her into a mess."

Running one hand over his chin, Simon thought for a minute. He could understand a restless spirit. He knew what it was like to wander with no purpose. And he could see how Cat's self-assured air could be covering up a disquiet hidden deep inside. But he was already in over his head spending so much time with Cecilia. Could he stand working with another woman for the next few weeks?

Lily stood with her hands on her hips, waiting for his answer. "Let me think about that, Lily. I'm sure there's a way to involve her in working with the children."

"Thank you, Simon, my boy. Now, you have a nice day and make sure you stop by my place sometime for a meal. Lily's Café, over on First Street. It'll be on me."

With a wink, Lily turned and walked away, a spring in her step that belied her age. Simon started to smile until he remembered that promising to find a way for Cat to help meant letting another woman into his space. Cat was the sort of woman who drew most men's attention, but Simon couldn't let himself get distracted by a pretty face. Yet the face that flashed in his mind wasn't Cat's. It was Cecilia's wide eyes and flushed cheeks that filled his thoughts.

With a shake of his head, he forced thoughts of women away. He had things to do. There were reports to write and send back to the Children's Aid Society. And he had to organize the paperwork the approval committee had completed when the children were placed out. Then he would take a few days to call on prominent residents of Spring Hill and enlist their assistance in helping the children acclimate to their new homes, as he did at every stop. It was one small way he tried to ease the transition for the orphans and the town.

With all he had to do, the week went by quickly. It was Monday before Simon was able to figure out how he could include Cat in his work. He sent the boy who ran errands for the hotel to deliver a message to Cat, asking her to meet him at the café for supper that evening, so he could explain his idea.

Simon had been able to spend some time exploring the town of Spring Hill and had found the café on one of his walks. Tonight, he took his time, ambling down the boardwalk to enjoy the crisp evening air. The town had captured his interest over the last few days. It was both wild and quaint, frontier and civilization rolled into one. He had seen many towns, large and small, on his travels with the orphan train, but none had grabbed his attention like Spring Hill.

This place had somehow gotten him thinking about what it would be like to settle down. To stop traveling the country, indulging his restlessness. He could almost see himself marrying, building a house, having children of his own. But every time the blissful vision played in his mind, it was interrupted by the memory of his best friend's youthful face covered in bruises.

He could feel the fear again when he remembered Michael telling him about the horrors of life with the cruel couple who'd taken him from the children's home they'd been in together. He couldn't help shuddering when the cold emptiness crept back in like it had the day Michael had died trying to escape them. And, every time, the overwhelming guilt renewed Simon's determination to help every orphan he could, even if it took the rest of his life. He refused to fail another person like he had Michael.

In spite of the pull he felt to remain in Spring Hill, he prayed his growing attachment didn't have more to do with a certain teacher than the town itself. Of their own volition, he'd found his eyes scanning the streets as he'd walked, watching for her familiar figure. At church the day before, he'd hardly heard a word of the sermon. His mind kept drifting to how pretty she looked sitting in the pew wearing a green dress with a delicate lace shawl wrapped around her shoulders.

But no matter how his heart betrayed him, Simon couldn't even consider staying on the frontier. He could visit the town now and then if his travels brought him to the area. But marriage was out of the question. He couldn't keep helping the orphans and settle down to married life at the same time. He'd never known a woman who would choose to travel the country helping abandoned and neglected children rather than having her own and he didn't expect to find one out here.

When Simon reached Lily's Café, he was surprised by how busy it was. But he managed to find a seat at a small table, the right size for two people. He had barely settled into his seat when the sound of footsteps close by grabbed his attention. Expecting Cat, he looked up and lost himself in lovely, intelligent eyes instead of flirtatious ones. Cecilia.

Her smile was a bit shy and Simon wondered if she felt as awkward as he did after the way they'd left things the week before. "Hello, Simon. It's nice to see you here at Lily's."

Simon stood to greet her. "Well, she introduced herself last week and invited me, so I thought I'd take her up on the offer."

Cecilia tucked her bottom lip under straight teeth. "Could I join you for a minute? There's something I'd like to say."

He gestured at the open chair with a shrug. Cecilia seemed to avoid his gaze as she seated herself while Simon did the same. An awkward silence fell between them. Simon glanced around the room, taking in the other patrons and trying to think of something to say that wouldn't make the moment more uncomfortable. But Cecilia broke the silence with a rush of words. "I think I owe you an apology. I know I was a bit rude last week when we parted and I'm sorry for that."

Her face was so earnest that Simon couldn't have held a grudge against her even if he'd wanted to. "Don't worry about it. I'm sure I pushed too hard. I've been told I can be overbearing."

Amusement crossed her face and he wondered if she would have made a joke about his words if he hadn't made her so uncomfortable before. The look passed and she shook her head. "No, I don't want any distractions or tension when we're out visiting the children, so I need to explain. It isn't that I didn't trust you to take me home or that I have anything to hide. I simply value my independence. Men so often treat single women like we're unable to handle ourselves, but I've been doing fine for several years on my own. I don't want you to think you need to take special care with me. I'm not weak and fragile."

The statement wasn't untrue. Cecilia didn't want to be coddled because she was an unmarried female. There was just so much more to it. But she couldn't tell him about the years she'd spent pining over men who were never interested in her. Or about how, after Mama died when the girls were small, Papa used to treat Cecilia like she was a china doll, so delicate he was afraid to touch her. He'd never treated her sisters like that. Coralee's strength always commanded respect rather than overprotection. And Cat's carefree confidence tended to keep people at arm's length. All too often, people treated Cecilia like she wasn't able to handle life on the frontier on her own.

Simon's tilted head and furrowed brow confirmed that keeping her deepest reasons to herself was the right choice. It was clear he didn't see why being treated as if she couldn't manage alone was a bad thing. And how could he? A man who had spent most of his life with no one to answer to would never understand why she had to work so hard to do things independently.

She was quite glad when he nodded and the confusion on his face cleared as if he'd considered all the angles and decided to accept her simplified explanation. She felt a little of the tight knot in her stomach relax. Spending hours side-by-side with him when they visited the children would have been unbearable if that awkwardness had persisted.

Looking across the small table at Simon, she was struck by the urge to stay and learn more about him. She'd seen him at the church service the day before, but she had wondered all week what he was doing and if she'd run into him around town. "Were you able to fill the rest of your week with any interesting activities?"

Before Simon could even open his mouth to answer her question, the room stilled and Cecilia turned to see Cat. After making her usual dramatic entrance, she sashayed to their table in a cloud of delicately flowered skirts. Every dark hair was in a perfect, flattering arrangement that looked like it had taken her hours. And had she pinched her cheeks before coming in? How else could she have such a charming pink flush on her skin all the time?

Cat's dusky voice grated on Cecilia's nerves as she flashed her favorite flirty smile at Simon. "Hello, Simon. Cecilia."

Cecilia raised an eyebrow at her sister. "I'm surprised to see you here today. You usually do anything you can to get out of helping at the café. There was no excuse Aunt Lily would accept this time?"

Cat's eyes flashed with humor. "Oh, I'm not here to work today. But can you believe she didn't think I really agreed to help rescue a child from a well outside town yesterday? There's no reason that couldn't be true."

A sudden cough brought both women's attention to Simon, who had his mouth covered with one hand. In spite of her irritation with Cat, Cecilia bit back her own laugh. He was trying so hard to be polite. Cat caught his concealed humor, as well, responding with an audacious wink. "Well, I suppose it could be a little far-fetched."

Cat and Simon burst out in laughter, but Cecilia couldn't help the sudden burn of jealousy that hit her heart. Every male eye in the room turned and locked on her sister as her tinkling giggle echoed. Cecilia was certain that nothing she did had ever garnered that kind of attention.

Simon's deep chuckle drew her gaze back to him and Cecilia was surprised to find that he was looking right at her, rather than watching Cat. She turned away, hoping the sudden flush in her cheeks wasn't showing as much as she felt it. Unlike Cat, she looked splotchy when she blushed. But she was soon distracted when Cat pulled an empty chair from the next table and joined them without even bothering to ask if she was welcome.

Cecilia plastered a smile on her face. "Don't you have any business that brought you to the café, Cat?"

Her sister nodded, oblivious to Cecilia's irritation, then turned to smile at Simon. "Yes, of course. Simon, won't you explain why you invited me for supper? I've been dying to find out what's going on since you sent that messenger."

Cecilia's gaze shot to Simon to see him blinking rapidly, his face blank. "Uh, well. Yes, supper." He was usually so self-assured. Had Cat's presence affected him more than he let on? Cecilia's heart sank. She would have loved to think that Simon was different, impervious to her sister's stunning beauty rather than enthralled by it. But he was as distracted by Cat as every other man.

Shoving her chair back with more force than she'd intended, Cecilia felt eyes around the room shift to her. Sure, they looked at her now, when her face must be redder than the flowers embroidered on Cat's dress. Fighting to maintain some dignity, she thrust her chin in the air and spoke so only Simon and Cat could hear. "Well, allow me to get out of your way so you can get to that important business."

She turned to walk away, but it didn't seem that a graceful retreat was possible for her. Her foot caught on the leg of a chair that was pushed out too far and she stumbled. And found herself falling straight toward Simon.

His hands shot out and grabbed her upper arms, holding her steady against him even as he stood to help her gain her footing. She had a horrible suspicion that he could actually feel the heat coming off her cheeks. She tried to shake off his hands, but he held her for a moment longer, leaning close to speak in a low voice. "Cecilia, you aren't in the way. There's nothing private about what I need to discuss with Cat."

Unable to pull her gaze from the intensity in his

eyes, she instead managed to pull her arms from his grasp and force false cheer into her voice. "Oh, I know. It's all right. The school term starts next week and I have so much to get done before then. I can't afford to waste a minute."

Cecilia hurried out of the café before she made another foolish mistake. Honestly, she'd almost fallen straight into Simon's lap. That was the sort of thing that made men think she wasn't able to handle herself and turn their attention right back to Cat, the graceful, confident one.

As she hurried around the corner of the building to the house she shared with Aunt Lily and Cat, Cecilia's steps slowed. What were they doing now? Had Cat started to giggle at Cecilia's abrupt and clumsy exit? Had Simon sat across from her and rolled his eyes at Cecilia's blunder? Or had he become transfixed by Cat's dancing eyes and perfect complexion and forgotten all about Cecilia?

Leaning against the side of the house, Cecilia let the ache wash over her for a brief second. Part of her quest for independence meant putting aside her previous habit of convincing herself that men shared her romantic notions when they didn't at all. Time after time, she'd put herself in a position to have her heart broken because she couldn't keep her feelings realistic. Changing that impulse was far from easy. It hurt every time she confronted the fact that she would never be sought after the way Cat was.

But that was her reality. Turning her face toward air laced with the hint of fall chill, she let her head fall back against the rough wood boards. Keeping her heart steady and unattached was harder than she imagined. But the scene with Simon and Cat was exactly what she'd needed to remind herself how important it was to her future. Her solitary future.

Rushing footsteps echoed from the boardwalk in front of the café. Cecilia looked up to see Cat hurry around the corner. A bright grin broke out on Cat's face when she caught sight of Cecilia. "I don't know why you had to rush off, but you'll never guess what Simon wanted."

It took all Cecilia's willpower to keep from snorting. She certainly could guess what Simon wanted. But, with supreme effort, she remained silent while her sister prattled on. "He asked me to come up with a way to help the orphans adjust to our community. I have several ideas, but I need to think about them a bit. Perhaps a sports tournament. Foot races? Or baseball? What sorts of things do the children like to do in school?"

The last thing Cecilia wanted to do at that moment was to help Cat. She was mortified to realize that Simon asking her to help with his visits had made her feel connected to him. As if he had asked her because he wanted to spend time with her. But now he was asking for Cat's help, too. He didn't have any special feelings for Cecilia. He only needed anyone who would step in and help the children.

She straightened and mentally shook herself. It didn't matter if Simon McKay wanted to spend his time with Cat. Cecilia had a clear goal to focus on: establish her independence.

Twisting her arm through Cat's, Cecilia forced a smile. "Let's sit down and come up with some ideas. Then you can decide what you want to tackle. I'm glad to see you so excited about helping the children."

Moving toward the house with her sister, Cecilia was more determined than ever. The school term would start next week and she would shine. She would prove herself indispensable as a teacher so the Spring Hill school board would agree to keep her on permanently. And her heart would remain firmly under control. She had to focus on that task until Simon finished his work and returned to New York, out of her way and out of her thoughts.

Chapter Four

Simon pulled the door of his room shut behind him and trudged down the empty hall of the hotel, feeling like the heavy emotions twisting his heart were also weighing down his steps. It had been a week since Cecilia had stormed out of the café when he'd met with Cat, but the hurt tone in her voice still echoed in his mind.

Knowing the school term had started, he'd found his feet heading in the direction of the schoolhouse at least five times in the past few days. But he didn't go. Every time he thought about trying to apologize for somehow hurting her feelings, worry stopped him. Bringing it up could make the situation worse. Then the time they had to spend together visiting the children would be strained.

As much as he wanted to see Cecilia, maybe it was for the best if he let her think he was the sort of man who would hurt her. Knowing they'd be spending so much time together, wasn't there less chance of either of them getting their hearts involved if she thought he was awful?

Pushing away from the door, Simon made his way outside and turned right. He had another bundle of paperwork ready to send to New York. In the last few days he had started calling on the most influential citizens of Spring Hill, educating them on the kind of life the orphans had come from. The people he'd spoken with had been interested and accommodating. He was sure this would be one of the orphan train's smoothest stops.

Except for Patrick. Simon's heart was still uneasy about the boy's situation. He prayed that he was wrong, that his fears were unfounded. But he couldn't shake the feeling that something was wrong out on that farm. He only hoped he could uncover the truth before it was too late.

A sudden voice behind him pulled Simon out of his anxious thoughts.

"Well, good morning, Simon. Out for an early stroll?"

He turned with a smile, recognizing Lily Holbrook's cheerful voice before he even saw her. But the warm greeting died on his tongue, melting into discomfort when he saw Cecilia standing next to her aunt. She looked beautiful. A breeze ruffled the lace that trimmed the neckline and sleeves of her dark red dress. She looked every bit the proper schoolteacher. A very pretty and intriguing one.

Although he couldn't take his eyes off her, she didn't speak a word in greeting. And she refused to meet his gaze, no matter how long he stared at her. He tipped his hat in her direction, anyway, then held up the bundle in his hand. "Good morning, ladies. I'm making a quick trip to send some of my place-ment paperwork back to New York."

Lily's grin widened and she looped her arm through his, pulling Simon into motion before he could react. "How nice. We're heading the same di-rection, so we'll walk with you."

Stifling the urge to look over at Cecilia again, he let Lily direct their steps. It didn't matter what her niece's reaction was, there was no reason Simon couldn't walk them to their destination. But Lily's next words almost took his mind off the pretty teacher trailing them. "Simon, have you heard about the rob-beries?"

A chill washed over him. "No. What's going on?"

The somber look on Lily's face only added to the instinctual worry rising in his chest. She wasn't given to being this serious, from what he'd experienced. "It seems there's been a rash of things gone missing. Mostly small items, some cash. I heard at least three businesses have reported thefts and several people said they've been pickpocketed. The sheriff seems to think they're all connected."

Tension drew Simon's spine straighter. "I'm sure there's a reason you're telling me this. Are people suspicious about one of the children being involved?"

The older woman released his arm, fidgeting with the small bag she carried as if she was reluctant to give him a straight answer. But she did, after a moment of hesitation. "I'm afraid so, my dear."

From her other side, Cecilia finally spoke up, surprising Simon. He had assumed after the cold reception that she wasn't going to acknowledge him at all. "Don't be too upset with them. When people are scared, they look for someone to blame. It doesn't always make sense."

Meeting her eyes, he shook his head. "Even if it doesn't make sense, those who can't defend themselves are always the ones they blame. I don't care if it's their fear talking. They're good children. I won't let this town cast judgment on them because of choices their parents made."

They had come to a stop in front of the barn that served as the stagecoach station, but Simon hardly noticed. Cecilia rounded on him, hands on her hips and those beautiful eyes flashing. "No one's casting judgment on the children, Simon. There have been a few whispers that maybe someone among all the new people in town could be responsible. With so many new faces here all the time, that could mean anyone."

It crossed his mind that this might be the time to calm down, to avoid another argument. But too much emotion was surging through him at the moment to worry about making her angrier. "So, no one has specifically said that one of the orphans could be the culprit? Not one whisper has implied that?"

She tilted her face away, biting one lip, and his heart dropped. In spite of her effort to defend Spring

Hill, people already suspected one of his children was guilty. "I see you don't have an answer for that."

When Cecilia looked up again, Simon was taken aback by the sheen of tears in her eyes. As much as he wanted to stay mad, his heart softened.

"I'm sorry, Simon. I hate that people react that way. But can't believe anyone will take it further than fearful talk and accuse one of the children."

Simon paused before responding, for once finding the strength to contain his frustration. It didn't hurt that he was distracted by her beauty after being apart for a week. But he pulled his thoughts back under control. "I can only hope they won't. But in case they do, I'm going to get to the bottom of this myself."

Lily rested one wrinkled hand on his arm. "Are you sure that's a good idea, young man? Maybe it's best left to the law to figure out what's going on."

But Simon's resolve was already hardened. "I only intend to keep an eye on the children, not interfere with the sheriff's work. I'll ask around a little when we visit the families and see if anything grabs my attention when I speak with them."

To his surprise, Cecilia nodded with enthusiasm. "Why don't you come by the school today and speak with the ones who are attending class? One of them might have some information to share."

Simon found himself responding with a genuine smile, caught off guard by her willingness to help after her reticence so far today. "I'll do that. And we should start visiting families sooner than planned. I don't want to put it off if we have a chance to find clues about this before it gets out of hand."

A lively sparkle lit her eyes. "Yes, that's a good idea. I can help in the evenings after school lets out. And we could make several visits on Sunday afternoon."

Lily was back to grinning. "Since we're all making plans, Simon, you just count on having Sunday dinner at our place. That way you two can ride out with full stomachs."

Simon nodded, grateful for allies in this town. It seemed like he was going to need them more than he'd thought. "That sounds great, Lily. Thank you. I'll let you ladies get on with your business now. Cecilia, I'll see you this afternoon."

Watching the women walk away, Simon shook his head at himself. All of a sudden he was looking forward to stopping at the school that afternoon more than he should be. And he had a feeling it didn't have much to do with talking to the children.

When the long hours of the day had finally passed, Simon walked to the schoolhouse filled with a mixture of nerves and excitement. He was a little worried about talking with the orphan train children. What if he found proof of exactly what he feared? What if one of them was responsible for the recent robberies?

But at the same time, visions of a certain teacher kept flashing in his mind at the most inopportune moments. Shaking away yet another memory of her eyes shining with tears for the children, Simon pushed open the door of the schoolhouse and silently found a spot in the back to wait. No one seemed to notice his presence, so he observed the class from his vantage point.

He counted fourteen children, appearing to be age five up to ten or eleven. It pleased him to note that nearly half the class was made up of his orphans. In fact, he saw all the school-aged children he'd traveled with, except Patrick. He had to hold back a deep sigh at that observation. He'd been hoping to see Patrick attending school with the others.

Toward the front of the room, the sight of Cecilia bending over a desk to work with one of the younger students caught Simon's attention. With gentle prodding, she reminded the little boy over and over how to pronounce letters as he tried to practice a line from his reader. After a few minutes she moved on to another student, then another. Simon was impressed by her endless patience. If only she could show a little more of that where he was concerned, maybe their relationship wouldn't be so strained most of the time.

Simon leaned against the door frame but must have scuffled his feet in the process. Several students turned to look at him. But he hardly noticed because, at the same moment, Cecilia looked up and met his gaze. The warm welcome in her eyes knocked the breath from his lungs.

Right then, Simon realized that he had been naïve to think he could let her believe he was a terrible person so he could keep her at arm's length. He cared too much what she thought of him. And that meant he was in serious trouble.

* * *

Although she was expecting him, Cecilia was startled when she turned to find Simon staring at her from the door. Her surprise was all too quickly followed by warmth. She'd been trying not to look forward to the end of the day and his visit, but it was clear that she hadn't succeeded.

Hoping she managed a pleasant—but not too excited—expression, she nodded in greeting, then returned to instructing the class. Ten minutes remained in the school day and she wasn't going to cut short her teaching time. That would give Mr. Collins more reason to convince the board they should dismiss her.

Once the lesson was finished, she addressed the class from the front of the room. "Children, will those of you who came to Spring Hill with Mr. McKay please come to the front for a moment? He'd like to have a word with you. The rest of you are dismissed. I'll see you tomorrow."

The sound of shuffling feet and excited chatter filled the room as half the class headed to the door and the others gathered next to her. Once the children were in place, Simon made his way to the front. "It's good to see all of you. I'm so glad you've decided to attend to your education."

Charles spoke up with a mischievous grin. "I don't know that we decided much, sir."

Simon chuckled. "No, maybe you didn't. But it's a good sign that the families you're with care enough to make you come. Trust me, it will be worthwhile."

Cecilia stood back and watched as Simon greeted

each child by name, asking how they were doing and how they liked their new families. Relief coursed through her with each positive report. But she had a feeling he was as disappointed as she was that Patrick wasn't attending school. She offered a brief prayer for the boy, as she did every time he came to mind.

After several minutes of discussion, Simon cleared his throat and looked around at the children, examining each face with serious intent. The mood in the room turned more subdued. "Now, I want you all to know that there's a situation in town. A string of thefts started not long after we arrived."

As the words sunk in, Cecilia noticed fear creep into most of the children's faces. A dull ache squeezed her heart. How much prejudice and judgment must they have already faced for those few words to scare them? If only she could reach out and wipe their minds clean of the memories that made trust so hard.

Without her willing them to, her eyes turned to Simon. Did he have the same sorts of memories? Did he act so gruff and cynical because his past made it hard for him to trust and hope?

Charles once again spoke up, putting into words what all the children must be feeling. "Mr. McKay, sir, you know we didn't do that. We're not dumb enough to go and ruin the good thing we've got going."

Simon rested a hand on the boy's shoulder, tone reassuring but still firm. "I know none of you would get involved with something like this and I won't let anyone go accusing you without solid proof, Charles. But if any of you have information, if you've seen or overheard something that could be related, I need you to tell me. I can't protect you unless you're all forthright with me. Is that understood?"

As one, the group nodded, wide-eyed and serious. But none of them came forward with anything to say. Cecilia couldn't help but wonder if it was loyalty keeping them silent, or if they really didn't know anything about the thefts. She chided herself the moment the thought crossed her mind. That was as judgmental as the nervous busybodies who were spreading ideas about the orphans being involved in the first place. If she wanted to help the children assimilate to their new home, she would have to watch her reactions, or they would never learn to trust her.

Simon reminded the children how they could get in touch with him if they needed to talk, then released them to head home. When the door closed behind the last one, he sagged against her desk with a deep sigh. "Well, I don't know what I'd hoped for, but I'm disappointed. I thought one of them might give us something to go on."

Cecilia rested her hand on his arm. She wished there was something she could do to relieve the pressure he must feel to protect the children who had arrived in his care. "I'm sure it won't take long for the sheriff to find out what's going on. Let's focus on visiting the children at home and getting a feel for how things are with their families. We could find some clues that way."

It looked for a moment as if Simon would argue. But then he nodded and met her eyes again. "I guess we should start as soon as possible, then, like we discussed."

"How about tonight?" Heat crept up the back of Cecilia's neck. Did that sound as bold to him as it did to her? It was probably only the direction her thoughts were taking. There was nothing wrong with the question, but spending so much time alone with him was starting to feel like quite a risk to her heart.

Simon straightened and dropped his hat back over his dark hair. "Tonight is fine. Do you mind going after supper? That would give the children time to finish their chores and eat before we stop by."

"Yes, that's a good idea."

"I'll rent a buggy at the livery and come for you later." His gaze caught hers and Cecilia forgot where she was for a second. Why did this feel so intimate, so romantic, all of a sudden?

Looking anywhere but at Simon, she fought the urge to cover her flushed cheeks and smoothed her skirt instead. "Do you know who you want to visit first?"

Taking a step toward the door, Simon paused in thought. "I'd like to go see how the three Watson children are getting on with their inexperienced guardians."

Cecilia barely stopped herself from shaking her head. He still couldn't accept that there were good, capable people in the world, people who would work hard and make a happy home for the orphans. Instead of starting another argument, she made herself smile. "That sounds fine. I'll see you tonight, then."

He tipped his hat and left the school without another word. Cecilia let out the breath she'd been holding in a slow stream. Spending so much time in close proximity to the handsome placing agent was going to be a challenge, for sure. But she had committed herself to it. She would have to keep a tight rein on her emotions. She could manage that for a few weeks. Couldn't she?

After tidying up the room, Cecilia locked the door and headed home. The entire walk, she tried to decide how to explain her evening plans without Cat or Aunt Lily teasing her about her interest in the placing agent. They knew Simon had enlisted her help weeks ago. But she was sure they would find a way to make the evening drive in the country sound more like romance than business. Those two saw romance in everything.

The key, she decided, was keeping her tone and expression neutral, as if the trip was nothing special. And it wasn't, she reminded herself. It couldn't be.

Pausing outside the door to compose her thoughts and put on a straight face, Cecilia smoothed her skirt. Then she entered the house and found Cat in the kitchen, starting preparations for supper.

Her younger sister stopped chopping vegetables to wave. "I'm glad you're home, Cecilia. Put on an apron and come help me. You know how much I hate cooking alone."

Cecilia couldn't help grinning at Cat, who was even exuberant about things she hated. "Sure, I'll help. But you hate cooking with company, too."

Cat giggled. "That's for sure. How was school? Are you ready to quit yet?"

Tying a neat bow with the apron strings, Cecilia nudged Cat out of the way and took over the chopping. "You know it doesn't matter if I want to quit or not. I need the job. Otherwise I'll be stuck helping at the café all the time like you are."

Heaving a sigh with her characteristic drama, Cat grabbed a towel and took the lid off a pot on the stove, using a long-handled spoon to stir the contents. Stew, from the smell. "I pray no one else gets stuck with that burden." Perking up, Cat dropped the spoon and returned the lid to the pot. "Did you hear the latest about the robberies?"

Cecilia's heart dropped. "No, I haven't talked to anyone except Simon."

Cat glowed at the chance to enlighten Cecilia about what she considered to be an exciting event. "There were two more today. Two! And no one ever sees a thing. It's like the items vanish into thin air. With so many new people streaming through on their way West, the sheriff could have a terrible time figuring out who it is."

The news, while not really good, could be positive for the orphans. Two new incidents occurring while most of them were in school would remove suspicion. And if people focused on the possibility that it was someone who had stopped in town on their way West, that could halt talk about an orphan being the culprit.

Cat prattled on about other news she'd heard that day, but Cecilia tuned most of it out. She poured the chopped vegetables into the stew then sliced a loaf of bread to go with their meal while it cooked. Once it was ready, she and Cat worked together to ladle out stew into bowls and set everything on the table. They would eat their supper and leave the pot simmering on the stove for Aunt Lily when she returned after the evening rush at the café.

Cecilia started to think she could slip out of the house when Simon came without giving much of an explanation. That is until Cat finished the last of her stew and leaned back, tilting her head from one side to the other to stretch her neck. "Aunt Lily's new stew recipe will be a hit at the café, I think. Oh, do you have much school preparation to do tonight? I could use some help with a new dress design I want to try."

The request wasn't unusual. Cat loved fashion and was always creating beautiful gowns based on the latest styles. But she hated detailed sewing work, so Cecilia often helped her. She didn't mind most of the time, but now she would have to tell Cat about her evening plans and face her questions. "I'd love to, but Simon wants to start visiting the orphans' homes tonight. He'll be here soon to pick me up."

Fighting to keep her expression as neutral as possible, Cecilia refused to meet her sister's eyes. She knew the smirk that would appear on Cat's face all too well. But when the younger woman didn't respond, she couldn't help herself and peeked up from her bowl. Ah, there it was. One delicate eyebrow arched, perfectly full lips turned up a bit at the corners. Cat's best smirk. "An evening out with the handsome Simon McKay? Sounds romantic."

Standing abruptly, Cecilia started gathering their dishes from the table. "It's not like we're going for a private ride in the country. We're going to visit the Shepherd family and talk with the three children. It's official business. That's all."

She knew the words came out in a guilty rush, but she couldn't stop them. Cat's light laugh followed Cecilia as she stomped out of the room. Even if Simon had showed any signs of romantic interest in her—and he hadn't—there was no doubt that he would leave town once his job was complete. He had already made it quite clear that he didn't have any desire to stay on the frontier. His life was in New York. But deep in her heart, a tiny seed of doubt made her wonder. Would he consider staying if he found a good enough reason? Of course, Cecilia would never be that reason. But what about Cat?

A loud knock sounded at the door, mercifully stopping her wretched thoughts in their tracks. Drying her hands, Cecilia removed her apron and took a second to smooth her hair while Cat answered the door. She did her best to ignore the way her heart jumped when she heard Simon's voice. Straightening her skirts, she squared her shoulders and stepped out to face an evening alone with Simon.

The buggy ride to the Shepherd house was quiet. Simon wasn't sure he trusted himself to talk much right then. When Cecilia stepped out of the kitchen to greet him, a bolt of awareness had struck him. She wore the same dark red dress she'd had on earlier, but now her hair was starting to come loose from its bun and her cheeks were tinged with pink. And the eyes that usually looked at him with storm clouds gathering were instead a shining blue like the sun glinting on water.

Of course, he had noticed her beauty the first time they'd met. But now something felt different. She was stunning. And he didn't know how to respond to the feelings rising in him without sounding like a fool. So he'd helped her into the buggy without a word and started out with the goal of getting to their destination as quickly as he could.

Relief washed over him when she gestured to a small farm several miles out of town. "That's it, right there."

He turned the buggy toward the neat little house. Light blazed from the windows, letting them know the trip wasn't in vain and they would catch the family at home.

After climbing out of the buggy, Simon went to Cecilia's side. He paused, knowing that helping Cecilia down would bring them far closer together than he wanted to be.

Trying to stay in control of his runaway attraction, he reached up and took her hand, holding her steady as she stood. He did his best to ignore how warm her hand was in his, but the softness of her skin was now branded into his memory. Distracted by the feeling, he didn't notice that as she started to step down, her foot caught on the edge of the buggy. Before he knew it, Simon's arms had wrapped around her shoulders and waist, catching her before she fell.

His eyes met hers and the air rushed from his lungs. He couldn't stop himself from leaning closer, drawn by her full lips. Then his mouth was almost touching hers—

A wild commotion came from the door of the house behind them as the three Watson children rushed outside to greet them. Simon jumped back, forcing himself to ignore the disappointment settling in his chest. He made certain Cecilia was firmly on her feet before letting go and stepping away. Two steps away. Yes, space would be good for him.

Turning to the children, Simon opened his arms and enveloped all three in a hug. Helen, the only one too young to attend school, grabbed his hand and pulled him down to her eye level. "Mr. 'Kay, I missed you lots."

He grinned and reached out to brush back the curls that framed her face. "I missed all of you, too. How is your new home?"

Ten-year-old Gertie spoke up, her voice full of wonder. "Oh, Mr. McKay, it's better than anything. Mr. and Mrs. Shepherd are so nice. And they like us, all three of us. I can tell."

Eyes sliding shut, Simon offered a silent prayer of thanks. Maybe Cecilia had been right and this placement would work out better than he'd thought. Standing, he looked at James. "And how about you? Are you getting settled in here?"

The boy offered a half smile with a shrug. "Yeah, I guess so. Mr. Shepherd lets me work with him in the barn. He likes to make furniture and last week he taught me how to whittle." He dug in his pocket. "He even gave me this pocketknife, so I can practice anytime I want."

The pride in the boy's voice warmed Simon's heart. This was what he always hoped for in placements: parents who tried hard and thriving children. Cecilia was hugging the children now, as the older two asked why she was at their house. "Mr. McKay and I came to talk with you and Mr. and Mrs. Shepherd. We're visiting all the orphan train children to see how you like your new families."

Happy chatter accompanied them as the children led Simon and Cecilia toward the house. James even held the door open for them to enter, with a dramatic flourish of his arm as Cecilia passed. Simon held back laughter and gave the boy a serious nod on his way in.

As the children's voices echoed around the small room, Eleanor Shepherd turned from the far corner, where a kitchen area was set up by the large fireplace. "Why, hello, Mr. McKay. Hi, Cecilia. We've been wondering when you would visit."

Robert Shepherd rose from a chair and crossed the room to shake Simon's hand after greeting Cecilia with a nod. "We're glad to have you both at our home. Come right on in."

Simon slid his coat off and turned to Cecilia, noticing that she was struggling to grasp the edge of her cloak where it had twisted over her arm. Resting one hand on her shoulder to let her know he was close behind her, Simon grasped the fabric and helped her untangle it. The pink that washed across her cheeks made her muttered thanks all the more charming. Could it be that she'd been as unsettled by the intense moment at the buggy as he had been?

Doing his best to focus on their visit, Simon found that it was a pleasant task. The Shepherds were kind people, easy to talk to and thrilled to have the children in their home. By the time he and Cecilia prepared to leave, Simon finally felt some relief. This placement, at least, gave him nothing to worry about.

While Cecilia said goodbye to the children, Simon pulled Robert aside. "I know we only just met, but I have a favor to ask of you, if you don't mind?"

The other man tilted his head, his expression open and interested. "Anything I can do, I'd be glad to. What do you need?"

Glancing at the children, Simon kept his voice low. "I suppose you've heard about the series of robberies in town recently?"

Robert narrowed his eyes. "Sure. I would think everyone has by now."

"I'm trying to keep an eye on all the children, to make sure none of them has gotten involved in the trouble. If you happen to hear anything from your children about another orphan that sounds suspicious, would you let me know?"

Visibly relaxing, Robert nodded and stuck out his hand to Simon. "Yes, I can do that. I'd hate to see any of the children's friends involved. They talk about the others all the time. They must have grown very close on the train."

Simon agreed. The children did bond when they were placed out at the same stop.

Cecilia joined them by the door as Simon pulled on his coat. The awkwardness was already returning between them and they weren't even out the door yet. "Are you ready? I don't want to keep you out too late."

She aimed a smile at the three children standing close by. "Yes, I believe so. Goodbye, again, children. I'll see you at school tomorrow."

They echoed her parting words as Simon rested his hand on her back and led her to the buggy. He helped her climb in, relieved when she made it into her seat without incident. The Shepherds and their children waved from the doorway as Simon steered the buggy back to the rutted path that would lead them to town.

Once they were out of sight of the farm, Simon risked a glance at Cecilia. She stared off across the dark prairie with a slight smile playing on her lips. He couldn't help wondering what thoughts made her look so happy. "How do you think that went?"

She looked up with wide eyes shining. "Oh, it's perfect. Robert and Eleanor couldn't be a better fit for those three darlings."

As she spoke, her expression softened even more, enough to make his heart ache. "You love the children, don't you?"

Her lips parted as she looked out over the horizon. "I do. I've always loved children. I used to think… well, it doesn't matter now."

Something in her tone caught his attention. "No, what did you think? It matters to me."

She turned and stared at him for a long moment.

Simon refused to break eye contact, wanting her to know that he was genuinely interested in what was important to her.

Finally she covered one pink cheek with her fingers and turned away. "I used to dream of having a houseful of children. When Coralee and Jake adopted their twins, I fell even deeper in love with the idea of one day having a big, happy family."

Simon watched leaves swirl across the path in front of them, spurred by a cool wind that made him pull his hat down more firmly on his head. "Why would you say that doesn't matter? Having a family is a fine dream. And you'll meet someone and settle down soon enough. You're a beautiful woman." Simon cringed. He'd been distracted by her loveliness since they'd met, but he hadn't intended to ever let the words slip out.

Cecilia's harsh laugh caught him off guard. He'd given her a compliment, after all, no matter that he hadn't meant to. "That's a nice sentiment, Simon. But, really, there's not one appropriate suitor in Spring Hill who would pursue me rather than Cat. That's become quite clear over the years. No, my future lies in securing my place in Spring Hill on my own."

Taken aback, Simon didn't respond for a moment. How could she think that her sister overshadowed her that much? Sure, Cat had the kind of beauty that drew men like moths to a flame. But she was also impulsive and often superficial. While he suspected that was partly an act, those weren't traits that made a man think of settling down and getting married.

Before Simon could find the words to tell her what he thought about that, a wagon crested the hill in front of them, heading straight in their direction. And traveling much faster than necessary. Acting on instinct, Simon pulled the reins hard, urging his horse off the path and out of harm's way just in time to avoid a collision. The wagon came to an abrupt stop next to them, revealing that the driver was none other than Mr. Hartley. Patrick was perched beside him on the seat, his small face pale and eyebrows drawn together.

The old farmer's bloodshot eyes traveled right past Simon and came to rest on Cecilia. "Well, well. Isn't this a cozy state of affairs? What, I'm not good enough for you to consider marrying, but this drifter is worth dallying with?"

Simon's hands clenched the reins, making the horse stir uneasily. Forcing himself to relax, he gave Mr. Hartley a hard glare. "I'll warn you once not to make such insinuations about Miss Holbrook. She's far too good for either of us."

Mr. Hartley finally turned to look at Simon. "Go back to your big city, McKay. Things are done a little different out here. A man needs a woman to run his home and women are scarce on the prairie. I'm sure this fine lady and I can come to a suitable arrangement, one way or another. If you'd just get out of the way."

The man's tone implied that his words were some

sort of threat. Simon ground his teeth together, holding back with every ounce of his being when all he wanted to do was to direct a solid punch at the fool's jaw. But Cecilia's hand moved to rest on his, her touch distracting him from Hartley's lack of sense and reminding him that he had to take the high road. He couldn't let his actions add to the bad name orphans already got from ignorant people.

With her hand still on his, Cecilia fixed a glare on the farmer. "Please don't speak to me of this again, Mr. Hartley. There will never be a good enough reason for me to even consider marrying you. Go hunting for your housekeeper elsewhere."

Warmth welled up in Simon's chest. This woman thought she had to fight for respect, but she was more than capable of demanding it when necessary.

A slight cough from Patrick drew his attention, even as Hartley fumed at Cecilia's words. Simon decided he might as well be direct. Mr. Hartley already knew they didn't trust him. "Patrick, are you safe? Do you want to stay with Mr. Hartley? You can come right back to town with us if that's what you want."

The boy refused to meet Simon's gaze, looking straight down at his feet and muttering so that Simon had to strain to hear his words. "No, thanks, Mr. McKay. I'm fine with Mr. Hartley."

Pressure filled Simon's entire body, making his hands clench into fists again. It was obvious that something was wrong. Patrick had been lively and funny during their travels. Now he appeared withdrawn and anxious. But Simon had instructions to let the orphans have time to bond with their new families unless he saw abuse or the children said they wanted to leave. He would have to bide his time and continue to be watchful. And pray that God would protect Patrick if Simon couldn't.

Chapter Five

Mr. Hartley urged his horse into motion, eyes boring into Cecilia as the wagon rolled past them. "So long, for now, Miss Holbrook. I'll be seeing you again, I'm sure."

A shudder passed through her. Cecilia did her best to restrain it, hoping Simon didn't notice. As close as they had to sit in the confines of the buggy, she could feel the tension in him. The last thing they needed was one more word from Mr. Hartley to push Simon over the edge and cause a physical altercation that would cast a bad light on Simon and the orphans.

She released a tense breath when the wagon continued on without further provocation. Mr. Hartley pushed the horse back to the breakneck speed he had been going when they'd first encountered the vehicle. Simon and Cecilia both turned on the seat to watch them go. Her heart whispered a prayer for Patrick's safety. The boy needed all the help he could get.

Simon stretched his clenched fingers several times

before flicking the reins and directing the horse back onto the dirt path. Cecilia found her gaze drawn to his profile, admiring his straight nose and wide lips, which were currently pressed into a tight line. The moment outside the Shepherd house flashed in her mind, that brief second when she'd thought he was going to kiss her. And, in spite of herself, she'd wanted him to. Almost more than she wanted anything else.

Shaking the memory away, she made herself examine the familiar landscape instead of her companion. The edge of Spring Hill was in sight ahead of them. Buildings that had been there for most of her life were now mixed with newer ones. Her world seemed to change on a weekly basis. Cecilia pulled her cloak further up her neck. The chill in the evening air hinted at the looming winter. "How fast do you suppose we'll fit in the rest of the visits?"

Simon's voice was tight when he responded and she wondered how long it would take him to relax after the encounter with Mr. Hartley. "There are seven more homes to visit, so I'd say a week or two. It depends on how much time your schedule permits."

Cecilia tried to ignore the way her heart leaped at the thought of the time they would spend together. She forced that little thrill away. "My schedule isn't very busy right now. And helping you make sure the children are all safe and happy is a priority."

They were passing the first few homes built on the outskirts of town. With his eyes glued straight ahead, Simon pulled the reins to slow the horse. "Do I get the chance to take you home this time or should we part ways here?"

Heat crept up her cheeks at the reminder of her previous behavior. She'd certainly made a fool of herself. "I hope you can forgive me for that, Simon. I overreacted and I'm sorry. I would appreciate it if you would drive me home."

He turned then, his eyes searching her face. As much as she should, Cecilia refused to break the intense stare. But she soon found herself falling into the pale depths, imagining that warm, even romantic, feelings were hidden in them. She had to look away. Her fickle heart was running wild without reason. And that would only lead to pain.

Clearing his throat, Simon urged the horse forward again and they drove the rest of the way home in silence. Cecilia allowed Simon to help her down from the buggy but took much more care in where she stepped this time. Her heart wouldn't be able to handle another incident like the one outside the Shepherds' house. Being so near to Simon again was sure to turn her into a puddle of out-of-control emotions.

But, even though she didn't slip, the air felt thick around them as her feet touched the ground. Simon stood close, holding her hand in his large, rough one far longer than necessary. Cecilia had to fight to keep her breath from coming in gasps when her lungs seemed short of air. Her gaze shifted, looking anywhere except into his face, which was far too near hers. She was almost tall enough to look straight into Simon's eyes, instead of up at him from a delicate height. One more thing that separated her from more desirable women.

"Cecilia."

His voice was deep and rough, drawing her gaze to his face against her better judgment. Sure enough, she was again looking right into his piercing eyes, so close to her own. She felt his free hand move to hold her upper arm and the small amount of air left in her body rushed out. Then she was leaning closer, even as her mind screamed at her to think about what was happening. Another second and his lips might touch hers.

Behind them, the door burst open and voices spilled out into the night. Simon instantly released her and stepped back, running a hand through his hair. Cecilia sagged against the buggy, eyes sliding shut. Twice in one evening, she'd thought Simon might kiss her. And both times, she was left feeling bereft when he didn't. Her heart was betraying her, wanting things she had vowed she wouldn't chase after anymore. As much as she wished otherwise, it was best that they had been interrupted both times.

Straightening her shoulders, Cecilia prepared to face her family. She heard children's voices, talking over each other and growing louder each second. Coralee and Jake must have come for a visit. Sure enough, it was only a moment before they started filing out the door, goodbyes ringing in the crisp evening air. Coralee spotted Cecilia and Simon first. "Oh, Cecilia, Simon. Hello. What are you two doing out here in the dark?"

Coralee's eyes traveled back and forth between them as Jake followed her out the door, the children coming behind him. "Coralee, what do you think they're doing? Let's leave them to say goodbye however they might want."

Cecilia watched in horror as Jake winked in their direction. Winked. Simon coughed sharply, causing Jake to burst out in laughter. Cecilia wished she could step backward and disappear underneath the buggy. To make matters worse, all three children were staring at the adults, trying to figure out what was going on. Phillip pulled on Jake's coat sleeve. "What's funny, Papa?"

Patting his son on the head, Jake chuckled again. "Oh, nothing you'd understand, son. Go give Aunt Cece a hug before we go home."

The twins ran to her and Cecilia crouched in front of them, accepting their exuberant hugs. Charles hung back, feet scuffing the ground. Simon went to him and held out one hand. "Well, young man. How are you enjoying your new home?"

The boy looked from Simon's hand into his face then tentatively reached out and shook hands. "Just fine, sir. I never had a sibling before. It's awful fun."

Simon grinned and ruffled the boy's hair. "That's good to hear. I'll be coming by to visit soon, so be ready to tell me all about it."

Charles stood a bit taller as he moved to follow Jake to their wagon. Cecilia and Simon smiled and waved until the family was loaded up and on their way. As soon as they were out of sight, Simon turned back to her, not quite meeting her eyes. "Thanks for going with me tonight. I'd appreciate if you could write out a few details of what you think about the placements after we visit. I'll add them to my reports to take back when I leave."

Cold reality hit Cecilia hard with his words. Of course, he wasn't wrapped up in a romantic fantasy like she was. This was how it always happened to her. Her heart got involved and she started imagining all sorts of scenarios where a man might decide to stay out here in a small frontier town just for her instead of returning to his home. But she should know better by now. Simon wasn't going to do that. He would finish his work, go back to his real life in New York, and forget all about her.

Fighting to hold back tears, Cecilia turned away before he noticed and started toward the door. "Of course, Simon. I can do that. Perhaps we can do the next visit or two on Sunday. I'm starting to feel a bit ill."

Confusion was clear in his voice but Simon didn't question her. "Sure. I'll talk to you on Sunday, then. I hope you feel better."

Nodding, Cecilia rushed into the house before she made a fool of herself. Again. She muttered more excuses about not feeling well as she hurried past Aunt Lily and Cat to her room. Leaning against the door, Cecilia gave in to the overwhelming emotions and let silent tears flow.

Simon spent a long night tossing and turning in his bed. Every time he closed his eyes, Cecilia's face filled his mind. The moments where he'd almost given in and kissed her played over and over. What on earth had he been thinking? He had responsibilities to get back to in New York. Not only was he putting his own heart in harm's way, the hopeful expression on Cecilia's face confirmed that the path he was on would hurt her, too.

The sun still hadn't crested the horizon when he stepped out of the hotel, pushing his hands deep into his coat pockets in response to the predawn chill. Everything was gray and dull, the perfect match for his mood. He had to find a way to keep his heart under control and some distance between him and Cecilia until his work in Spring Hill was complete.

Looking up and down the street, Simon tried to decide how to start his day. He felt restless and hoped a walk would clear his head. But before he could take a step, Jake exited a shop nearby and waved in his direction. Simon returned the greeting and waited until the other man reached his side. "Good morning, Simon. I was hoping to find you. Want to get a bite to eat with me at the café?"

Simon would rather have some time to himself, but he wondered if Jake needed to talk about their placement with Charles. "Is there something I can help you with?"

Jake clapped him on the shoulder with a smile and practically pulled Simon with him when he started walking. "I want to have a chat with you, that's all. This early, there won't be quite as many people at the café as usual, so we can have a few minutes for private discussion."

There was nothing for Simon to do except go along with Jake. But his defenses were up as they entered the warm, bright café a few minutes later. The scents of fresh bread and coffee hit him as soon as they stepped through the door, making his mouth water. He had skipped breakfast at the hotel, craving solitude over small talk with the other guests.

Looking around, Simon saw that Jake had been right about the number of patrons in the café. It was almost deserted. Two men shared a table toward the front while another sat by himself reading a newspaper several tables away. Jake went straight to a table in the back corner, so Simon followed along.

A cheery young woman took their order as soon as they sat down. Once she left, Jake turned to Simon, expression serious. "I'll get right to the point, I guess. I may have teased you and Cecilia a bit last night, but I need to be sure you're aware of a few things where my sister-in-law is concerned."

Heat washed over Simon's face. "Jake, you don't need to tell me anything. There's nothing between me and Cecilia. What you saw was a moment of weakness that I won't allow again."

Jake's jaw tightened. "So, you're going to sit there and tell me she means nothing to you?"

Simon's hands flew up, palms open. "That's not what I meant."

"Well, that's sure what it sounded like to me."

Running his suddenly damp hands over his pants,

Simon hesitated, trying to gather his thoughts before speaking this time. "Cecilia is beautiful, smart and kind. I enjoy spending time with her, I can't deny that. But my life is in New York. I have a job that means everything to me. There are still dozens of orphans on the streets there that need help. *My help.* I can't abandon the position God's placed me in."

Jake leaned back in his chair, considering the words. "I understand that. I faced a similar situation myself when I moved back here last year. I had to figure out how to do right by Coralee while also following God's leading. I assure you, it's possible to do both."

Simon shook his head. "I'm sure it is. But staying here is not in my plans."

"Then I need to say the rest of what I intended to. Since William Holbrook isn't here to watch out for his daughters, I feel it's my responsibility to see that Cecilia and Cat are treated with respect. I can't allow you to hurt Cecilia. I know the two of you planned to make the rest of your visits together, but I'm not sure that's the best idea."

It was all Simon could do to remain in his seat and keep from clenching his hands into fists. What was Jake implying about him? "Listen, I understand you're trying to protect your family. But I don't intend to harm Cecilia in any way. However, I do need her help with the placements."

Jake's eyebrows shot up. "So, you think you can use her to get your work done and then run off like there's nothing between you? I'm sorry, but even I can see that she's falling for you. If you keep this up and then leave, she'll be heartbroken."

Somehow, Simon went cold and hot at the same time. He dropped back against his chair, mind racing, trying to decide if he believed Jake's assessment or not. "Are you sure about that? She wants her independence more than anything." But even as he spoke the words, Simon remembered the wistful look on her face when she'd told him how she used to dream of having a large family. And the spark of hope in her eyes when he'd leaned in and almost kissed her. Who was he kidding? It was clear that he was on thin ice.

The feeling must have showed on his face. Jake shot him a grim smile. "Feels like getting hit by a train, doesn't it? I think it would be wise for you to put some space between you and Cecilia. There's got to be something you can do to keep from getting closer while also finishing your work. It's up to you to decide what you do then."

Simon was considering whether he should be offended by Jake's meddling or happy for the advice when the young woman returned with their food. The two men ate in silence. Once they finished, Jake pushed his plate back and stood. "Well, thanks for joining me, Simon. I hope you'll consider our discussion. Because I can't stand by and let Cecilia get hurt."

Before Simon could reply, Jake turned and walked out of the café. Shaking his head, Simon took one last, long drink of his coffee and stood to leave. At that moment the door burst open and Cat swept into the room, drawing every eye in the place. That seemed to happen often when she was around. Maybe that's why Cecilia thought men were more interested in her sister than in her.

Tipping his hat, Simon greeted Cat as she approached. "Good morning. What brings you out on such a gloomy day?"

Cat's smile beamed. "Thankfully, nothing to do with working here."

Simon chuckled along with her. Cat seemed to enjoy making herself appear flighty and careless, but he had seen glimpses of the real woman underneath that mask. Cat was dedicated and passionate when she wanted to be. While Simon thought she was entertaining, he didn't see what Cecilia must see. Cat paled in comparison to her smart, kind sister.

Gesturing to the table, he looked at Cat in question. "Would you like to join me?"

Her eyes brightened as she perched on the seat Jake had vacated. "Actually, I would. I have an idea that I think will help the orphans transition into the community and this is the perfect time to discuss it."

Curious, Simon leaned back in his seat. "Go ahead. What's your idea?"

As she gripped the edge of the table, Cat's whole face lit up. "I recently read about larger schools in the east putting on recitals where the children perform musical pieces and readings. The article said the young people developed quite the camaraderie through performing together. Isn't it a grand idea?"

She paused and offered a brilliant smile. "Of

course, coming from New York, you must have much more experience than I do with this sort of thing. But I thought, what better way for the children to get more comfortable in Spring Hill than to put on our own little recital? Something lighthearted that the whole town could enjoy."

Simon's gut tightened in response to the idea of his children getting up in front of the town, exposed to their judgment. He shook his head. "The Children's Aid Society holds that hard work and the influence of a good family are what will guide a child to be successful. I'm not sure dabbling in the performing arts would meet with approval."

Cat's lips rose in a mischievous smile. "Who says anyone has to approve? It can be a town effort. And I'll take charge. Officially, it won't have a thing to do with you or your society."

His gaze swept over her, taking note of the hint of excitement hidden behind her casual expression. She believed in this idea. He wasn't so sure the people of Spring Hill would support her, but maybe the children would enjoy learning pieces and performing. They rarely got the chance to dream about cultural experiences when they were fighting for their livelihood on the streets. "All right, Cat. You're in charge. But I'll help out where I can as long as I'm here."

Her squeal brought curious looks from every person in the room. "Oh, thank you. It's going to be such fun. It'll be good for the children and the town, you'll see."

Simon chuckled. "With you leading the charge, I have no doubt it will be fun."

The last response he expected was for Cat to go still, staring at the empty dishes on the table. "I know fun is all anyone thinks there is to me. But I do care deeply about Spring Hill." Now her gaze rose to meet his, more serious than he'd ever seen her. "Without any other goal in life, I've decided I want to help this town become the jewel of the territory, a place everyone wants to live. And I want those children to be happier here than they ever imagined they could be."

Her personal revelation caught him off guard. He shouldn't be surprised that there was such depth to her, but he was. And he knew that he had to support her recital, no matter what the society might think about it. She was right about how good a town project would be for the orphans. "I'll have you know, I never doubted that you're more than fun and games. I've seen how committed you can be when you care about something."

A hint of her usual bright expression started to peek back through the gravity. "And I'm thankful for people like you. But most don't bother to look deeper. Especially men. They get distracted by a pretty face." Her eyebrows arched and she tilted her head as if trying to figure him out. "Except for you. Although, it occurs to me that if you were going to be distracted, it would be by my sister, not me."

He shook his head. Did every member of Cecilia's family think there was something romantic between them? "Cecilia is helping me in a time of need. It's nothing more than that."

Cat shrugged one shoulder and ran her finger around the edge of an empty plate. "Well, I don't think Cecilia sees it that way. She was awfully upset when she came in last night after you brought her home. And don't think we weren't aware of how much time you two spent out there. We heard the buggy drive up."

"That was…well, it wasn't what you're thinking." But in truth, wasn't it exactly what Jake and Cat had both implied? He had come within a breath of kissing Cecilia last night. Twice.

Cat's sly smile told him she didn't believe the words any more than he did.

"Fine, maybe it was. But it was a mistake. I don't want to hurt Cecilia, but I can't stay in Spring Hill. I have to put some space between us before I end up breaking her heart."

Cat watched him through appraising eyes as he spoke. "I hope you find a way to do that, Simon. She probably won't talk about it, but Cecilia's been hurt too many times before." She rolled her eyes. "Unfortunately, I've been the cause more than once."

Hoping he didn't sound too eager to learn more about Cecilia's past, he tried to keep his tone neutral. "How is that?"

She met his gaze with a rueful smile. "Men always pay attention to me, even with her standing right there. And my attitude about her feelings has been careless in the past. Most recently, the manager of our bank, Charlie Albridge, had an interest in me. He's a flirt, so I played along for a bit. I never seriously considered him marriage material, more of a friend. But later I realized that Cecilia had real feelings for him. My cavalier attitude kept me from noticing that I was hurting my own sister."

Simon watched a harried mother with three small children enter the café and claim a table toward the front. The room was starting to fill up, but he hardly noticed the faces of the people. All he could see was a vision of Cecilia, face streaked with tears. He hated to think of her feeling betrayed by her own sister and rejected by a man who couldn't see a good thing when it was right in front of him. "Still, now that you're aware of it, I'm sure you'll do whatever you can to keep from hurting her again. I can see that the whole thing upset you."

Her bright smile and teasing expression were back in full force. She reached out across the table and patted his hand. "I don't intend to stand in the way of her happiness ever again if I can help it. But what about you? Are you sure you don't want to at least consider staying in Spring Hill to prove to her that she's worthy of a good man?"

"Simon? Cat?" Cecilia's voice startled Simon. He hadn't noticed anyone come into the café. But there she stood, lips drawn into a tight line and arms wrapped around her waist. Out of context, he had a feeling the current situation looked more intimate than it was. And for possibly the first time in his life, Simon blushed.

* * *

After practically crying herself to sleep the night before, the last thing Cecilia wanted to see was Simon and Cat sharing breakfast at the café. Walking in to see her sister leaning across the table and holding his hand with that flirtatious expression had been bad enough. But the guilty blush that covered his face when he saw Cecilia really raised her ire. How could he go and almost kiss her one day—twice—and then have a cozy breakfast with her sister the next?

In spite of the pain in her chest, even as she fumed, her heart did a funny flip when he stood and gestured at the table. "Hello, Cecilia. Cat happened to come by after I had breakfast with Jake this morning and we were discussing an idea she had for the orphans. Would you like to join us?"

Drawing her spine up as straight as possible, Cecilia searched for the words to refuse the offer. Even if a small corner of her heart wanted to accept. That little corner reminded her that maybe she'd read the situation wrong and Simon hadn't planned an intimate breakfast with Cat. But the rest of her heart hurt. She decided she wasn't going to sit there and watch Simon flirt with her sister, even if it was related to helping the children. "No, thank you. I only stopped to grab a lunch Aunt Lily packed for me. I need to get to the schoolhouse and start the stove so it will warm up before my students arrive. I hope you enjoy your chat."

Cecilia regretted her tone as soon as the words came out of her mouth, but she didn't know what to do besides turn and stomp to the kitchen. Trying to avoid talking to anyone, she escaped out the back door as soon as she grabbed the basket Aunt Lily had left on a table. She wasn't about to walk back through that dining room.

Unfortunately the drudgery of the school day provided far too much time for her to think. Every time she finished helping a student and returned to her desk, thoughts of Simon played in her mind. She even found herself looking at the door from time to time, half expecting to see him standing there watching her as he had yesterday.

She examined the room, wondering what Simon had thought of their little school. She was sure it couldn't compare to the bigger, more established schools in New York. The town had constructed this little building during the spring term and Cecilia had done her best to set it up like the successful eastern schools she'd read about. When he looked around, did Simon see a frontier town trying hard or did he see a school that could stand up next to those he was used to?

By the end of the day, she was more than ready for the children to leave so she could pull herself together. After the last student shut the door behind him, she sat utterly still until the tension drained out of her. Then it was time to start cleaning up. She relished the silence, broken only by the swishing of the straw broom on the floorboards.

Cecilia was so deep in her thoughts that when the door opened behind her with a sudden bang, it caused her to jump and drop the broom. She bent to retrieve it, holding back a frustrated sigh when she saw Mr. Collins heading toward her. A visit from him was hardly what she needed to add to this terrible day.

"Hello, Mr. Collins. What brings you by this afternoon?"

The stout man came to a stop in front of her, glancing around the room as if he expected a skeleton to fall out of a closet and give him a reason to fire her on the spot. "Miss Holbrook, I have a quick matter to discuss with you. The school board had our monthly meeting last night, as I'm sure you're aware."

"Yes, sir. Is there some change I need to know about?"

His beady eyes focused on her again. "Yes, as a matter of fact, there is. The board members have finally come to their senses and agreed that Spring Hill needs a male teacher to meet the needs of our students. We'll be placing advertisements in several papers and interviewing candidates soon."

Cecilia did her best not to react. The man would feel quite justified in his assumptions about female teachers if she showed any sign of the tears that threatened to fall. "Thank you for informing me so promptly. I wish you the best in the search. But if you should be unable to find a replacement, you can be sure I'll stay as long as you need."

"But, of course, Miss Holbrook. I had no doubts you would."

Clenching her fists, Cecilia turned away to lean the broom in the corner, mostly to keep herself from slapping that mocking grin off his face. She was relieved to find that he was almost out the door when she faced him again.

"Good day, Miss Holbrook. And I do mean that it's a good day. For me, anyway." A cackling laugh echoed through the room as he shut the door on his way out.

Cecilia counted to twenty before grabbing a book from her desk and letting it slam onto the floor with a satisfying bang. Only then did she sag against the desk and let her tears fall.

When she heard the creak of the door opening again, Cecilia tried to stop sniffling, wiping at her wet cheeks and hoping Mr. Collins didn't notice. But the voice behind her was deep and sincere, not nasal and mean.

"Cecilia, what's wrong? Did something happen?"

Spinning around, she found herself staring into Simon's sincere eyes instead of Mr. Collins's mocking ones. And before she realized what she was doing, she leaned into his arms, her cheek pressed against the rough fabric of his coat. The tears fell again, although she tried to fight them. But Simon ran his hand over her back and let her sob until the tears ran dry.

As her crying slowed, Cecilia's face started to burn. She'd thrown herself into Simon's arms mere hours after resolving to keep her heart shut away from him. Pulling back, she took a few deep breaths to bring herself under control. But her heart thumped hard when he reached out and raised her chin with two fingers, eyes searching her face.

"Now, can you tell me what happened? Is it one of the children?"

Stepping back to put a little distance between them, she shook her head. "No, the children are all fine as far as I know. Mr. Collins stopped by to threaten my job again, this time with the school board on his side. It's only a matter of time before they find the male teacher he wants so badly."

Simon took a step closer to her. "I'm sorry, Cecilia. What does that mean for you?"

She tried to move back again but bumped into the desk. "It means I only have until they find a man willing to take over the school. Then…well, I don't know what I'll do."

"I guess we'll have to pray that they don't find anyone, then."

She couldn't help a tiny smile at that. But it was soon followed by churning in her stomach. It wasn't often that her first reaction was to pray, rather than to worry. That was one more thing she couldn't do well. "I guess you're right. Now, I doubt you stopped by to let me cry all over you. Is there something you need?"

Simon's expression tightened and tension settled heavy on her chest. She almost regretted asking. But at least the strain kept her emotions from taking over her actions again.

"Actually, I came to talk to you. About this morning at the café."

Of course, it had to be about that. She forced herself to meet his gaze. "What about it?"

"It wasn't at all what it looked like. Jake found me

this morning and invited me to have breakfast with him. He wanted to…well, he had a few things to say to me. Right after he left, Cat came to me to discuss an idea she has for helping the orphans settle in here. That's all it was."

Was that red washing over Simon's cheeks again? If it was as innocent as he claimed, what did he have to be embarrassed about?

"And what is Cat's grand idea this time?"

The man had the gall to chuckle in spite of the tension permeating the room. "Well, I asked her recently to help me find a way for the children to bond with the community. She wants to plan a recital where the children perform various musical acts or recitations for the town."

Leaning back against her desk, Cecilia's hurt feelings warred with her desire to help the children and curiosity about what Cat had planned. Her sister hadn't mentioned this idea when they'd talked about the project before. "And what do you think about it?"

Simon paced to a window and straightened an uneven curtain. "It's not what the Children's Aid Society would normally encourage. While stage performances are quite popular in New York, the society's stance is that good, honest work alongside a solid family is what will keep the children out of trouble. Entertainments are somewhat discouraged."

She caught the cautious edge in his voice. "But you don't agree?"

Turning to face her, he leaned back against the wall. "I think anything that gives them an outlet for their energy will help. And I wish there had been more time for dreaming and culture in my own childhood. It could do them some good."

Nodding, she watched intense emotions race across his face and wondered what deeper thoughts were behind his words. "So, you're going to organize it?"

A small smile stretched across his lips. "No, Cat is. She insisted that she wants to put her time into something that will help the town. And she thinks this is it. I think she'll do an excellent job running the program."

That soft expression on his face sent red-hot pain through her heart. Cecilia slid away from the desk and walked over to pick up a loose scrap of paper from the floor, giving herself a minute for the familiar frustration to fade. "I see. You're right, she will be good at it. Convincing people to do what she wants is one of Cat's best skills."

Behind her, she heard Simon take several steps closer. "You have to admit that it's a good plan. Cat cares about the children more than she lets on. And they could use some practice in being children, in doing things other children get to do. Don't you think the town will rally around that?"

Of course, he would uphold wonderful Cat and her perfect idea. Cecilia gritted her teeth, trying to sound as normal as possible when she responded. "I'm sure the whole town will be thrilled to take part."

Silence filled the room. She could feel that he was waiting for her to say more, but what else was there?

Cat was pulling him into her usual web of flirtation and he seemed quite willing to go along. Determined to stand her ground, she waited until she heard his footsteps move toward the door. "I guess I'll see you Sunday afternoon. We can head out to visit some families after lunch like we planned."

"Yes, I'll see you then."

Several long moments passed but Cecilia refused to turn from the window to see what Simon was doing. If she had to look at those handsome eyes, ones that would rather be staring at Cat than her, she would start crying all over again. Finally the door opened and closed and she risked a glance over her shoulder. The room was empty, the silence stifling. Much like the weight that settled on her heart.

Chapter Six

Sunday came far quicker than Simon had hoped. While he was anxious to check on more of the children, his conversation with Jake had added a layer of worry about spending hours alone with Cecilia. And her abrupt change in demeanor at the school on Tuesday had bothered him all week. One minute she was crying on his shoulder. The next she was refusing to speak to him. It seemed that no matter what he did, he continued to hurt her.

After spending the morning service failing to focus on the message, Simon stepped out of the church building into bright sunlight. He saw Lily nearby, gesturing for him to join her, so he started walking that way. But the large clump of people standing next to her almost made him stop and turn around. As an orphan who grew up on the streets, Simon was never very comfortable with large families. And Cecilia's family fit that category, in his mind.

In spite of the crowd, he couldn't ignore Lily's gestures. When he reached her side, she leaned in close, speaking low enough he had to strain to hear her over the chatter from the others. "Simon, Cecilia told me you're calling on some families this afternoon. You'll join us for lunch first, like we talked about?"

He smiled, not sure he could tell Lily no if he tried. She was such an open, welcoming person. "Sure, Lily. Thanks."

Cat separated herself from Jake and Coralee's twins and walked over to stand close by Simon's other side, greeting him with a teasing smile. "I'm glad to see you're willing to brave our crazy family for Cecilia."

Refusing to join her game, he shook his head. "You know better than that, Cat. Your aunt invited me to lunch days ago."

Shrugging, Cat's smile only grew brighter. "Deny it all you want. Cecilia might be able to convince herself that you don't care, but I can see that you do. You're uncomfortable, but you're still here instead of making excuses to get out of lunch."

"Lily asked me and I see no reason to refuse a kind invitation. That's it."

Winking, Cat shrugged again. "Sure, whatever you say, Simon. But you aren't fooling me. Or Jake." She glanced meaningfully toward her brother-in-law, who stood at the other side of the group, staring straight at Simon over the children's heads.

Well, this was shaping up to be a fun afternoon.

The women started gathering the children and moving away from the church with the men following close behind. Simon found himself walking next to Charles, the boy shuffling along with hands in his pockets. "Good morning, Mr. McKay."

"Good morning, Charles. How have you been the last few days?"

"Just fine, sir."

The boy's downcast expression caught Simon's attention. "Is there anything you want to talk about?"

Keeping his eyes glued on the side of the road, Charles shrugged without answering. Simon decided to try again. "Is something wrong at home?"

The only response this time was a slight shake of his head. "Or maybe with one of the other children from the train?"

Charles's shoulders stiffened and he answered with a slow nod. Okay, Simon was on the right track. "You know you can tell me what's going on. I'm here to look out for all of you until I'm certain everyone is in a good place."

Looking ahead of them at his family, Charles slowed his steps. Simon kept pace with him until they were separated from the others a bit and the boy decided to talk. "It's Patrick."

Simon's heart dropped. "What's wrong with Patrick? When did you hear from him?"

"Well, that's the problem. Yesterday, Coralee sent me to the mercantile for a few things. I saw Patrick outside, peeking around the corner of the store. I know he saw me, sir. He smiled a little and almost waved. But then he turned and walked away and wouldn't answer when I called him. Something's wrong, I just know it."

The incident did seem strange. The two boys had grown close on the train and hadn't seen each other much since arriving. It stood to reason that Patrick would have been glad to see his friend and at least would have said hello. But Simon didn't want to worry Charles any more than necessary. "Thank you for telling me about it. I'm keeping a close eye on Patrick. If there's something wrong, I'll find out soon."

Charles's entire body relaxed and a genuine grin lit his face. "Thanks, Mr. McKay."

Simon watched the boy run off to join the twins, worry over Patrick mixing with relief that Charles was doing so well. If only every family could be as kind and loving as this one.

Cecilia dropped back to walk next to him. "Is everything all right with Charles?"

Before he could answer, Cecilia stumbled and started to pitch forward. He caught her arm, finding her pressed close against his side by the time she regained her footing. "I'm sorry, Simon. I don't usually trip over my own feet."

He smiled and pulled her arm through his before continuing after the rest of her family. Maybe encouraging the closeness wasn't wise, but he told himself he was keeping her from stumbling again. "It's nothing. I'm glad I caught you."

She tensed and he thought she might pull away. But she just caught her bottom lip between her teeth, gaze darting away from him. "Well, yes. Thank you for that. Now, is something wrong with Charles?"

The warmth of her arm entwined with his was distracting. Simon forced his thoughts back to the two boys. "He had a run-in with Patrick yesterday, saw him sneaking around by the mercantile. He was upset that Patrick refused to acknowledge him."

A little furrow formed between her eyebrows. "Oh, that's terrible. I got the feeling that they were great friends."

"They were. I'm a little worried about it, myself. I've seen this before. Often a child withdraws from everyone he cares about because of something bad happening at home."

They had arrived at the house behind the café and Cecilia's family had already gone inside. Pausing at the door, she pulled her arm from his. "We'll find out what's going on, Simon."

"I'm sure we will. I only hope we don't find out when it's too late." He pushed the door open and stood to the side, gesturing for her to go in first. A pretty flush colored her cheeks and it was all he could do to keep from wrapping his arms around her. The urge caught him by surprise. Had her family's comments about their obvious attraction made him more aware of her? He would have to be careful. Both for his sake and Cecilia's.

They entered the house to find it filled with conversation and activity. Coralee and Lily went back and forth from the kitchen to the dining room, laying out food on the table. Cat played with the twins and

Charles in one corner of the parlor while Jake visited with an older couple. Simon hadn't met them, but he thought Cecilia had pointed out that they were Jake's parents. The scene was loud and chaotic, but somehow also completely wonderful.

Simon felt Cecilia's gaze on him and turned to her as she spoke. "Do you wish you had a family like this as a child? Or is this more confusion than you would ever want?"

He looked back over the activity in the rooms. "I've always found groups of people to be overwhelming. But right now, this feels nice."

Light filled her eyes and he saw her shoulders release tension. Had she been worried for him? "Well, that's good. Because you're not getting out of here without a strong dose of family chaos."

Cat noticed them standing in the doorway and called Cecilia over, so Simon settled himself in a seat near Jake and his parents. Jake's father leaned closer and stuck out his hand. "I've heard about you, young man, but I don't believe we've met. Ezra Hadley. Glad you're joining us today."

As they shook hands, Simon noticed that the man's other arm ended in a stump at the wrist, barely noticeable at the edge of his sleeve. He couldn't help wondering what had happened, but he'd learned long ago not to ask too many questions. People usually didn't respond well to a stranger prying into their personal life. "Simon McKay. It's nice to meet you."

The older man leaned back against the settee he shared with his wife. "How are the orphan placements going? We've enjoyed getting to know Charles. He's a good boy."

Simon smiled at that, pride welling up. "Yes, he is. The other children are doing well with their families. We have one situation of concern, but I hope that will be resolved soon."

Jake spoke up from his place in a chair next to his mother. "If we can help at all, you know Coralee and I don't mind taking in another child."

His mother, Beth, laughed warmly. "Jake, dear, I hardly think you need to jump right in again. You already have three children and Charles has only recently joined the family. I'm sure Simon has this situation under control."

Jake and his parents continued in relaxed chitchat, but Simon didn't hear it. Did he have anything under control anymore? At least one of the orphans in his care was in a perilous situation. He didn't have any idea if one or more of the children could be involved in the recent thefts. And he couldn't seem to control his own thoughts or feelings when Cecilia Holbrook was around. Everything was spiraling out of his control, rather than staying in it like he would prefer.

He was thankful when Lily stuck her head into the room and announced that the meal was ready. Simon followed behind the family, watching as they flowed around the table. They talked and teased each other as they took seats. Then one would switch so someone else could sit by who they wanted. And then another child would whine about sitting by someone else. Finally they were all seated and Simon took the last chair, stuck tight between Cat and Charles, with Cecilia right across from him.

Jake prayed for their meal and everyone started right back up with their conversations while dishing out food. Simon was surprised by how much he relished the banter between Cat and Charles as they spoke over him. Snippets of conversation from around the table reached his ears, most of it rushing past until one comment about a robbery caught his attention. Leaning forward to look past Cat, he interrupted Jake and Ezra. "Has there been another incident?"

The table fell silent and Jake nodded. "This time it was a house on the north edge of town. The family had been out and came home late to find a broken window and some valuables missing."

Something about the incident struck Simon, but he couldn't put his finger on it. "When was that? Last night?"

"No, it was Monday. I just heard about it this morning from the sheriff before church."

Simon glanced at Cecilia and his heart plummeted at the sight of her worried gaze. They had been out visiting the Shepherd family on Monday evening. And they had met Mr. Hartley and Patrick racing north out of town like they were running from something. Could it be that they were connected to the break-in?

Simon could only pick at his food as the family members went back to their meal. One by one, they left the table as they finished. Cat and Cecilia finally started clearing plates, so Simon pushed his away. He wished they didn't have plans for the afternoon. He would much rather try to find out exactly what was going on out at Hartley's farm.

Cecilia stepped into her room as soon as she and Cat finished cleaning up from the meal. She took off her apron and peeked in the mirror by the door, smoothing back a few strands of hair that had come loose. Then she straightened the checkered shawl she'd wrapped around her shoulders. Yes, she was stalling. But this afternoon's outing was likely to be a disaster. It was as if her heart had decided to ignore every rational command her mind tried to make when it came to Simon McKay.

Tilting her head to each side, she examined her appearance in the mirror one more time then settled a bonnet over her hair and left the room, working to bury the trepidation that filled her. Simon waited by the door, looking far too handsome. Cecilia started toward him, but before she even reached his side, Cat appeared in the hallway. Also dressed to go out. It struck Cecilia as odd since Cat hadn't mentioned any afternoon plans for that day.

But the truth sank in when the three of them left the house and Cat walked straight to the carriage Jake had let them borrow. "It's a lovely afternoon for a ride, although that wind might get cool. Cecilia, are you certain that shawl will be warm enough?"

Unable to answer, Cecilia nodded. Simon took Cat's hand, but before she stepped up into the carriage, Cat turned back to Cecilia, like her own sister was an afterthought. "Oh, Cecilia, you were in your room when Simon and I decided. I'm going along to talk with the families about helping the children prepare for the recital."

With that, Cat bounded into the carriage and started arranging her skirts and straightening her bonnet. Preening, Cecilia decided. Simon turned to Cecilia and offered his hand, eyebrows raised in question. As if she would refuse his help after the last time. As if she would acknowledge that something had happened between them when he'd helped her before.

Straightening her spine, Cecilia raised her chin and took his hand, refusing to meet his gaze as she stepped up and settled on the seat. He hesitated then went to the other side of the carriage, climbed into his own spot and flicked the reins to spur the horse into motion.

There was silence for the first few minutes of the ride and Cecilia could almost feel Cat's nervous energy building. Her sister couldn't stand to be quiet for long. She thought about counting the seconds until words burst out of Cat, but it turned out that she was already too late. "Simon, tell us about New York. I've heard it's amazing."

Cecilia tensed, waiting for Simon to snap that he didn't want to talk about it like he had when she'd asked him before. To her shock, an easy smile crossed his face. "It is amazing. The buildings stretch on forever and there are so many people. They're everywhere. But at the same time, you can feel very alone.

You would love the theaters, though. Not only are the actors quite glamorous, but the architecture of the buildings is beautiful."

Turning away, Cecilia pretended to study the flowers along the edge of the road. Their leaves were starting to wilt, thanks to the chilly nights. Her stomach churned. So, Simon would tell Cat all about his home and how beautiful it was, but when Cecilia asked, he got upset?

Behind her, Cat sighed in delight at his description. "That sounds wonderful. Have you been to any theatrical productions?"

"No, I haven't. I keep pretty busy with the orphans and functions for the Children's Aid Society. But I've heard all about them from several of the society's benefactors."

"Oh, I would love to go to a real theater. To see the fantastic costumes and hear the music."

Cat's voice was dreamy and Cecilia half expected her to start humming a tune right there. "Really, Cat. How likely is it that you'll ever go to a theater in New York City?"

Her sister's words cut short with a little gasp and Cecilia felt a slight stab of guilt at her sharp tone. Until she heard Cat's tense response. "I suppose about as likely as it is that you'll keep your job, Cecilia."

Raising her chin, Cecilia bit back an angry retort. She deserved that. Cat had only been daydreaming, but Cecilia had let her hurt over Simon's preference for Cat spill out in her words. She turned to lock eyes with her sister. "I'm sorry, Cat. I didn't mean to hurt your feelings."

Cat sniffed and pursed her lips. "Well, all right. I forgive you." Her bright smile returned instantly. "Now, who are we going to visit today?"

Cecilia looked at Simon, startled to find that he was watching her with intense eyes. He paused to clear his throat before answering. "We're going to see Ada, who is with a Mrs. Felder."

Cat's light laugh rang out from the back. "Oh, Simon, you're going to love Mrs. Felder. She's quite the interesting woman. I hope to be just like her when I'm old."

Staring at Cat, Cecilia tried to give her the glare Coralee used when their sister acted up. "You shouldn't go around calling people old, Cat. Mrs. Felder is a strong, respectable woman."

Shrugging, Cat flopped back against the seat. "I know, Cecilia. I don't mean any disrespect. In fact, I'm trying to say I admire the woman for those exact qualities. If she's anything like me, I'm sure she would be the first to call herself old without one bit of shame."

Cecilia shook her head and turned to look forward again. They were very near Mrs. Felder's property. Her mind turned to how the widow and Ada might be getting along. Mrs. Felder had very strong opinions and usually voiced them. She had even insisted her son go West without her when he got an itch to hunt for gold, claiming she was perfectly capable of managing by herself. And it seemed she was right.

When the little farm came into view, Cecilia could see it was tidy and well run.

While Simon helped her and Cat down from the carriage, the door opened and Ada stepped out. The girl looked the picture of health with pink cheeks and pale blond hair blowing in the breeze. She nodded at the visitors. "Hello, Mr. McKay. Mrs. Felder and I were wondering how soon you'd make it out here to see us."

Simon tipped his hat in greeting. "I'm glad to see you looking so well, Ada. How are you enjoying life in the country?"

She shrugged. "Oh, it's fine, I suppose. It's so different from the city, awfully quiet and still. And it takes so much work to run a farm like this. I never realized how hard it would be."

Something that sounded like a snort came from Cat's direction. "I'm with you, dear. Manual labor tends to sneak up on you."

Ignoring her sister's rude behavior, Cecilia leaned closer to Ada. "And how do you like Mrs. Felder?"

A genuine smile slipped over Ada's face for a brief moment. "She's kind to me. I'm glad she asked me to come live with her."

Simon nodded, his shoulders losing their tension as if her answer was all he needed to hear. "We'd like to visit for a bit, to give you both a chance to ask questions or discuss any problems."

Ada flipped her loose curls over one shoulder. "Why don't you all come in, then? Mrs. Felder was getting some tea ready anyway and I'm sure she'll be glad to have guests."

They followed the girl into the bright, clean cabin. Mrs. Felder greeted them from the stove in the back, waving them toward several chairs with broad motions. "Welcome, friends. Have a seat and we'll chat once I get this tea ready. Ada, get that bench over there so our visitors can have the chairs."

Once they were all settled and Mrs. Felder poured tea for each of them, Simon asked how things were going. Mrs. Felder spoke so kindly about Ada that it warmed Cecilia's heart. It looked as if the two were good for each other.

Cat explained the details of her recital then she and Ada spent some time discussing what she could perform.

They spent a good hour chatting until Simon stood and reminded them that they had planned to make another stop before it got too late. Mrs. Felder grabbed on to Simon's arm as Cat and Ada walked ahead to the door, chatting like old friends. "I must thank you for trusting me with Ada. She's delightful. I had two sons, you know, but always wished I could have had a daughter, too. And now God's blessed me with one in my old age. I can't thank you enough."

Cecilia's eyes filled with tears as she listened to the woman's earnest words. This was a beautiful testament to what God could do when people stepped out and followed where He led. In spite of the difficulty she had with making her faith a priority, her heart stirred. Maybe there was hope for her to have a good life without a husband, after all.

Mrs. Felder threw a quick glance toward Ada, lowering her voice to keep the girl from hearing from where she was talking with Cat by the carriage. "There is one thing I'm a bit concerned about. The dear child has become rather infatuated with a young man. He's been by a few times, but I haven't let him in. She's far too young for romantic entanglements, don't you agree?"

Simon turned to face the older woman, all seriousness. "I do agree. And that's always one of my concerns with older children. They've had to shoulder such responsibility at young ages and they tend to have trouble adjusting to being part of a family. The girls are often quick to marry. Who's this young man?"

"His name is David and he's a farmhand over at the Johnsons'. They're the couple that baby Clara is with. Ada loves that baby and she visits often, which is how they met."

Meeting the woman's gaze with his lips pressed into a tight line, Simon patted Mrs. Felder's hand. "I'll keep an eye on the situation and speak with the two if necessary. You keep doing what you feel is best. I trust that you have Ada's best interests in mind."

Relief filled the woman's expression. They said their goodbyes while Mrs. Felder wrapped her arm around Ada's waist. They waved until the carriage traveled out of sight of the little cabin.

Simon met Cecilia's eyes and spoke with firm determination. "I think we ought to pay the Johnsons a visit next. Maybe I'll pass on a request to keep their farmhand away from a certain young girl."

Cecilia was a little taken aback by his intense reaction. "Simon, I don't think that's necessary. Aren't you making a little too much out of a youthful infatuation?"

Cat was quick to add her opinion, as always. "I have to agree. Young people like the idea of love. Let them enjoy the feeling while it lasts."

Shaking his head, Simon flicked the reins with more force than needed, making the horse speed up with a jerk. "You ladies don't have much experience with orphans who have lived on the streets. If Mrs. Felder believes there's cause for concern, so do I."

Cecilia fought to keep her frustration under control. "We may not have much experience with street children, but we have much more than you with young ladies. Ada seems like a young woman who wouldn't take well to being told what to do. I'm afraid that trying to pull them apart will only have the opposite effect."

Simon's expression hardened and Cecilia wondered how often his tactics with the children were questioned. She got the impression that he wouldn't even consider her words. "I don't want them getting into trouble. Ada deserves to have at least a few years of childhood before she commits to marriage."

Knowing she wasn't going to convince him otherwise, Cecilia let the comment go. But staying quiet didn't mean she was going to let him make the situation worse. What did he know about the hearts of young women, anyway?

Simon's knee bounced against the side of the carriage, keeping a rapid beat that matched his racing thoughts. He worried that he could be right about Mr. Hartley and Patrick. If he was, what should he do about it? And now he was also anxious about Ada. How was it that Cecilia couldn't see how serious the situation was? Simon didn't doubt at all that the girl would run away with her young man if he asked. It happened far too often with older orphans.

But at the same time, could Cecilia have a point? He didn't know much about what motivated a young woman. Would his involvement push Ada closer to her beau rather than turning her away? He rubbed a hand over the back of his neck until the skin stung. They had to visit the Johnsons at some point and according to Cecilia's directions, their home was nearby. They might as well go now and Simon would gauge the situation as the day went on.

The Johnson farm was much newer than the others they had been to. There was a small house with a lean-to and not much else. But when they drove into the yard, Simon could see that they had made a start on clearing some fields on the other side of the farm. A large plot of dirt behind the house was filled with rows of brittle, drooping plants, indicating that the couple had worked hard in their garden that summer.

Everything was still as Simon helped the women from the carriage and went to knock on the door. The smell of dirt wafted by on the breeze while he waited, listening for movement inside the house. It surprised him to realize how pleasant the scent was. He wasn't sure he'd ever noticed the smell before, much less enjoyed it. After several long moments the door finally creaked open and Mrs. Johnson peeked out.

"Well, hello, Mr. McKay. We weren't expecting company and Clara just fell asleep for her nap."

The woman looked tired. He hoped the smile he tried to give her wasn't a grimace. The last thing she needed with a baby to care for was to think he didn't approve of her. "That's all right. We only need to talk with you and your husband for a few minutes, if you can spare it."

"I'll get him and we'll come right out." She disappeared from the door and Simon stepped back to wait with Cecilia and Cat. Soon enough, the couple joined them, Mrs. Johnson closing the door behind her with great care.

Mr. Johnson greeted each of them in turn before getting right to the point. "I suppose you have questions for us, Mr. McKay?"

Simon appreciated the man's open attitude. "Mostly, I need to hear how you're adjusting to having Clara here and if you're all happy with the arrangement. When the children are older, I always speak privately with them, but since Clara's too young to talk, I'll let you tell me how it's going."

The young mother's face lit up through the obvious exhaustion. "Oh, we're so pleased to have Clara with us. I can't tell you what a blessing it is to finally have a precious baby in our home."

Mr. Johnson slid his arm around his wife's shoulders, tucking her close to his side. A sudden burning sensation filled Simon's chest. They were so happy and in love. It was almost enough to make him sick. But he had a job to do. He didn't have time to dwell on why their contentment made him cranky.

Forcing the unwanted response to the back of his mind, he tried looking past the couple instead of straight at them. Focusing on the rough boards that covered the house helped ease the burning a little. "And how are you adjusting to life with a baby? I know it isn't always easy."

The two new parents shifted uneasily and shared a glance as if there was something they had talked about together but didn't want to reveal to anyone else. Cecilia stepped closer to Mrs. Johnson. "Please, you can be honest with us. We aren't here to make any trouble. We want to make sure all three of you are happy and doing well with this new situation. I have some experience with babies. I might be able to help."

Mrs. Johnson's shoulders fell and, for a moment, Simon thought she might burst into tears. But she inhaled a deep breath and answered in a rush of words. "It's much harder than we expected. I thought we would settle in and be happy right away. We wanted a baby for so long. But she cries all the time and I can't get her to stop."

Cecilia tilted her head, expression thoughtful.

"Does she seem to be in discomfort? Does she arch her back or act like her stomach is tender?"

The words drew Mrs. Johnson's head up in surprise. "Why, now that I think about it, she does arch her back quite a bit. I'm afraid I'll drop her sometimes, she does it with such strength."

Resting her hand on the other woman's arm, Cecilia smiled reassuringly. "Then I have several ideas for you. Why don't we go in for a moment and you can show me what she's been eating? It could be that she's having trouble digesting something."

Deep in conversation, the two women headed to the house with Cat trailing along, looking bored.

Simon turned to Mr. Johnson. "And how are you handling the stress of a new baby and a tired wife?"

The man grinned, running a hand over the back of his neck. "I've ended up on the wrong side of a few emotional outbursts, that's for sure. But we're getting the hang of it. She's just afraid, worried she'll do something wrong."

"You'll both learn and grow more confident with time, I'm sure. I can tell that you care about Clara and you're trying to do your best. You can rest assured that I'll be giving this placement a positive report."

Clapping Simon on the shoulder, Mr. Johnson grinned. "Thank you for that, Mr. McKay. It means a lot that you trust us with that sweet girl."

When silence fell between them, Simon wondered if he should say anything about their farmhand and Ada. He wanted to. That was how he would have handled this type of situation on any other trip. But

Cecilia's words still rang in his mind. And he had to admit that her objections made sense.

So instead he asked about the farm, which led to a discussion of the various crops and livestock that were common in the area. They exhausted several subjects of small talk before the women finally returned, baby Clara perched in Cecilia's arms. "Look who woke up, Simon. Isn't she precious?"

As she spoke, Cecilia brushed her cheek against the baby's silky hair. Every nerve in Simon's body seemed to freeze at the same time. Although he'd spent years stifling the desire, all of a sudden he couldn't control it any longer. He wanted more than helping orphans find families: he wanted a family of his own. And that awareness was terrifying.

Backing away, hoping that no one saw him, Simon tried to pull himself together before anyone noticed that his entire world had shifted. Thankfully, the women were all distracted from their conversation when Clara started fussing.

Mrs. Johnson took her from Cecilia with a smile. "I think someone is hungry. And thanks to you, Miss Holbrook, I do believe we'll have a happier evening tonight than we have had for some time."

With a cheerful wave, Cat climbed into the carriage while Simon said goodbye to Mr. and Mrs. Johnson. Cecilia's eyes shimmered as she said goodbye to Clara and her parents. Her parted lips and faraway gaze as they pulled away from the farm made him certain she wished she could go back and snuggle the baby one more time. At least he wasn't the only one who was suddenly envisioning the future.

On the way back to town, Cat and Cecilia talked nonstop about baby Clara and the problems Mrs. Johnson had been having with her. Simon barely heard any of it. Everything he knew about his life had become blurred. That momentary vision of Cecilia holding a beautiful baby girl brought to the surface desires he used to be able to control. And they were strong enough to make him reevaluate his entire purpose in life.

How could his priorities change so suddenly that he would even consider dropping his work with the Children's Aid Society? He'd always known without a doubt that God had led him to work there because He wanted Simon to help children in the same circumstances he had experienced as a child. That was Simon's life, his direction.

It couldn't be God's plan for Simon to leave it all behind and settle down on some little frontier farm to get married and raise a few children. What about the orphans? God wouldn't take Simon away from that calling, would He? So few people cared for their plight as it was. But that longing that pulled Simon's heart in a different direction wasn't going to be easy to ignore.

Glancing at Cecilia out of the corner of his eye, Simon wished Cat wasn't there. He wanted to confide in Cecilia about the things he was feeling. As always, she would see the problem from an angle he couldn't. But Cat was there and he didn't want to tell her about his deep, heart-wrenching dilemma. It was for the best, anyway, he finally decided. He couldn't risk opening his heart to Cecilia and getting distracted with so many young lives on the line. He would have to find a way to smother that unrealistic dream on his own.

Chapter Seven

Cecilia held back a sigh as she corrected Edwin's spelling for what felt like the hundredth time. The dreary weather combined with the fact that the whole week of school was still looming before her made the day seem as if it would never end. And it didn't help that she kept thinking about Simon rather than giving the children her full attention. A distracted teacher made mistakes and mistakes would give the school board more reasons to replace her.

Forcing her mind back to the work before her, Cecilia gave each child a word to spell out loud in turn. Most of them were doing quite well, but Edwin and Charles were both struggling to keep up with their lessons. She would have to spend some extra time with each of them while the others were reading after lunch.

The hours dragged by but, finally, the last student left the building and Cecilia could tidy up. She grabbed a cloth to wipe the frames lining the walls.

She started with the picture of President Buchanan and moved around the room until she finished with a map of the territory that hung on the wall behind her desk. The mindless work allowed her thoughts to turn back to Simon.

She thought about the delightful, warm feeling that filled her when she realized Simon had taken her advice yesterday. He had refrained from confronting the Johnsons about their farmhand and Ada, even though he was convinced doing so would help.

As she locked the door and started home in the cold October air, the warmth of knowing he respected her opinion spread through her again.

She ambled along the boardwalk, not ready to go home in spite of the chill in the air. Stopping in front of a window display at one of the millinery shops, a bonnet covered in flowers caught her eye. Would that look appealing on her? It was the sort of thing Cat would look marvelous in.

The question of what Simon might think of the bonnet formed in her mind at the same moment that a touch on her shoulder pulled her out of her thoughts. She turned to see Coralee smiling gently at her. "Hello, Cecilia. I'll walk with you if you're headed home. Cat has the twins and I'm on my way to get them."

Cecilia agreed as her older sister leaned close and wrapped an arm around hers. "How did your visits go yesterday? Cat didn't have much to say when I saw her this morning."

"Oh, they went very well. The Johnsons were

struggling a bit with little Clara, but we came up with some ideas that will help them. Mrs. Felder and Ada are quite the pair. They seem to be getting along very well."

Coralee sighed in contentment. "I love seeing so many darling orphans finding good homes. I'm so pleased that Simon was able to bring them all the way out here to Spring Hill, aren't you?"

All Cecilia could do was nod. She wasn't certain that was true for her. Simon McKay had brought some wonderful children to their town, but at the same time he'd brought her a good deal of heartache. Would she ever wish he hadn't come? No, she couldn't say that, either.

Coralee caught the hesitation and her eyes narrowed. She never missed a thing when it came to her sisters' feelings. "I know you're happy for the children. So what caused that dour look?"

Shrugging, Cecilia took a try at evading the question. "I had a difficult time with some of the students today, that's all."

But Coralee, motherly oldest sister that she was, wasn't about to accept that excuse. "You and I both know that isn't all. Is Simon treating you well? You know that Jake and I will step in if he's been disrespectful in any way."

Cecilia sighed. "I don't need you and Jake to defend me, Coralee. And Simon has been a perfect gentleman." Well, for the most part. But she wasn't about to tell her sister he had almost kissed her. Twice. If she so much as hinted at that, Coralee was certain to notice how much Cecilia wished those moments hadn't been interrupted.

But Coralee was more observant than she had expected. Her eyes flashed with interest. "Perhaps you wish he would be a little less of a gentleman, then?"

A hot flush washed across her cheeks. "No! I don't… I wouldn't…that's hardly ladylike, Coralee."

Her sister's knowing laugh made her blush all the more. "That doesn't mean the thought hasn't crossed your mind. I guess it's a good thing Simon is enamored with you, too."

Cecilia's head shot up, her heart clenching as she met Coralee's steady gaze. "How would you know that?"

"My dear, it's clear as day to the rest of us. It seems you're the only one who can't see it."

Turning away, Cecilia's eyes swept over the storefronts without really seeing them. "I know you mean well, but you must be wrong. Simon is dedicated to returning to New York as soon as he's satisfied with the placements here. Even if he did have some romantic interest in me—he doesn't, but if he did—that wouldn't be enough to make him stay."

Coralee stopped as they reached the house. "I suppose I could be wrong. But Jake and Cat agree with me. I doubt all three of us are seeing something that isn't there."

Cecilia hesitated outside when Coralee stepped through the door and disappeared into the house. They had to be wrong. He couldn't be drawn to her the way she was to him. Time and again, it turned out that men she thought might see her in a romantic light were only using her to get to Cat. Not one time in her life had a man looked at her and truly wanted to spend time with her, to find out who she was. And Simon was no different. He needed her help to finish his job here, then he would be gone without a backward glance.

Shaking off that thought, Cecilia squared her shoulders and joined her sisters inside. The twins had run to their mother and were talking over each other in an effort to be the first to tell her what they'd done while she was gone. Phillip managed to be the loudest. "Mama, Aunt Cat took us to the creek, but no frogs. Why?"

Before Coralee could respond, Louisa cut in. "Aunt Cat said, Phillip. It's cold."

Bickering broke out between the two little ones and Coralee pulled them aside to settle the matter. Cat smiled at Cecilia, a self-satisfied light in her eyes. "We had a visitor this afternoon."

"Oh? Who was that?" She tried to keep her tone uninterested. Cat was taking far too much pleasure in her secret, a sure sign that she intended to tease Cecilia once it was revealed.

"Our old friend Charlie Albridge. I haven't seen him in ages. Apparently he left his cousin in charge of the bank and returned home to care for an ailing family member. That's all the details I could dig up, but it makes a sweet story, don't you think?"

Trying not to wince at Charlie's name, Cecilia responded with a tight smile. "Is he back for good now?"

Cat grinned, eyebrows raised. "He is. He was asking about you, if you're still teaching and how you are. Maybe he realized he missed you while he was away."

Cecilia searched her sister's face, wondering what made her think that comment was welcome. The last thing Cecilia wanted was to be teased about the disaster of her feelings for Charlie. But she saw only genuine hope in Cat's eyes, with no hint of unkindness. Cat must really think Cecilia still had feelings for Charlie.

"Thank you for telling me, but I have no interest in trying to get his attention. Or anyone's, for that matter. I'm doing fine on my own and I plan to continue that way."

Forehead scrunching, Cat looked as if she was trying to figure out a difficult puzzle. "What do you mean? You've always talked about getting married and having babies. I can't believe you'd give up on all your dreams for no reason."

Coralee picked that terrible moment to return and sit by Cecilia. "What's this about giving up on dreams? Cecilia, you're young and so lovely. In God's perfect time, the right man will appear and sweep you off your feet. There's no reason to get discouraged."

Biting back an angry response, Cecilia threw up her hands. "It has nothing to do with discouragement. I've come to realize that I pinned too many of my hopes on a man showing up. And maybe he won't. You don't know for sure that I'm meant to marry. There are spinsters out there who lead happy, fulfilling lives. There's no reason I can't be one of them."

Cat and Coralee both looked aghast at her words.

Cecilia couldn't hold back her frustration one more moment. She stood and threw up her hands. "I get it. We've all expected to marry since we were little girls. But not every childhood hope is realistic. I'm satisfied with the path my life seems to be on. So, please, let this go."

Even as her sisters started to protest, Cecilia retreated to her room. If they were so convinced that exchanging her girlish hopes for more realistic goals was so terrible, then they could speculate about her future without her.

Simon hesitated with his hand raised to knock on the door of the little house behind the café. He had spent a long night with little sleep, worrying about what God wanted from him and if what he suddenly longed for was going to get in the way. But he'd come to the decision that all he needed was to finish his work in Spring Hill as soon as possible and get back to New York. Once he was there, he knew his path would become clear again.

But to get done, he needed Cecilia. His only option was to stay firmly in control of his own feelings and actions long enough to complete his task. It should only take a few more weeks. He could do that.

Pulling his spine straight, Simon rapped his knuckles on the door. It took longer than he expected, but finally the door cracked opened. Two little round faces peered at him from inside. Grinning, he crouched down so he could look Louisa and Phillip in the eyes.

"Well, how nice to see both of you today. I'm calling for your aunt Cecilia. Is she at home?"

Louisa giggled when he waggled his eyebrows at them, but Phillip remained serious with his little brow furrowed. "Mama say see who it is. Can't let people in."

Standing, Simon nodded, trying to maintain an equally solemn expression. "Ah, well, that's a problem. Could you get your mama? Or tell her who's at the door and let her decide?"

The boy thought for a minute then ran off suddenly, yelling as he went through the house. Simon couldn't help a chuckle. Louisa looked up with a shy smile. "Are you here to court Aunt Cece?"

Something about her innocent words hit him like a punch to the stomach. It was several seconds before air started filling his lungs again. "Well, no, I'm not. She's helping me with some work I have to do here." But he couldn't stop thinking that it would be nice if he was there to court Cecilia. Sitting in the parlor next to her, talking and laughing with her welcoming family sounded like a dream.

Phillip appeared at the door again, this time with a smile. "Mama say come in."

Simon followed his two small guides into the house and to the parlor where Coralee and Cat sat. They watched the twins run off to play and Simon turned to Coralee. "Your children are very obedient. Phillip wasn't going to let me in for anything short of your say-so."

To his surprise, she laughed. "They're obedient

at times, yes. But they can be ornery, too. Please, take a seat."

Greeting Cat as he sat, Simon decided to get right to the point. "Is Cecilia here? I wanted to plan a time to finish our visits. It would be nice to have them done sooner rather than later."

Cat pinned him with an arched glance. "You mean, so you don't have to spend more time with Cecilia than necessary? Really, Simon. You ought to give her and Spring Hill a chance. You might like it here and decide not to go back at all."

Shifting in his chair, Simon wondered why the room was stifling all of a sudden. His mind scrambled for a response that wouldn't seem like an insult to Cecilia while still telling Cat in no uncertain terms that he would return to New York. Thankfully, Coralee took pity on him.

"Cat, don't push the man. He has a job to do and he wants to get it done. There's no reason to tease him."

Shrugging, Cat turned her attention back to the sketchbook in her hands. "I'm only pointing out the obvious. There are more than a few sparks between those two. It would be a shame for such an interesting combination of personalities to be wasted when it would make an enthralling story. The big-city humanitarian falls for a frontier teacher."

With a shake of her head, Coralee sent Simon an apologetic look. "Never mind Cat's vivid imagination. Cecilia's in her room. I'll go get her and you can make your plans together."

Simon tried not to cringe. He'd been a little relieved when he realized Cecilia wasn't in the room, thinking he wouldn't have to come face-to-face with her in his present state of mind. The more time they spent together, the greater the risk that he would give in to his fickle emotions and do something that would put their hearts in danger. But all too soon, Coralee returned with her sister following behind. Cecilia looked tense. Was she unhappy to see him? And why did the answer to that question matter so much?

Cecilia perched on the edge of a chair and all three women looked at him expectantly. Simon cleared his throat, which had gone dry. "Hello, Cecilia. I came to see if we could arrange a time to go do a few more visits. I'd like to complete them as soon as possible."

"Which you already mentioned, Simon." Cat had the audacity to wink at him in full view of Cecilia.

Ignoring her, Simon looked at Cecilia. "When would your schedule allow for several more visits?"

Her fingers twisted a thread on the edge of her lace shawl as she avoided his gaze. Her voice was quiet. "My evenings are free this week. How many visits do we have left?"

Simon counted up in his head. "Three, plus another trip out to Mr. Hartley's place to see Patrick."

She finally looked right at him. The sight of her red-rimmed eyes hit him in the stomach like a physical blow. She'd been crying. He wished he could ask what was wrong, but with both her sisters present, he couldn't decide how to go about it without making her feel awkward. She bit her bottom lip. "I suppose you want to leave that trip for last?"

He nodded and she looked away again. He swallowed around the thickness in his throat before responding. "If you're able, we could do one each evening this week, saving Patrick for Friday."

When Cecilia agreed, Cat clapped her hands loud enough to make the twins look up from their play across the room. "Sounds like we have a plan. That wasn't so hard, was it?"

Cecilia's gaze shot to her sister. "You're going again?"

Almost wiggling with excitement, Cat spoke in a rush. "Of course. Simon and I decided it would be best for me to discuss our recital with each family, remember? You two are going, anyway. I might as well tag along."

Noticing the way Cecilia's cheeks paled as Cat spoke, Simon rose. Something about his presence was upsetting her, so he should leave before she got to the point of becoming ill. "Thank you, ladies. I appreciate your help. I'll be glad to have the visits complete and know all the children are in good care."

Coralee waved from her seat and then gave the youngest sister a pointed look. "Cecilia, why don't you walk Simon out? I need to speak with Cat for a minute."

Cecilia nodded after a long hesitation and rose to lead the way.

Trying to ignore the tense pitching of his stomach, Simon followed Cecilia to the front door. The silence stretched between them as they stood awkwardly in the hall. She kept her gaze glued to the floorboards, giving Simon a moment to admire the shiny curls of her hair, which had all been twisted together in an intricate style.

Finally, Simon cleared his throat again. "I suppose I'll come get you and Cat tomorrow after dinner like we did last week?"

She crossed her arms, wrapping them around herself as if to ward him off. "Yes, that's fine. We'll see you tomorrow."

He turned to the door then turned back, finding that she had taken a step to follow and was now standing very close to him. Her stormy eyes were only inches away, still looking anywhere but right at him. He caught a whiff of a floral scent and barely held his hand back from brushing over her hair to see if that's where it was coming from. "Are you all right? You seem upset about something."

Shaking her head, Simon saw Cecilia's shoulders rise and fall as she drew a deep breath and released it. But still, she didn't speak.

He couldn't take it anymore. "Please talk to me. Is it something I've done?"

Tipping her head only a bit, she finally met his eyes. A weight settled over him at the resignation lurking in her expression. "No, Simon. It's nothing you've done. It's nothing at all, to be honest."

Silence fell again and the moment grew, stretching longer as he searched her face for some clue as to what that meant. Before he could think about what he was doing, his hand rose and his fingers brushed her chin. She angled her head away, her eyes leaving his again, and Simon's heart clenched. That had been a mistake. He had to finish his business and return home to figure out what God had in store for him. He needed to stop this behavior before it was too late for one of them. Or both.

Simon took a step backward and reached behind himself to push the door open. "I'm sorry, I shouldn't have done that. I'll see you and Cat tomorrow night."

He walked away from her without looking back, but it took every ounce of self-control he could muster. Protecting her heart might be the most honorable choice, but doing the right thing wasn't easy this time. And it was completely opposite of what he wanted to do.

Cecilia closed the schoolhouse door with a loud bang that echoed across the prairie. This day couldn't have been much worse. Mr. Collins had poked his nose in throughout the hours, claiming he was gathering information for the next week's school board meeting. More like he was spying to try to catch her at a bad moment.

When she hadn't been pointedly ignoring his beady little eyes, her rebellious mind kept turning to Simon. For all her sisters' words about how he had some romantic interest in her, she couldn't stop thinking about the moment he had walked away from her yesterday. He'd almost run from the house and his retreating back had spoken with complete clarity: he wouldn't allow himself to care about her, even if he wanted to. Simon McKay was returning to New York no matter what.

Walking in a distracted haze, Cecilia stifled a cry of surprise when a figure blocked her path as she passed the butcher shop. It was Mr. Hartley, standing in front of her with his arms crossed, that familiar, leering grin in place. "Miss Holbrook, allow me to walk you home."

Mustering all the sincerity she could manage in the face of that awful man, Cecilia tried to step around him. "No, thank you. I can get home fine on my own."

But the farmer wouldn't take no for an answer and moved to block her again. "Tsk, tsk, Miss Holbrook. A pretty lady like yourself shouldn't be out and about alone. You never know what can happen to a woman by herself."

He took hold of her arm with a stronger grip than she expected from him. Practically dragging her along with him, he set off down the boardwalk as if she hadn't refused his offer.

Gritting her teeth, Cecilia went along to keep from having her arm separated from her shoulder. "Mr. Hartley, I would prefer for you to let me go. I'll walk with you, but you're hurting my arm."

The lewd smile she got in return chilled Cecilia's heart, but she was relieved that he loosened his grip on her arm a fraction. "I couldn't call myself a gentleman if I didn't keep you out of harm's way, my dear."

"What is it you want from me? I don't believe for a moment that this is about making sure I get home safely."

He feigned an injured expression, but it didn't hold for long before he started cackling. "You got me. I need something from you. Something you'll be glad to agree to."

She flinched at his awful tone. The man had no shame and she could hardly stand being so near him. "I doubt that. But what is it you think I'll help with?"

"I want you to put off visiting the farm again."

Looking at him through narrowed eyes, Cecilia tried to figure out his goal in making such an outlandish request. Did he want to hide something untoward that was going on out there?

"That only makes me want to surprise you with a visit sooner. Why on earth would you think I'd ever agree to that?"

His face tightened strangely, almost as if he was trying to look sincere but wasn't sure how to. "Me and the boy are getting to know each other, but it's taking some time. I hoped with a little longer, we'd bond more before you come out and judge us."

Cecilia's head started to ache as she tried to decide if he was being honest with her. Or was this a ploy to cover up what he was really doing out there? "I'll talk to Mr. McKay, but I have a stipulation for you."

His red-rimmed eyes regarded her with interest. After a moment he nodded. "And what is that?"

Her heart jumped. It seemed he might take the bait. "Send Patrick to perform in the recital my sister is organizing for the children in town."

Leaning back, his head tilted as he considered her request. "Don't know why anyone would want to do that, but sure. Why not? I'll send the boy. But you have to delay coming out. You agreed."

"I agreed to talk to Mr. McKay. I can't guarantee he'll be willing to wait long, but I'll do what I can."

He nodded, surprising her with sudden enthusiasm. "Yes, yes, that's fine. I knew I could count on you, my dear."

She tensed again. "Please stop calling me that. I'm not dear to you."

The nasty tone was back when he responded. "Ah, that will change with time, Miss Holbrook. My offer still stands. Eventually you'll come to find that I'm an excellent option for a single woman who doesn't have any other prospects."

Shivering again, she finally managed to pull her arm away from him as they approached the café. Putting several feet of space between them, she edged toward the door. "I'm sorry, Mr. Hartley, but you'll never be the sort of man I'd consider. Good day."

She rushed into the café, peeking over her shoulder to see him standing there with his face red and angry. That last statement might have been a mistake. As the door closed behind her, she said a quick, silent prayer that he wouldn't take his anger at her out on Patrick.

Twisting her hands together, Cecilia turned and scanned the room for an empty table. She and Cat had decided to eat at the café before heading out with Simon, but her sister would be late. She was always late. The room was already rather full. But as she craned her neck to look for any spots toward the back,

Cecilia heard her name. There was Simon, sitting at a table by the door to the kitchen and waving her over.

Steeling her heart against the sudden thrill that coursed through her, she walked to the table. "Hello, Simon. I didn't expect to see you here. I've heard the hotel has a very good cook."

He pulled out an empty chair and offered her the seat. "The food at the hotel is fine, but I like the change of pace in coming here sometimes."

Lowering herself onto the edge of the seat, Cecilia felt tension building in her chest and tried to relax. It wouldn't help anything if she let herself get emotional in front of Simon. He had proved his priorities when he'd walked away from her last night. If she had any sense, she wouldn't waste any more emotion on him.

Doing her best not to stare across the table at him like a lovesick puppy, she let her eyes dart around the room. Her attention settled on a family near the large front window. "Simon, isn't that Sophia and her family over there?"

He followed her gaze and a smile broke out on his handsome face. "Why, it is. We can save a trip if we talk with them before they leave."

Rising from the table, he moved to the side and let her go in front of him. She was startled when his hand rested on her back as they walked across the room, the touch feather-light but potent. Distracted, she almost bumped into several tables on the way. Her face was thoroughly flushed by the time they reached Sophia's family.

The seven-year-old noticed them first and grinned

as she waved. "Hello, Miss Holbrook. Are you having dinner here, too?"

Cecilia smiled in spite of the chill left behind when Simon's touch disappeared from her back. "My aunt owns this café, so I eat here often. It's nice to see you and your family enjoying an evening out."

Sophia politely introduced her new parents, Mr. and Mrs. Ames, who also had a five-year-old named Howard. This was the first school term he had been in her class, so Cecilia didn't know his parents yet. She smiled at each of them. "It's so nice to meet you. I'm Sophia and Howard's teacher, Miss Holbrook. And you might have met Mr. McKay, the orphan train placing agent."

Cecilia let Simon take over the conversation. He asked his questions and chatted with the family members while Cecilia watched them respond. The family seemed happy. And she had some clue of how Sophia was adjusting from her good behavior in school. She couldn't be prouder of how well most of the placements were going.

It didn't take long for Simon to come to the same conclusion. They said goodbye to the family and returned to their table after only a few minutes of conversation. Still, Cecilia was surprised her sister hadn't yet arrived. She wasn't usually that late. "I do wonder when Cat will get here. I feel bad eating without her, but we need to get going soon."

Simon cleared his throat as he settled in his chair. "Actually, she was here before you came in. She said

Coralee needed her help tonight and she can't come along."

Heat burned in Cecilia's chest, bursting out to spread further up her neck the longer she considered his words. This was obviously her sisters' way of interfering. They thought Simon wanted to spend time with her, so they'd taken it upon themselves to arrange it.

Gritting her teeth, Cecilia managed to respond with a tight smile as Aunt Lily approached their table. "Dearies, we've got a nice roast with potatoes tonight. How does that sound?"

They both agreed and Aunt Lily gave them each a glass of water. "I'll be right back with that, then." And she marched away to the next table with her usual broad smile.

Simon watched her go, then turned back to Cecilia. "Cat takes after her, doesn't she?"

Tilting her head, Cecilia examined her aunt for a moment. "You know, I think you're right. To be honest, I never noticed. But they do have the same endless energy and social personality."

Sipping his water, Simon's tone was dry. "And they both speak their mind about…well, everything."

Cecilia couldn't help a chuckle at that. "Very true."

"It reminds me of a woman at the orphanage when I was a child."

Glancing at him, Cecilia almost gasped. He so rarely offered any information about his life before working with the Children's Aid Society. "How's that?"

His eyes glowed with humor. "Oh, she was lovely. She would always flit around like a little bird, clucking over the youngest children. But she didn't take any talking back from the older ones, either. Miss Laurence. I think most of the boys had a crush on her."

Cecilia laughed again. "Including you?"

Was he actually blushing? "Maybe a little. She got married not long after she started working at the orphanage and we never saw her again. But there were other kind people who took her place." He grew serious and his eyes locked on hers. "I know I tend to see the worst in people. But I want you to know, your optimism and the good people here in Spring Hill are helping me see that my quick judgments aren't always warranted."

It was an effort to keep her mouth from dropping open. Now he was talking about his feelings with her? Gathering her wits, Cecilia searched his face. "What brought on this soul-searching?"

She watched Simon take a deep breath before he responded. "I don't know. Seeing most of the children in happy homes reminds me of the good in this world. And that I don't notice that good often enough."

A warm, fuzzy feeling spread through her as his gaze held hers. He looked more peaceful than she had ever seen him. "Well, I'm glad Spring Hill has had that effect on you. There are very good people here." The walk with Mr. Hartley flashed in her mind. There were also some who weren't so good.

His eyes were still on her, myriad emotions that she couldn't quite identify rolling beneath the surface.

The intensity in that look made a fluttering sensation start up inside her. Pulling her gaze away from his, she fiddled with the napkin in front of her until Aunt Lily returned with their food.

The meal was delicious, but a lump in her throat made it hard to swallow. The look in Simon's eyes, the way he'd opened up to her, made her wish with all her heart that he wanted to stay in Spring Hill. And that he would do it for her.

But that was a silly fantasy. Simon had left no doubt about his plans. He would finish his work—as fast as he could—and return to New York. And even if, by some chance, he felt led to stay, there was no reason to think it would be because of her. Cecilia had never been enough to draw a man's eye and she wasn't enough to keep Simon in Spring Hill.

Chapter Eight

Simon pushed his plate away and leaned back in his chair. Lily's roast and potatoes had been much better than the meals he'd had at the hotel. But he hadn't been able to concentrate on the food because he couldn't take his eyes off Cecilia. The pretty flush on her cheeks and the way she tilted her head the slightest bit when she was thinking through something tugged at his heart. And he knew that, for all his efforts, he was losing control of his feelings for her.

The problem was, Simon didn't know what to do with that revelation. His heart screamed that he should act on it. He could almost feel the relief and excitement of giving himself permission to woo her. But the little voice of reason deep in the back of his mind kept reminding him of his need to return to New York and the importance of his work with the orphans. He still didn't feel right about abandoning them or the calling God had given him.

He was so torn between the contradictory longings, he almost missed Cecilia's words as she folded her napkin and laid it over her empty plate. "Are you ready to go? Since it's just the two of us, we can get this done in no time."

She seemed anxious about the time they would spend together. Was she the one worried about their reputations now? Somehow, Simon couldn't muster the energy to care about that anymore. And he didn't care what her brother-in-law had to say, either. Simon liked spending time with her and he was pretty sure she enjoyed it, too.

But did she understand that they couldn't have a romantic relationship? No matter what his heart longed for, it wasn't realistic to think they could ignore all the issues that held them both back. She'd alluded to her desire to stay independent on several occasions, so she must feel the same way.

Deep down, though, his heart urged him to think about what that really meant. What could it hurt to spend time together as two people working to help the children? If they both understood the necessary limits of the relationship, what harm could come from enjoying the time they had before he went home? It had been so long since he'd had a friend to confide in and the personal talk they'd had over dinner felt good.

His confusion started to fade, leaving him feeling better than he had in days. Yes, they could be friends.

Simon smiled as he stood and offered his arm to Cecilia. "Sure, I'm ready. I thought we'd go see Patrick's sister, Jane. Since they're right in town, it won't take long."

Taking his arm, she let him lead the way out of the café. "That's a good idea. I know she's been missing him and a little worried because he isn't in school. Maybe we can help ease her fears."

Simon wasn't so sure since he was still plagued with his own fears about Patrick. But they would do what they could. If the boy had contacted his sister at some point, she would be able to give them a little insight into his situation.

As they strolled arm-in-arm along the boardwalk, Simon found that the pressure in his chest that came with thoughts of Patrick was less than usual. He wondered if it was Cecilia's presence at his side that made the situation seem less daunting. When she was with him, he often found his internal worries calming. Where that tension used to make him irritable toward those he worked with, her easy optimism seemed to brighten his own outlook.

They had a good visit with Jane's new family, who already had two boys older than her and a girl who was younger. Jane seemed content with her family, but Simon could see the sadness Cecilia had mentioned when the girl told them she hadn't heard from her brother. He offered her what little consolation he could, but the visit solidified in his heart that he had to get to the bottom of what was happening with Patrick. As soon as all the other visits were complete, he would devote his full attention to the boy.

In spite of their efforts to make the visit short, the stars were starting to peek through the curtain of darkness when they left the small house. Cecilia tilted her face up, eyes scanning the twinkling lights. "It's getting dark much earlier now."

Simon agreed. "It will be winter before we know it."

Her voice was hesitant when she responded. "Will you try to get done and return home before the snow settles in?"

He inspected the stars with her, finding a few familiar constellations that his mentor in New York had taught him. "I'm not trying to beat it, specifically. But it would make the return trip a lot easier if I can leave before winter is in full swing. Once I'm confident all the children are happy and safe, there won't be any reason for me to stay, regardless of the weather."

As soon as the words left his mouth, Simon realized how crass they sounded. He kicked himself when her cheeks paled and she turned away. Maybe she wasn't keeping her feelings in check as well as he'd thought. All his confidence from earlier evaporated. Letting any kind of relationship develop between them, even friendship, was too risky.

Correcting his words now would only make the situation more awkward. He certainly couldn't tell her the truth—that she was more than enough reason for a man to stay. Sure, he wished he could give in to the desire to remain in Spring Hill and discover if there were more ways that spending time with her made him a better man. But he had to remain committed to the children who needed him. If a fellow orphan like him didn't make the street children a priority, who else would?

The weight of the situation settled heavy between them for the rest of the walk to Cecilia's house. As they turned the corner by the café, he hesitated, feeling as if there were things they both wanted to say but neither could. Finally he looked at her, wishing her eyes weren't so beautiful and her skin so perfect. Wishing his arms didn't ache to wrap around her.

Clearing his throat, Simon glanced away before he did something he would regret. "It looks like we have one visit left in town and then another trip out to see Patrick."

Her voice was soft and low. "Tomorrow night, then?"

He nodded. Before he could say more of what weighed on his heart, she walked to the door, glancing back at him over her shoulder. "Have a good night, Simon."

"You, too, Cecilia. And thank you. For all the time you're giving to help me."

Responding with a long look, she went into the house, leaving him wondering what had made the situation feel so intense. Had he finally fulfilled Jake's prediction and hurt her? Or had his careless words earlier reminded her of the reality of their situation?

The night was restless for Simon. His sleep was filled with dreams that he couldn't quite remember in the morning. He was agitated during breakfast, anxious to do something more than paperwork that day. Maybe he would take a walk around town. He could talk to a few people to see if there was any more information about the robberies or if anyone had seen

Patrick sneaking around. It was high time he got to
the bottom of what was going on at Hartley's farm.

Energized by his renewed sense of purpose, Simon
marched right to the mercantile. Dozens of people
walked in and out of there during the day, making
it the perfect hub for gossip. Stepping into the warm
interior, Simon took a quick glance around. In one
front corner, several ladies were chatting over a table
as they examined bolts of fabric. On the other side,
a long counter ran the length of the room, display-
ing small wares and holding the paper and boxes Mr.
and Mrs. Collins used to wrap purchases. The rest of
the room was filled with shelves, crates and barrels.

Simon decided to start with the most obvious
place: the store owners. He was pleased to see no
one was waiting at the counter. He didn't want to in-
terrupt their business in his quest for news. Leaning
against the solid wood, he waited. He spent a moment
trying to determine the source of the delicious scent
that surrounded him. Tea leaves? Or a whiff of cin-
namon clinging to the containers by the counter? Finally, Mr. Collins walked out from behind a display
across the store and noticed him.

Extending his hand to shake Simon's, the store
owner greeted him with enthusiasm. "Mr. McKay,
wonderful to have you stop by. I trust all is going
well with those children you brought us?"

"Yes, they're adjusting nicely. For the most part,
they have wonderful families. I'm still making visits and determining the success of the trip, of course.

But in general, I'd say the placements in Spring Hill will last."

Mr. Collins rested both hands on his side of the counter. "I heard an interesting bit of information about you the other day. Lily Holbrook said that you used to be a teacher in New York."

Surprised, Simon wondered why that had caught the man's interest. "That's correct. I taught for several years before moving on to work with the Children's Aid Society full time."

Rubbing his chin with one hand, Mr. Collins leaned a little closer on his other elbow. "Now, this isn't something that the whole town knows, but our school board has been looking for a male teacher since our previous one took ill and died. Miss Holbrook was his sister-in-law and took over temporarily, you know."

The man's conspiratorial tone put Simon on his guard. Cecilia had mentioned that Mr. Collins was angling to get a male teacher for the school in her place. But why was he bringing it up to Simon now?

"Yes, I'm aware of the circumstances."

Mr. Collins chuckled in a way that made Simon want to punch him. "I'm sure you are, young man. It's all over town how much time you've been spending with her. But my question for you pertains to whether or not you would be interested in staying here instead of returning to New York. And if you'd also be interested in teaching our fine young scholars. With the school board's full support, of course."

For a moment Simon was stunned at the man's

audacity. After insinuating that Simon had a close relationship with Cecilia, he would still offer Simon the chance to take her job right out from under her? It was beyond unbelievable.

But even as Simon opened his mouth to give this man a piece of his mind, he realized that he had an opportunity here to help Cecilia before he left town. Clamping his lips shut, he thought it through for a moment. If he told Mr. Collins that he would consider the position, it would delay the school board's search for another candidate. That would buy Cecilia more time to prove herself and change the board members' minds.

Clearing his throat, Simon tried to look sincere. "I'm honored by the offer, Mr. Collins. If you don't mind, I'd like to take some time to think about it. Moving clear out here from New York is a big decision."

The other man clapped him on the shoulder with a grin. "Of course, of course. Take your time. Now, what brings you in this morning?"

In his surprise, Simon had nearly forgotten his purpose for stopping at the mercantile. "Right. I'm keeping tabs on all the orphans while I'm here, to make sure they're adjusting well. But I haven't seen much from one boy, Patrick. He lives with Mr. Hartley. I believe you know him?"

"Yes, I know him. He comes in now and then for supplies. As many people do, you know."

Simon could almost see the store owner's vest buttons popping, his pride was so obvious. Well, that was something he could use to his advantage. "With good reason. You run a fine establishment. I'm wondering if you've seen Mr. Hartley or Patrick in the last few days. Maybe you have a general sense of how they might be getting along?"

Pursing his lips, Mr. Collins thought for a moment. "I don't believe I've seen them for some time, come to think of it. Let me ask my wife if they've been in."

He disappeared into the back of the store. Simon turned to look around again. His eyes were sweeping over shelves holding various sizes of shoes when movement outside a window in the back drew his attention. The top of a small head was slowly creeping into view. Simon averted his gaze before the face appeared in the glass so the child wouldn't know anyone had noticed. He was sure that head belonged to Patrick. He had to get out there before the boy disappeared.

Thankfully, Mr. Collins returned at that very moment. "My wife hasn't seen them lately, either. I'm sorry we can't be of more help."

Distracted now, Simon turned toward the door before he even finished speaking. "That's fine, Mr. Collins. Thanks for trying."

He went the long way around the building, hoping to take the peeper by surprise. Sneaking up to the corner near the window, he paused, held his breath and slowly turned his head around the edge. Ah, there he was. Patrick was still crouched under the window, fingers gripping the outside trim as he peeked in. He hadn't noticed Simon at all.

In one smooth movement Simon stepped around the corner and grabbed the back of Patrick's shabby coat before the boy could run. "Hello, there, Patrick."

A small gasp escaped the boy's lips. "Mr. McKay, sir. I, uh, I was just looking at the store. Sir." Guilt was written on every inch of the dirt-smudged face.

"There's no harm in that unless you intend to do something to be guilty about."

He released Patrick, who squared his shoulders, straightened his coat and met Simon's gaze defiantly. "No, sir. No guilt here. I like looking at all the things in the store, but they don't want us orphans loitering about inside."

Resting his hand on Patrick's shoulder, Simon tried to let his expression convey his willingness to listen. "I know all about that. Too many times, I did the same thing. I'm sorry they aren't being as kind as they should be."

The boy shrugged off his touch and Simon's heart ached for all Patrick had experienced and the fact that it might not get better, even if he found a good home. "I guess I'll be on my way, sir. Mr. Hartley'll be looking for me soon."

Simon couldn't waste this opportunity to help get Patrick back on the right path. "One more thing, Patrick. I'd love to see you tomorrow at the rehearsal for the recital Miss Holbrook's putting together. I'm sure you'd enjoy spending time with the other children again."

Patrick shuffled his feet in the dirt. "I'll think about it, I guess."

The words no sooner left Patrick's mouth than they heard a gruff voice bark his name and both turned. There was Mr. Hartley himself, hobbling across the dirt toward them. "McKay, you bothering my boy again?"

Trying to maintain his composure, Simon raised both hands, palms up. "I'm not bothering anyone. I saw him on my way by and stopped to ask how you're both doing. I'm sure you're busy, so I won't keep you."

Mr. Hartley's eyes narrowed as he gripped Patrick's shoulder with a gnarled hand and pulled him closer. "You're right about that. I'll thank you not to be nosing around us anymore."

The old farmer dragged Patrick to the front of the building before Simon could react. It took him a few minutes of silent prayer before he felt calm enough to walk away. He didn't care what danger there was to his heart, he would not leave this town until he knew Patrick was safe.

The air was thick with excitement in the schoolhouse all morning and the children were rowdy, anticipating their first rehearsal for the recital that afternoon. Cecilia had to admit, she was eager, too. Especially with the hope that Patrick would be there.

Around midafternoon, Cat slipped into the room and stood at the back until Cecilia had finished the lesson she was working on with the older children. She could only grin at the shouts of excitement when she told the class it was time to go outside to learn about their exciting venture.

Chatter filled the air as they filed out of the school one at a time. Cecilia stood by Cat at the door, wishing she could shout and run like the children did once they reached the outdoors. "Are you ready for this? They're so enthusiastic, I'm sure they'll be far more energetic than usual. Corralling them is going to be a challenge."

Cat straightened her shoulders with a grin. "I'm more than ready to keep up with them. Let's go out there and get this started."

Cecilia sat on the schoolhouse steps and watched as Cat gathered the children around. With almost palpable excitement, Cat explained to the children that they were going to put together a program of musical acts and recitations, all chosen and performed by the students. The community would come together to organize details like food for the guests and decorations. It would be a town-wide endeavor.

In spite of the exclamations of joy and eager chatter surrounding her, Cecilia's heart ached when she realized Patrick wasn't there, after all. Of their own accord, her eyes kept sweeping the edges of the grassy area next to the school. She was so wrapped up in examining the tree line for any sign of a small boy sneaking in that she didn't hear the approaching footsteps from her other side.

"Looks like rehearsal is under way. Is there room for one more?"

Turning, her heart jumped when she saw Simon standing by the steps with Patrick at his side. Unable to resist, she rushed to give the boy a quick hug. "Patrick, I'm so glad you came. Run on out there and Cat will catch you up on what they're doing."

Lightness filled her chest as she followed Patrick's progress across the field. Simon spoke quietly from her side. "I ran into him on the way over here. He said you had something to do with getting Hartley to let him come."

Trying not to draw his suspicion about how the conversation had taken place, she searched for an honest response that would satisfy him. "I happened to run into Mr. Hartley and asked him to consider sending Patrick. I hardly dared to hope that he actually would, though."

They fell into silence. The children's laughter and banter filled the air as they discussed their performances, bringing a smile to Cecilia's face. It was wonderful to see the orphans bonding with the other children, working together toward a common goal. And to think that Patrick was able to join in that wonderful connection, after all.

Simon rocked back and forth on his feet, pulling her attention away from the children. "I'm glad to see this is going so well. And a little ashamed that I doubted Cat when she assured me it would. She was right."

Clenching her jaw, Cecilia did her best to let the comment pass without getting upset. Why did everything with him have to come back to Cat? "Yes, it's good for the children to have this opportunity."

Without warning, Simon reached out and lightly gripped her upper arms, turning her toward him. She looked up to find his expression serious, eyes intense. "Cecilia, I hope you understand that I'm only here to see that the children are happy and safe. All my actions are to ensure that they have the best chance for a good life here."

What had caused that sudden outburst? It felt as if he'd read her thoughts, like he could sense her fears that he was interested in her sister and not at all in her. "Of course, Simon. I wouldn't think otherwise. You've mentioned more than once that you'll be leaving as soon as you see that they're settled."

"Yes. Well, I'm glad we understand each other." His tense posture relaxed and she was dumbfounded when a huge, genuine smile broke out on his face.

Her heart felt tattered and sore, but he was happy? The realization hit her with an almost physical blow. She had opened her heart to him more than she thought. Even when her mind had reminded her over and over to protect herself, she'd let emotions get involved. But he was still committed to leaving and now his absence was going to be terribly painful.

Loud voices across the field drew their attention, pulling Cecilia back from the brink of tears. They looked over to see Cat struggling to pull Charles away before Patrick's raised fist connected in a blow. Cecilia followed Simon at a run across the yard to where the children had clumped around, all shouting and jostling to see.

Pushing through them, Simon stood in front of the two boys, arms crossed and eyes blazing. "What's going on here? I thought you were friends, but now you're fighting?"

Charles yanked his arm from Cat's grasp and brushed at the dirt on his pants. "He started it. Ask him."

Turning to Patrick, they all waited for him to speak. His eyes remained trained on a hill of dirt at his feet as he muttered, "I didn't do anything to him."

Cecilia's heart ached for the boys, who had been friends but now had a wedge driven between them. She looked up and caught sight of her sister, standing behind Charles with one firm hand on his shoulder. Was Cecilia doing the same thing, letting Simon come between her and her sister? She'd had more spiteful thoughts about Cat recently than kind ones.

Charles grumbled under his breath but Simon wasn't going to let the matter rest. "Charles, tell me what happened, please."

Eyes blazing and red staining his cheeks, the boy nearly shouted his answer. "He said my pa was a no-good vagabond. It ain't true. Pa was a good man. He had to leave Ma and us kids to find work."

Without thinking, Cecilia turned to Patrick. "Why would you say such a hurtful thing to your friend? You need to apologize."

She realized her mistake when Patrick's face hardened. "I don't have to do what you say. Coming here was a bad idea, anyway."

Before anyone could stop him, Patrick turned and ran. Cecilia took a step to follow him but Simon's warm hand gripping hers stopped her short. "Don't.

He needs to calm down. Following him now will only upset him more."

Emotions welling, Cecilia faced him as Cat led the rest of the children back to their work. "Simon, this recital might be the only chance we have to make sure he's all right with Mr. Hartley. We need to do anything we can to keep him involved."

Shaking his head, Simon stood rooted between her and the direction Patrick had fled. "I've seen this before when a child falls in with someone who's a bad influence. Pushing too hard will make him afraid and he'll run even farther. For now, let him go. He'll come back."

His advice went against every one of her instincts. She taught children every day. Surely her experience gave her insight into what they needed, the same as his. But Simon's gaze held hers, pleading with her to do it his way. She sighed. "Fine. But if he comes back, I'm doing everything possible to keep him here."

Relaxing, Simon led the way back to the steps, where he sat next to her. Far closer than she wished. Her heart kept doing funny little flips in her chest and it was all his fault. Keeping her gaze trained on the children and Cat as they returned to their work, she rested one elbow on her knee and leaned forward.

Simon shifted next to her, the movement bringing him incrementally closer. She licked her lips, which felt too dry. Honestly, she was acting like a silly girl instead of an independent woman in a respected position. But she couldn't help imagining that the brush of his arm against hers was intentional. Or that he leaned a tiny bit closer to her when he chuckled at one of the children's antics.

Suddenly it was all too much. Cecilia jumped up, not sure what to say when Simon looked at her in surprise. He had made his intentions known in no uncertain terms. For the sake of her heart, she had to put some space between them, both physical and emotional. In a strangled voice, she managed to croak out, "I need to go. I have…something to do." And, with as much dignity as she could muster, she retreated.

Unsure what had happened, Simon watched Cecilia rush away. He was tempted to go after her, but what good would that do? He couldn't let himself get more tangled up in her affairs or leaving in a few weeks would be that much harder.

But her panicked expression lodged in his mind, refusing to leave. He stared out at the children, who were now running around the field with Cat. He should stop by the Holbrook ladies' house later. He and Cecilia still needed to make another trip out to see Patrick and Mr. Hartley again. Simon could confirm their plans for that visit and see if she was all right without making it seem like he was checking up on her. Yes, that might be his best option.

The children started leaving the schoolyard in groups of two or three. Simon's heart softened when he saw Charles walking alone, scuffing his feet in the dirt, his head hanging low. Pushing up from the step, Simon hurried to catch up to the boy.

"I'm sorry about what Patrick said to you earlier."

Charles shrugged, head drooping even lower. Simon tried again. "Listen, I know how hard it is to see your friend going down a bad path. If you want to talk, I'm always here for you."

The boy's dark head shot up, his eyes red-rimmed. "That's not true. You're leaving soon. Leaving us here to fend for ourselves."

Taken aback, Simon blinked. "Yes, I have to leave eventually. But I'll stay as long as it takes to make sure you're all happy here. I want to help you."

"Then don't go. Stay here with us. I need you. Patrick needs you. We all do."

Moving to the side of the boardwalk, Simon grasped the boy's shoulder, pulling him around so they were face-to-face. "You have a good family now. You can rely on them. I need to go back to New York to help other children who don't have anyone. I know you understand that."

He shrugged again. Simon's eyes slid shut as pain sliced through him. He'd had no idea that the children felt abandoned when he left. Once again, he had to make a choice that would force him to let down someone who needed him. "I'm so sorry you feel that I'm deserting all of you, Charles. But that's part of my job. Please believe that I won't leave until I know you're all safe."

Pulling away, Charles glared at him. "Like you're making sure Patrick's safe? That old man isn't a good person. But you left Patrick alone out there with him, anyway. Doesn't seem like you're as worried about us as you say."

Simon stepped back as the pain in his chest intensified. Charles took off running, but Simon couldn't go after him. Because what could he say? It was true. He'd left Patrick with Hartley for weeks, knowing in his gut that something was going on. How could any of the children trust him when they saw what was happening with Patrick?

His resolve hardened. He had to get back out to that farm and find out what was going on with Patrick right away. It couldn't wait any longer.

He stopped at the hotel long enough to eat a quick supper before heading to the house tucked behind Lily's Café.

Tapping a firm knock on the door, Simon rocked on his toes while he waited for an answer. His mind was moving so fast, he was startled when the door opened. Cecilia's expression tightened when she caught sight of him and Simon's heart sank. Whatever had upset her earlier, she was clearly not feeling better.

But he wanted her with him when he went back to Hartley's farm. Yes, he was expected to have another adult with him for the visits. But more than that, he found that he needed her by his side for personal reasons.

"Cecilia, can you drive out to visit Patrick with me tonight?"

Her eyes narrowed. "What's the urgency? If Patrick returns to rehearsals, we'll be able to keep an eye on him and we can wait for the right time to go visit."

The shuttered look on her face exasperated Simon.

Was she closing herself off from him on purpose? He never knew if she was going to be friendly or not. And he could use a friend at the moment. "It's urgent because I say it is. I'm responsible for these children and I have to take that seriously. If you don't, maybe you're not the right person to help me, after all." Simon regretted the words as soon as they left his lips.

Cecilia drew her spine straighter, chin jutting out at him. "Well. I think perhaps you're right. I hope the rest of your visits go well." And she shut the door in his face.

He stood frozen for a moment, stunned. But it didn't take long for angry heat to course through him again and spur him into motion. Turning, he stomped away from the house and around the corner of the café. Then he paused. He spun around and looked at the door Cecilia had slammed. His attitude had been heavy-handed and an apology was reasonable. He couldn't blame her for being upset with the way he'd acted.

He shook his head and took a few steps down the boardwalk in front of the café. If she'd taken him at his word and agreed to go along, he wouldn't have had a reason to respond with frustration. She knew he needed her.

He got three steps before pausing again. As much as he wanted to, the burning of his conscience wasn't going to let him walk away. It might be easier to finish his work and leave town if she was mad at him, but that wouldn't be fair to her. She deserved to be treated better. Retracing his steps, Simon took a deep breath and knocked on the door again.

She yanked it open before he'd finished knocking, as if she'd been standing right there waiting for him. Swallowing hard around the lump of pride in his throat, Simon forced himself to speak with humility.

"I'm sorry for how I acted. I spoke with Charles a bit ago. He's upset because to him it looks like I'm letting Patrick down by leaving him with Mr. Hartley. I can't stand that the children would think that of me."

Her expression softened. "Oh, Simon. I'm sorry you have to shoulder that burden. As they mature, the children will understand why you've had to give Patrick and Mr. Hartley time."

He searched her face, wondering why her eyes made him feel as if his very soul was exposed. The thought caused him to look away. The last thing he needed was to feel a stronger connection to Cecilia.

"Maybe you're right. Even so, I would like to visit them as soon as possible. And I hope you'll still go with me."

"Of course, I will. But you told me earlier that he needed time after the incident with Charles. We should stick to the plan and visit him on Friday. We can go see Edwin and his family tomorrow night."

Her words made sense. As much as Simon wanted to hurry right out there and rescue Patrick, the emotional exchange earlier might cause him to run again if they attempted anything now. Reluctantly he nodded. "I suppose you're right. We'll wait. I'll come get you tomorrow evening and we'll walk to the Meyers' house to see how Edwin is getting along."

The sun was hanging low in the sky and long shadows were falling all around them. But Simon found himself staring at Cecilia's expressive face. How could she believe her sister was more beautiful than her? She'd said it several times and it always shocked him. Her loveliness was perfect. But more than that, she had a kind, caring heart that made her stand above all the women he'd known, including her sister.

Time stretched between them, but Simon couldn't pull his eyes away from her. He wondered if his longing for marriage was really so far-fetched. She'd made it sound like she didn't want to leave Spring Hill, but had he ever asked her? Was the answer to his heart's dilemma as easy as one question?

Leaning against the door frame, hoping his voice wouldn't give away the quaking in his stomach, he said, "Cecilia, you have a wonderful way with the children. I know you don't love teaching. Have you considered working with the Children's Aid Society? You could do so much good for the orphans."

Several long moments passed as she stared toward the horizon. Then she blinked several times and shook her head. "Oh, no. I—"

Her response was cut short by a commotion on the street. Exchanging a glance, they rushed toward the front of the café to see what was happening. A crowd was gathered around the tailor's shop across the street. Simon leaned in to listen as a man nearby took advantage of the crowd to rave about what he'd seen. "It was another break-in. I was walking past and saw the whole thing. The sheriff snuck in that side door to catch the thief. Rumor has it it's the same fellow that's behind all those other robberies."

Simon's heart thumped wildly in his chest as the crowd parted and the sheriff appeared. He nearly sagged back against the wall when he saw the tall, broad figure of a young man being pulled along behind the sheriff. Not Patrick. Not even Mr. Hartley. His orphans were safe.

The crowd cleared as the sheriff walked his prisoner down the street. Cecilia turned and walked back to her house, so Simon followed. Pausing in the open doorway, she looked past him toward the tailor's shop. "None of the orphans are to blame for the thefts, then. What a relief."

"Yes, it is." Simon heard himself say the words but he wasn't sure he felt them. There was still a knot of worry for Patrick lodged in his stomach. Something was going on with him and Hartley. Simon just couldn't figure out what.

Looking at Cecilia, Simon thought that she didn't seem too relieved, either, in spite of her comment. He ran one hand over his face, hoping the tangle of emotions tightening his chest didn't show in his eyes. "Well, I guess I'll see you tomorrow."

She responded with a brief quirk of her lips, eyes focused on the ground at her feet. "Yes, tomorrow."

He could only nod as he stepped back out of the doorway. He watched as she slowly closed the door. The weight of the emotional day settled on Simon's heart as he walked back to the hotel. Never in his life had he felt so many contradicting things at the same time. Something kept drawing him to Cecilia and Spring Hill, but his heart refused to give up on the orphans who needed him. He'd hoped she would jump at the chance to help on the orphan train, but her eyes had shuttered and she'd clearly been ready to say no when he'd asked. No matter how much he tried, there didn't seem to be a way for him to have both the things he so longed for.

Chapter Nine

Cecilia didn't realize she was pacing until Cat laughed at her. After another long day at school, it was a relief to eat supper and clean up early. Now she was waiting for Simon to come so they could visit little Edwin and the Meyer family. But she refused to think about why that caused her to mindlessly wander the room.

"Why don't you sit down, already?" Cat had paper and a pencil and was sketching a dress she had seen and wanted to copy. Which meant that it wouldn't be long before she asked Cecilia to do the more intricate stitching that Cat didn't have the patience for. As if Cecilia didn't have enough to manage.

She shook her head in response to Cat's distracted command. "I'm not in the mood to sit and read or draw or sew. It seems that's all life is anymore, sitting down and doing what people expect."

Her sister's head shot up. "You're not happy doing what everyone expects? I thought you liked your life as it is."

Cecilia heaved a sigh as she peeked through the front curtain again. "You think I like teaching because it's the only thing I can do? Or having the Ladies' Aid Society fill my free time with endless work and meetings? No, I have to say that I'm not all that pleased with doing what other people want all the time."

She heard Cat drop her sketch on the table by her chair and join her at the window. "Then why do you do all those things? Why don't you find something that makes you happy?"

Facing her sister, Cecilia was horrified to find tears welling in her eyes. "And what might that be? I'm not sure there's anything in this town that makes me happy." *Except for Simon.* Her heart echoed the words loud and clear. When they weren't fighting, she loved spending time with him, discovering all the little pieces that made him the intensely caring man he was. But he wasn't going to be in town much longer, while she would be stuck there forever.

Rocking on her toes, Cat touched Cecilia's arm. "You could travel. I would go with you. We could go anywhere we wanted, Cecilia."

The ache of longing tore through Cecilia's heart. "No, we couldn't. Two single women can't go traveling alone. Everyone says it isn't safe. And where would we get the funds, even if we could? It's terribly expensive. We have to face it, we're stuck here."

Even to her ears, the words sounded a bit harsh. But the conversation with Simon the day before had reawakened a desire she'd tried for years to extinguish. She wished there was a way she could travel, see new places, do something important. When Simon had asked if she would work with the Children's Aid Society, her heart had cried out to say yes. But there was no way that could happen in reality. A young, single woman traveling with a male placing agent? It would never be allowed.

No, her only chance at supporting herself was to keep her job teaching in Spring Hill for as long as possible. Even if she hated being confined in the stuffy schoolhouse doing what everyone expected of her. She would just have to find a way to stuff that longing far back into a corner of her heart again after Simon left. When she was old, her dreams of adventure, of doing something to help others, or even of falling in love, would remain cherished memories. But that's all they would ever be: dreams and memories.

Simon's knock sounded at the door, cutting off any further discussion. Cecilia arranged her ribbon-trimmed bonnet over her hair and glanced at her sister. Cat had settled back in the chair with her paper but wasn't drawing. Cecilia felt bad for dashing Cat's hopes, but they had to be realistic. Unmarried women couldn't just do things like that.

At the door, Simon offered his arm. It was warmer that evening than the last few days had been, lovely weather for a walk. If she hadn't been so aware of guarding her heart, she might have thought the moment romantic. But she forced that wish away. Romance and Simon could not go together. Not for her, anyway.

It wasn't far to the Meyers' home, but the walk felt interminable to Cecilia. Simon asked about Jake and Coralee, so Cecilia told him how they had ended up marrying and adopting the twins the year before. That led them to talk about Charles and a little of his life before the orphan train. The conversation would have been wonderful, if not for the cloud of sadness hanging over her. It wouldn't be long and these conversations with Simon would be a distant memory.

When they reached the door, Simon paused before knocking. "I hope you know how much I appreciate your help. And how sorry I am for my harsh words yesterday. I couldn't imagine this would go as well with anyone else accompanying me. To be honest, it never went this easily with any other agent I worked with."

Her defiant heart fluttered at his kind words. She watched several dry, brown leaves whip down the street on a gust of wind and felt as if she was being carried away with them. She'd lost all common sense. But when she looked back into Simon's eyes, his comments rattling around in her mind, she could imagine looking into those eyes every day. She could feel what it would be like to have him by her side as they built a life together.

She had never been more thankful than when he turned and rapped his knuckles on the door. Pressure rose inside her as they waited for an answer.

After what felt like an eternity, the door creaked

open and ten-year-old Ann Meyer peeked out. Catching sight of Cecilia, she pushed the door open further. "Miss Holbrook, I'm so excited you're here. Mama and Papa said you'd come soon." Still holding the door with one hand, she turned and yelled into the house, "Mama! Miss Holbrook and Mr. McKay are here."

It was all Cecilia could do to hold back her laughter when they heard the faint reply from inside. "Don't make them wait, girl. Bring them in."

Ann stood back to let them through the door, Cecilia going first, then Simon. Closing it behind them, the girl kept up a steady commentary as she led them down a long hall to the living area in the back of the house. Ann's sister, Ida, and little Edwin were playing a loud game together in front of the fire while Mr. Meyer read a newspaper nearby.

Mrs. Meyer wiped her hands on her apron as she approached from the cookstove in the corner. "Well, it's a pleasure to finally see you both. Welcome to our home." She turned to her husband and raised her voice over the chaos. "Albert, won't you come greet our guests?"

With a start, Mr. Meyer looked up, clearly unaware guests had even entered the room. He folded the paper and jumped from his seat. "Hello, nice to see you. Sorry I didn't notice when you came in."

Mrs. Meyer quirked an eyebrow with a smirk. "He's very good at tuning out all the children's noise. Too good, I'd say."

Cecilia didn't know whether to laugh or nod. Glancing at Simon out of the corner of her eye, she noted that he looked just as uncertain. A giggle welled up in her throat and almost burst out, but Simon got right to business. "We won't keep you folks long. We'll need to talk for a little bit, to see how you all feel about the placement."

At Mrs. Meyer's direction, they took seats near the fireplace. Ida and Edwin stopped playing to join Ann in chatting about everything they could think of, talking over each other most of the time. Cecilia spent all day with these children in school, but they were always much quieter there. She had no idea they could be so talkative.

They managed to get several questions in edgewise to find out how the family members were adjusting to each other. But they hardly needed to ask. It was obvious that Edwin was perfect for this family and that they were all quite happy with the arrangement.

Once they said goodbye to the family and stepped back out onto the boardwalk, Cecilia paused, savoring the quiet outside the house. She turned and found Simon watching her, eyes wide. They both burst into laughter. Between giggles, Cecilia gasped, "I've never heard so much noise out of three children in my life."

Simon rested his hand on her back and steered her across the street, still laughing. "Neither have I. All that time with Edwin on the trains and I couldn't have imagined he would have so much to say."

Cecilia sobered as she thought back on the visit. "But he's so happy, Simon. God brought him here just for the Meyer family, I'm sure of it."

Stopping in the middle of the boardwalk, Simon

looked up into the clear, sunset-streaked sky. "Sometimes it's hard for me to believe that God can bring good out of anything. I've seen so many terrible situations. Children who are abused or neglected by their own parents. How can anything good come from that?"

Watching his profile as he stared into the evening sky, Cecilia searched for something to say that would soothe the pain she heard in his voice. But some wounds couldn't be healed with mere words. So she simply leaned closer to his side.

Simon looked over at her and she could almost see the wheels turning in his mind. "Earlier, I told you how important it is to me that I'm always there when the children need someone. But there's more to it than that. I'd like to tell you about it."

The conversation stalled while an older couple passed on the boardwalk behind them. Once they were out of earshot, Simon looked back up at the bright stars. "You know I was orphaned at a young age. But I had a close friend, Michael, who was always by my side on the streets. When we were around ten, he was taken in by a couple. They were cruel and only wanted him for free labor."

As if reliving the events of his childhood made him restless, Simon started walking again. Cecilia slid her arm through his and kept pace beside him. "Did something happen to him?"

Simon's head drooped for a moment then he looked at her with pain-filled eyes. "Those people forced him to do all their work and anything else they wanted.

Eventually, it got so bad that they wouldn't let him eat if he didn't act like they expected."

Voice cracking, Simon rubbed one hand over his face. His next words were slow and quiet, forcing her to lean in closer to hear. "He ran away one night but fainted from hunger before he reached shelter. He didn't survive the frigid night out on the street."

With her heart breaking, Cecilia wished there was some way she could ease his pain. But it was too deep, too raw, even after so many years. "Oh, Simon. I'm so sorry."

Pulling his arm away from hers, Simon stopped to lean against a post, looking like his body was worn out from telling the tale. "I knew how bad it was. The few times he was able to sneak away, Michael told me how they were treating him. I tried to tell workers at the children's home, but they didn't believe me."

When he turned back to her, his eyes were intense. "I could have saved him if I'd tried harder to get them to help. I could have done more. But I didn't. I never thought it would get that bad, so I didn't try harder. After he died, I promised myself and God that I would never let down an orphan in need of help. I devoted my life to them, right there at ten years old."

"It's terrible that you had to experience that, but it wasn't your fault he died."

Her words didn't seem to penetrate the haze of pain surrounding him. "I can't let that happen to another child, Cecilia. I can't sit by watching and later realize there was more I could have done. I have to make sure Patrick is all right."

Nothing she said was going to make him feel better. Cecilia's mind formed a silent prayer for Simon to find peace in his past as she moved closer to him. "And we will. We'll go tomorrow night and visit the farm. Maybe by now they've had time to adjust and things will be much better than before."

Simon wished he could have the same certainty that Cecilia had. She was so confident that all the placements would work out, even Patrick's. But Simon had seen too many bad outcomes to have that much hope. Patrick would need to be rescued. Simon just had to be sure he was there when the time came.

After walking Cecilia home, Simon took a longer route back to the hotel, reluctant to go inside when the evening was so warm and clear. He found himself wandering past the schoolhouse and paused, looking out at the field where the children had met for their rehearsal. Patrick's sudden change in attitude from a sweet, kind boy to the angry child he'd seen two days ago wasn't the only reason Simon was concerned. His gut told him something was wrong and he had learned to listen to that instinct.

Wandering back through town, Simon noticed a group of older boys gathered by the mercantile, none of whom he had met. Except for the familiar small figure in the middle. Patrick. Sliding around the corner of the building, Simon strained to hear what they were saying.

One boy's deep voice grew louder. "My pa said you

orphans are no good. Now you're sneaking around in the dark? Looks suspicious to me."

Another voice chimed in. "Yeah, what're you doing out here, anyway, orphan?"

Simon winced at the cruel tone. Growing up, he had mostly kept company with other street children. But on occasion he had experienced the sting of judgment from those who were considered more respectable. The voices were getting louder and angrier, and Simon knew he needed to step in before the situation deteriorated into a fight.

Stepping out onto the boardwalk, he approached the group as one boy, who looked far old enough to know better, shoved Patrick with both hands. The orphan sprawled on the ground with a grunt and several of the others laughed. Simon barely restrained his anger in time to keep from responding in kind. "Excuse me, boys. Is something wrong?"

Patrick caught sight of Simon and his head drooped. Aiming a scowl at the other boys, Simon planted his feet and crossed his arms. "Well, is anyone going to answer? What's going on here?"

The largest boy mimicked Simon's stance, a rebellious look on his face. "Nothin' going on here. Just a few friends havin' fun."

Simon shook his head. "I doubt that. Why don't you all head on home."

For a moment he thought several of the boys would refuse. But, one by one, they filed past him and headed in different directions. Simon waited and watched until Patrick was the only one left, still sitting in the dirt, picking at his threadbare pants.

Crouching next to the boy, Simon took in the dark circles under his eyes and his stringy hair. No one was taking care of this child. Simon's chest burned with frustration. "Patrick, what happened with those boys?"

Patrick leaned forward, resting his arms on his knees. "It's like they said. We were having a little fun. It was all a joke."

Standing, Simon paced the patch of dirt. "I saw that boy push you. I heard them talking. That didn't seem like friendly teasing."

Rising and brushing uselessly at the dirt on his pants, Patrick shrugged. "Well, it was."

Simon tried again. "What are you doing in town this late? Is Mr. Hartley around?"

The boy refused to meet his gaze. "He's around somewhere, I guess. He likes to spend some time at the saloon in the evenings."

"And he leaves you alone when he does?"

Patrick shrugged again. "Sure. He says I'm old enough to handle myself. He's taught me some tricks for handling bullies like those fellows."

He started to walk away but Simon grabbed his arm. "Patrick, please. Let me help you."

The boy's eyes flared with anger. "Help me? Mr. Hartley's helping me. I don't need your help anymore."

He wrenched his arm out of Simon's grip and ran off, leaving Simon standing in the dirt with his heart at his feet. Patrick didn't need him anymore? What did that mean? And how exactly was Hartley helping him? More than ever, he was glad Patrick was next on the list to visit.

Tension wound Simon tighter and tighter as the hours passed the next day. He tried to finish his report on the visit to Edwin's home the night before, but he found himself staring at nothing for longer than he spent writing. He tried to take a walk around town to clear his head, but he couldn't stop peeking into every nook and cranny, vaguely hoping to run into Patrick again. Finally he forced himself to eat a few bites of supper at the hotel before renting a horse and carriage from the livery and heading to the Holbrook home.

Cecilia was coming out when Simon arrived. He jumped down and went to greet her, a little uncertain how to act after the way he'd revealed his childhood secrets to her the night before. But the gentle, sincere smile she sent his way melted the tension right out of him.

They didn't say much as Simon helped her into the carriage and went to his own seat. Urging the horse into motion, he trained his eyes on the swaying prairie grass, wishing he didn't have to tell her about his run-in with Patrick. But she should know. He took a deep breath before speaking up.

"I saw Patrick last night."

Cecilia sat close enough on the narrow seat that he felt her tense at his words. "Where? What was he doing?"

Shaking his head, Simon sighed. "I'm not sure what he was doing. He was with a group of older boys by the mercantile. They were teasing him and would have started a fight if I hadn't stepped in."

Her hand flew to her lips. "Oh, poor Patrick. Wasn't Mr. Hartley there to help him?"

"No. Patrick said Hartley likes to spend time at the saloon in the evenings, leaving him free to wander the town."

He glanced at Cecilia, unable to keep from noticing how lovely her profile was, even with sorrow written on her features. Her eyes focused on some far-off spot and her voice was soft. "I feel terrible about the situation he's in. Jane and Charles are distraught about the fight the other day. I hope we'll get some answers tonight. We all need them."

Nodding, Simon let silence fall. He wanted to turn to look at her again, to examine her soft skin and the perfect line of her nose. He couldn't seem to keep his thoughts focused on the coming visit like he needed to. It would be a relief to get done with their work together. He couldn't afford to be distracted by her for much longer.

But, as it turned out, it didn't matter that he couldn't get his thoughts in order. They pulled into the dusty yard at Hartley's farm to find the place still and quiet. Heart sinking, Simon waited and waited at the door, knocking several times. But there was no answer. Turning to Cecilia, he shook his head. "Looks like we won't get any answers tonight, after all."

She tiptoed to the windows at the side and back

of the cabin and tried to peek in, but she returned looking disappointed. "No, I guess they're not here."

They walked back to the carriage. As he was helping her onto the seat, her face lit up. "Simon, you said that Patrick told you Mr. Hartley spends his evenings at the saloon. They're probably in town now. Let's go see if we can find them."

Standing below her, Simon looked up into her glowing eyes. "I don't think that's a good idea. Hartley's not pleasant to begin with. I don't want to see how he'd treat you with alcohol in him."

But she wasn't going to let the idea go. "Then we can look for Patrick. If we can approach him without any demands, he might talk to us. You have to admit, most of the times we've tried, emotions have been high."

He wanted to say no. It didn't seem like a good idea at all. But she was so earnest, so pleased with her plan. He couldn't find it in himself to disagree again. Climbing up into the carriage, he turned the horse toward town. "All right, we'll go hunt for Patrick."

They decided the task would be better accomplished on foot, so Simon drove to the stable and returned the horse and carriage. Then he offered his arm to Cecilia and they started down the street. But deep down, he hoped the search would be fruitless. He didn't feel good about walking into this without knowing what they would find.

The evening was much cooler than the previous night had been. Simon felt Cecilia shiver and leaned closer to help her stay warm. At least, that's what he told himself. But walking so near her was even more distracting than watching her in the carriage. Adjusting the collar of his coat, he trained his eyes on the shadows between buildings, places where he knew, from experience, that a small boy could hide.

When she spoke, Cecilia's voice was quiet. "Simon, I'm glad you told me about your friend Michael last night."

He cringed when she said that name. No matter how much time passed, thinking of his dear friend always brought a wave of guilt that he couldn't control. "It's not something I like to talk about."

She rested one hand on his arm. "I can imagine you wouldn't. That's why it means so much that you chose to confide in me."

Simon's chest tightened. He wished now that he hadn't said anything about it. He didn't want to make her feel close to him, like they shared their deepest secrets. They shouldn't have that kind of relationship. But even as the thoughts crossed his mind, his heart thumped in disagreement. Why couldn't they? He rarely got the chance to develop friendships when he spent so much time traveling. But one sideways look at her reminded him why. She was beautiful and distracting. And when there were young lives at stake, he couldn't let anything distract him.

They had turned the corner near the ornate bank building when Cecilia gasped and grabbed his arm, pulling him to a stop. Simon glanced in the direction she was looking and then took a quick second look. Mr. Hartley and Patrick were walking along the boardwalk on the other side of the street, the farmer's hand on the boy's shoulder in a friendly gesture. They certainly looked as if they were getting along fine.

Simon and Cecilia hurried to cross the street in time to intercept them. "Well, Mr. Hartley, Patrick. We drove out to visit you and we were disappointed to miss you at home. But now here you are. How convenient."

Hartley's face reddened as he scowled, beady eyes darting to Cecilia even as he spoke to Simon. "What do you want, McKay?"

Planting himself in front of the man, Simon used himself and Cecilia to form a barrier across the board-walk. "It's time for us to assess how you and Patrick are adjusting to your placement. Let's find some-where to sit and talk for a bit and we'll get the questions out of the way."

Hartley looked like he wanted to protest, but, to Simon's surprise, he responded with a curt nod. Glancing around, Simon saw a bench in front of the darkened barber shop. He started in that direction with Cecilia at his side, praying the other two would follow. And that they would finally find out the truth behind Patrick's behavior.

Cecilia watched as Mr. Hartley heaved himself down on the bench. Patrick leaned against the wall next to him with his arms crossed. If there had been any other spot, she would have taken a seat, too. But Mr. Hartley's suggestive grin as he patted the bench beside him gave her every reason to remain standing by Simon.

Simon didn't hesitate to start questioning the pair. "Mr. Hartley, how do you think the placement is going for you and Patrick?"

The older man leaned back and rested his hands on his protruding stomach. "Oh, fine, fine." He looked over at Patrick. "Right, boy? We're happy as can be."

Without moving from his own casual pose, Patrick responded in a tone heavy with sarcasm. "Sure. It's a dream come true."

Simon's jaw tightened. "Patrick, I have to ask questions, for your own good. It would benefit you to take me seriously."

The boy shrugged and Mr. Hartley barked out a harsh laugh. "That would be easier if there was a good reason for you to ask so many questions. We're doing fine. What more do you need to know? Me and the boy make a great team."

The two shared a look and chuckled together in a way that made Cecilia's stomach churn. She had been hopeful that a sincere conversation with both Patrick and Mr. Hartley would calm the fears she and Simon had been dealing with. But instead something about their behavior made her more suspicious. If only she could root out what was going on under the surface.

Simon must have felt the same way. His next question was direct and forceful. "I'm sure you've heard about the string of thefts occurring in town since our arrival and the recent arrest. Patrick, were you involved? Did that man somehow convince you to be his accomplice?"

Cecilia wasn't sure if it was a trick of the falling darkness or if a hint of guilt flickered in Patrick's eyes. "Of course not. I don't need to take things from people. Mr. Hartley takes good care of me."

Simon's lips tightened and she was aware of his fist clenching near her side. "I hope that's true. Because I intend to stay in town until I'm sure nothing illicit is happening. I won't let it rest until I can guarantee each child I brought here is safe and happy. Including you, Patrick. I'll be watching both of you the whole time."

Turning and pressing one hand against her back, Simon propelled her along with him as he stomped away from the barber shop without another word.

She tried to slow down, to make him see reason before they lost their chance to talk with both Patrick and Mr. Hartley. "Simon, wait. Shouldn't we try to talk to them more? This might be our only opportunity."

Shaking his head, Simon lessened the pressure on her back but kept walking with long strides. "The way those two are acting, if I spend one more minute there, I'll end up punching that man. And losing my job."

Cecilia's heart clenched when she glanced back over her shoulder and saw Patrick and Mr. Hartley still lounging where she and Simon had left them. The boy's face was hard and tense. She was still certain there was more going on than they could see but, without proof, they couldn't help Patrick.

Sensing that Simon wasn't in the mood to chat, Cecilia trudged along next to him until his steps slowed and his stiff posture relaxed. "I'm sorry for rushing away like that. The look on Hartley's face almost did me in. Somehow, I think they were both involved with those thefts."

Threading her arm through his, Cecilia patted his hand. "How could they be involved when the sheriff already has the thief in the jail and there haven't been any more instances? It must be something else. We can only bide our time and keep a watchful eye on both of them. We know more of their usual activities now than we did a few days ago, so it should be easier to see what they're doing."

She was pleased when his tense face relaxed a little. "Maybe you're right. Whatever's going on with those two, I'll stay as long as it takes to get to the bottom of it."

The surge of hope that raced through her was immediately followed by disappointment. His words reminded her that he might stay in Spring Hill, but only as long as it suited his need to protect the orphans. It had nothing to do with her.

Stepping away from Simon to give herself a little space to think, Cecilia forced her head to remain high. He hadn't promised her anything. Just because her heart got carried away, that didn't mean reality would match her wishful thinking. She would get through his time in Spring Hill and when he left she would be able to focus on her job. Her heart sank a little further with the reminder of her other problem.

She could only focus on her teaching position if she still had it.

She felt Simon studying her and turned. His eyes searched her face. "What has you so deep in thought? Patrick?"

Fighting the tingling in her limbs that accompanied his steady gaze, she shook her head. "No, it's the problem with Mr. Collins and his insistence that the school board doesn't want me teaching."

His eyes darted away and he rubbed one hand over the back of his neck. "I see. Well, you never know. It could all work out on its own. You talked about God bringing Edwin here and placing him with the Meyers on purpose. I think God's placed you at the school for a reason, too."

To her horror, a rude snort escaped her before she could contain it. Simon's eyes widened and his mouth dropped open. She pulled at the neckline of her dress, which was irritating her skin all of a sudden. "I do apologize for that."

Simon actually laughed at her. Heat flushed Cecilia's cheeks and she wished she could disappear into the shadows of a building and be alone. Why were they still so far from home? Feeling like a petulant child, she found herself muttering a response in an arched tone Cat used on a regular basis. "I don't find it funny."

He sobered instantly. "I'm sorry, Cecilia. That was so out of character for you. You're usually so… proper."

She was tempted to snort again, just to show him

how wrong he was. "I'm not always proper. I can be spontaneous."

He shook his head. "That sounds more like Cat. I know you said teaching isn't your preference, but maybe you need to give it more of a chance. You're perfect for it. Involved in the community, caring with children, always responsible. Spring Hill couldn't ask for more from their teacher."

His words once again stirred up the longing she always tried so hard to snuff out. She didn't want to be responsible and well-behaved. At least, not all the time. Why couldn't she do something spontaneous, like Cat would? Why did the town's schoolteacher have to be so boring?

Coming to a stop in the middle of the boardwalk, Cecilia planted her hands on her hips. "Does the whole town see me that way? Boring and proper? Never measuring up to fun, carefree Cat?"

Simon's eyes widened and he stammered over his words. "No. I mean, well, yes. Not in Cat's shadow. But you have a reputation of always acting appropriately. That's a good thing. Right?"

It all became clear. She would never be free of the yearning for adventure until she took a chance and did something completely for herself. Something out of character. Something to prove she could be more than a well-behaved schoolteacher. But what? Cat was spontaneous in a way Cecilia had never been. If everyone was going to compare her to her sister, anyway, maybe she should try to figure out what Cat would do.

Simon was staring at her, bewildered. "Did I say something wrong?"

She lost herself for a moment in his eyes before the answer hit her. Cat wouldn't worry about Simon leaving in a matter of weeks. She would jump right in and enjoy every moment of his presence. Could Cecilia do the same?

He was still standing in front of her with raised eyebrows. She mustered a smile that she hoped looked like the flirtatious one Cat used to get her way and not a strange, painful grimace. "No, Simon. You said just the right things." Wrapping her arm around his, she looked into his eyes with another smile. "I suppose we should move along."

He hesitated, watching her with narrowed eyes. Then he nodded and started walking, leading her with him.

A rush of energy raced through her. No wonder Cat acted like this all the time. It was exhilarating. But Cat wouldn't head home like an obedient child at bedtime. Cecilia racked her brain, trying to come up with something daring—but not too risky—that she could suggest.

Inspiration came when they rounded the corner near Jake and Coralee's property. "Simon, there's a spot by the creek past Jake's medical practice that I'd love to show you. It's beautiful there. Why don't we take a little detour?"

She refused to let her eyes turn away, even when his filled with doubt. "I'm not sure that's a good idea. It's getting rather late."

Sliding her hand into his and tilting her head, she tried out Cat's signature playful manner. "Oh, it'll only take a minute. It's a sight you don't want to miss, especially under the stars on a clear night like this." Then she waited, breath caught in her throat, praying he wouldn't laugh in her face.

Chapter Ten

Simon's gut told him wandering the outskirts of
town at night with Cecilia was a bad idea. But he
was sure something he'd said earlier had hurt her feelings, and he felt terrible about it. A quick stop at her
pretty spot might help smooth things over.

So he let her lead him past dark businesses and
down to the edge of the shallow creek that wound
through the town. When she came to a stop, Simon
paused to glance around. The spot was more secluded
than he'd expected. There was a rise in the creek
bank that shielded them from the sight of the town.
A clump of trees blocked the other side and several
large rocks were clustered a few feet back from the
water. Cool moonlight filtered through the almost-
bare branches, making angled shadows across everything.

Cecilia released his arm and dropped onto one of
the rocks, wrapping her arms around her knees. She
sent Simon that smile she'd used back in town, the

one that hit him like a bullet in the chest. He perched on another rock, not too close to her, hoping the space between them would be enough to keep him from dreaming of how nice it would feel to wrap his arms around her. But to his surprise, she scooted over until their shoulders were pressed together.

"Isn't this so beautiful? When I was young, Papa used to bring me and my sisters here now and then to fish by moonlight. He always said the fish bit better when the moon was full."

Trying not to think about her closeness, he stared at the still water. "How long ago did you lose him?"

Her voice turned quiet. "Two years ago, now. I think Coralee took it hardest of all of us. She spent so much time with him at the apothecary shop. But we all miss him."

Simon's heart ached from wishing he could understand that kind of connection. "You must have been very close."

She shrugged, eyes taking on a far-off look. "I suppose we were. But it often felt to me like I got lost in the shuffle. Coralee and Papa were the closest, probably because she shared his love for medicine and the apothecary shop. And he doted on Cat from birth. She was such a tiny baby and always so pretty and fun. No one could help it."

The words didn't sound bitter as they might coming from anyone else. The matter-of-fact way she said it spoke volumes to Simon. She had spent much of her life overlooked, sandwiched between her two more noticeable sisters. Or rather, her needier sisters. Because Simon would never understand how anyone could think Cecilia's beauty and kindness weren't remarkable. Her sisters must have demanded the attention.

Sure, Coralee had a strong, confident air and Cat was beautiful. But Cecilia was fascinating. Even across a room full of people, his eyes were drawn to her. She had a depth and softness that Cat rarely showed. Soaking in the sight of her gazing at the water in the dappled moonlight, Simon realized that leaving this place unattached was no longer possible. Part of his heart would remain here, with her.

Somehow that thought didn't scare him, although it should. Instead he felt a sense of relief. He didn't have to fight his feelings anymore. It was too late for that. He would have to deal with the pain of leaving later.

Unable to stop himself, Simon leaned closer to her. He watched her head turn and those lovely eyes find his. Her lips parted. And that was his undoing. Bending his head closer to her, Simon let his fingertips graze over the soft skin of her cheek. The air rushed from his lungs when her eyes slid shut and she tilted her head closer to his hand. His eyes closed as his lips lowered.

And then they were on hers. The softness pulled him deeper. He heard her breath catch and his heart beat a crazy, racing rhythm. Without realizing he was doing it, the hand that had been stroking her cheek buried itself in the hair at the nape of her neck, drawing her closer.

She murmured his name against his lips, pulling

him out of the haze. Reluctantly he lifted his head away from hers, mourning the loss of the contact with her as soon as it was over. But her eyes almost drew him right back. They shimmered with emotion, so full that he could get lost in them forever and not mind one bit.

Shaking his head in hope of clearing away the lingering warmth, Simon tried to force himself back into a more proper frame of mind. At least, he tried until she rested her head on his shoulder and sighed as if her world was finally complete. Before he could stop it, his hand rose and rested on her thick hair.

They sat in silence for several long moments. But reality crept back all too soon, sneaking in and stealing the delight he had felt when he'd kissed her. They had to talk about what happened. He had to be sure she didn't think that kiss had been a commitment of any sort. He couldn't afford to make promises, not when he had nothing to offer a woman who deserved the world.

"Cecilia, I—"

A sharp clap of thunder cut off his words, and they both turned to look up at the sky. Dark, heavy clouds roiled overhead. A bolt of lightning flashed, illuminating Cecilia's beautiful face. She brushed a drop of rain from her forehead and stood. "I guess we better go before we get drenched."

There were so many things he needed to say to her, but a gust of wind sprayed more raindrops over them. Simon rose, ready to follow her until Cecilia stopped him with a wave. "I can make it home by myself. I'd hate for you to get caught in the rain on my account."

She started up the bank, then paused and looked at him, her voice soft enough it was nearly lost in the rising wind. "This was a nice end to the evening, Simon. Good night."

Although everything in him screamed to follow her, Simon stood rooted to the spot, letting her go. It was clear that she needed space right then. He would find the right time to talk to her later. But he couldn't shake the feeling that the relationship between them would never be quite the same.

For the next week Simon purposefully avoided Cecilia. He knew it was best to keep space between them. And she didn't seem eager to seek him out, either. He didn't blame her. The intensity of what he'd felt that night by the creek made it almost laughable that he'd thought he could leave Spring Hill without either of them getting hurt. It was far too late for that. So he was determined to keep away from her. The visits were finished; he only needed to find out what was going on with Patrick and then he could go home and try to let his heart heal.

But no matter how sensible his reasons were, it was a miserable few days. He spent most of his time watching Patrick's and Mr. Hartley's activities around town. Over and over, his mind forced him to relive the moments by the creek. The moments that made him want to run and find Cecilia and recreate that evening.

Finally, the day of the children's recital dawned. Simon rose early so he could get breakfast before heading to the school to help some of the men put the finishing touches on the stage. When he got there, people were already streaming in. Excitement filled the air and he couldn't help being impressed with the work Cat had done to build up the event. It seemed like people had appeared out of every corner of the county.

Around midday, Cat started gathering the children behind the stage. Simon wasn't sure he'd ever been prouder than the moment he caught sight of the group standing in two straight lines. The orphans were chatting away with the other children as if they'd lived alongside each other their whole lives. Maybe this had been what they'd needed, after all.

Simon found a place to stand near the rows of chairs that had been set out for the audience. They were all occupied already and many people were standing or sitting on the grass. His eyes found Cecilia sitting with Coralee and her children moments before Cat climbed the steps onto the stage. The crowd hushed, every eye on the youngest Holbrook sister. Simon had to grin. She glowed from the attention.

Grinning and spreading her arms wide in a welcoming gesture, Cat spoke in a clear, confident voice. "Thank you all for coming today and supporting our children and their hard work." Cheers rose from the gathered spectators and Cat stood smiling until the noise died down. "The first part of our program will be a few words from our mayor. Then the children will perform their musical numbers and recitations. After that, the ladies of Spring Hill have put together an impressive meal for all of us to share. It looks like everyone is in place, so let's welcome the mayor."

As the mayor stood and the audience applauded, Cat ended with a flourish of her arms. Then she bounded down the stairs, ignoring a man who stood nearby with his hand out to help her. The noise of the crowd hushed as the mayor began to speak, but a few pockets of conversation remained.

In spite of his determination to avoid her, Simon started to make his way over to Cecilia. But he found Mr. Collins in his path before he could reach her. "Nice day for such a fine event, wouldn't you say, McKay?"

Nodding, Simon tried not to crane his head to look past the man at Cecilia. "It sure is. I'm pleased to see such a good turnout, as well."

"Yes, yes. The people of Spring Hill are proud of their community. Say, I'd like you to meet some of the other school board members. Why don't you come sit with us for a bit?"

Unsure how he could gracefully decline, Simon followed Mr. Collins to a group of chairs at the far side of the stage. Introductions were made around the circle and Simon took the seat Mr. Collins offered, wishing he was across the audience next to Cecilia instead.

Conversation flowed around the group for most of the mayor's speech. Simon would rather have listened, but he found himself pulled into the chatter.

The wives of the school board members had questions for him about the orphans and the long trip by train. They wanted to know all about living in New York.

The men were more interested in his teaching qualifications, which made Simon a little nervous. He didn't want to lie to them, but he couldn't commit to anything, either. He only wanted to give Cecilia time. To his frustration, Mr. Collins led the conversation as if it was a job interview. "Mr. McKay, how do you like Spring Hill? Can you see yourself deciding to stay and live in our growing town?"

"Spring Hill is quite different from New York, of course. But I enjoy the open space. And the people here are caring and kind. It's been an honor to work with so many wonderful families on this stop. This is certainly the sort of place where a man could settle down and be happy for many years."

Even as he said the words, Simon was surprised to realize how true they were. He was coming to love this frontier town. He wouldn't just leave a part of his heart with Cecilia when he returned to New York, he would leave a piece in the town, too. He had found a place that fulfilled all his secret childhood longings, but he would have to leave it.

After missing Simon for days, Cecilia's heart started pounding the moment she saw him walking toward the spot where she sat with her family. Without even a greeting, he dropped onto the blanket next to her and heaved a sigh of relief. Aunt Lily chuckled and patted his shoulder. "Having a good time with the school board, were you?"

Shaking his head, Simon grinned up at her. "Hardly. They don't have any interest in the program at all, so I didn't get to hear much of what the mayor said. I'm glad I got a chance to sneak away before the children started."

Cecilia swallowed hard around the lump that filled her throat and hoped her words didn't betray the uncertainty she felt. "I spoke with them earlier. They all seem excited and prepared. This should be a delightful afternoon."

Silence fell over the crowd and they all turned to watch as Cat took the stage and introduced the first performer. Edwin. Knowing the boy could be shy in crowds, Cecilia held her breath until he began. He spoke too quietly for people in the back to hear, but she was quite proud that he managed to get through his entire recitation. Next, Alice and Mary Boyd sang a duet, then Howard Ames read a long poem from his reader.

The program continued, some children performing with gusto, some much more nervous. But they all tried hard and the crowd applauded each one as if they were famous performers on a world-class stage. Cecilia wasn't sure she'd ever been so proud to be their teacher.

During a short intermission between the younger and older children, Cecilia leaned close to Simon and spoke for his ears alone. "Was Mr. Collins trying to dig up something he can use against me to sway the school board?"

She'd been sure he was going to sit with them before the mayor had spoken, but then he'd ended up with the school board members and their wives. The scene had made her stomach clench, leaving a hard weight in the pit of her stomach that wouldn't go away. Why had they spent so much time talking with Simon? And why had Mr. Collins kept looking over at her pointedly the entire time?

Before answering, Simon licked his lips, his eyes darting away to follow some of the crowd as they milled around. "Uh, no. He only wanted me to meet some of the other board members. It's always good to have influential people in town advocating for the orphans."

Nodding, she looked back at the stage but left her shoulder pressed against his. Simon didn't have any reason to lie to her about his conversation with the school board. She would have to assume that Mr. Collins was only trying to keep her guessing. Relieved that they hadn't questioned Simon about her, she did her best to pay attention to the rest of the performances.

But his nearness was distracting. She found her mind drifting into memories of the night by the creek, the moments his lips had touched hers. And she wished that there was some way she could get him to kiss her again.

She'd been too nervous wondering about Simon's feelings after their kiss to give in to the desire to find him that week. She'd caught glimpses of him now and then. But anytime she thought to get close enough to talk to him, he was either helping Cat with details for the recital or her courage had failed. It had been an endless week, dreaming of him but unable to be near him.

With extreme effort, she forced her attention away from the spot where their shoulders still touched and listened to the last few children perform. As the crowds started rising and gathering up their belongings, her family remained seated, talking and laughing. But Cecilia didn't hear a word of it. She turned to Simon and her heart raced when she found his pale eyes were already watching her.

Jumping to his feet, Simon offered his hand to help Cecilia rise. She held his gaze the entire time, hoping the pressure that tightened her chest didn't show on her face. Mustering all her boldness, she even clutched his hand after she stood instead of letting go as she should have. Now that she was with him again, her courage returned. She still wanted to be more like Cat for the time he was here. She cherished every second she got to spend with Simon and she didn't want to waste a single one acting like her timid, people-pleasing self.

Cat walked up to the group, greeting each member of her family cheerfully. The moment her eyes swept across Simon and Cecilia and their clasped hands, her eyebrows shot up. Heat crept up Cecilia's neck but she refused to act guilty. Holding hands wasn't anything to be ashamed of. Cat herself had probably done far worse more than once.

But Simon tensed when he noticed Cat's stare. He released Cecilia's hand and leaned away. Her heart froze solid. Was he embarrassed that someone had noticed how close they were? Or had he moved away because it was Cat in particular?

Lily approached them and spoke to Simon, oblivious to the tension. "We're going to have a picnic by the creek. We'd love if you'd join us, my boy."

Before he responded, Charles and the twins stepped out from behind Lily. Phillip grabbed his hand. "Please come? We like you."

Louisa nodded with great enthusiasm and Charles shuffled his feet in the dirt, glancing up at Simon with his head lowered. Cecilia's heart melted. The children would be so disappointed when Simon returned to New York. And she would be more than disappointed, but she'd worry about that when the time came. This was a day to celebrate and enjoy what time she could get with him. Even if he was embarrassed to be near her with Cat around.

Looking at the children, Simon finally smiled. "Thanks, Lily. I'd be glad to join you."

Cecilia decided she couldn't let Cat get between her and Simon so easily. Cat would never let someone get in her way. So, Cecilia wouldn't, either. She slid her arm around Simon's, relieved when he bent his arm so hers was tucked close to his side. Maybe he didn't mind her presence.

Her family had started moving toward the creek,

with Jake carrying a large basket and leading the group. Charles and the twins fell into step on either side of Cecilia and Simon, the little ones skipping along with nonstop chatter. Cecilia closed her eyes as they walked, letting the feeling of Simon at her side and the scent of drying grass and leaves fill her senses. She felt a desperate need to lock those impressions away in her memory. They would give her something to dream about when Simon was long gone and the winter stretched out before her, cold and lonely.

By the time the last of them reached the creek, Coralee had already spread blankets on the grass. Lily was setting out plates of boiled ham, fresh bread and vegetables from the tables of food families had brought to share. Once they were all seated, Jake turned to Simon. "Would you mind giving thanks for the meal, Simon?"

Heads bowed and Cecilia waited for Simon to start, chest swelling when his voice rang out, clear and confident as he offered up thanks. "Lord, thank You for this fine meal and for good company. Please bless the food and each of us. Amen."

Almost before the echoed amens faded away, conversation started up and plates were passed around. Cecilia watched emotions flash across Simon's face as he observed the rush of activity. He was quiet as they ate, taking in the children eating with loud voices and messy hands while the adults tried to talk over them and each other. Did he still enjoy the chaos of a family like hers, as he'd said he did weeks ago? Or was the noise and activity starting to wear on him?

Once they finished eating, she leaned closer to him, her heart thumping hard when his eyes swung to meet hers. "Do you want to take a walk?"

It might not be the most prudent idea to wander off with Simon in front of the whole town. Even knowing that, she wasn't sure she cared. She didn't know what had changed in her the week before, but something had shifted. She couldn't shake the feeling that this might be her one chance to do something just because she wanted to.

Cecilia was still committed to maintaining her independence. She had no intention of waiting around for the perfect man to walk into her life. After all the years she'd waited for that, there was little hope it would ever happen. But she still longed to experience love. And why shouldn't she get to?

That's why this opportunity was too good to pass up. Simon would only be in Spring Hill for a few more weeks at the most. It was the perfect chance for her to feel what it would be like to have a man courting her, without settling for someone she didn't care for. She would deal with the consequences later when he returned to New York.

There would be talk. Being the schoolteacher in a town like this, there was no way to stay clear of it. She could say that they'd considered courting, but he'd called it off before leaving. Maybe then the town would show sympathy rather than judgment. But even if rumors about them flew for years, giving herself permission to revel in the feelings Simon stirred in her was worth it.

With a nod, Simon offered his hand to help her up, pulling her out of her thoughts and back to the walk she'd offered. They kept a bit of distance between them until they were past a hill and shielded from her family's eyes. Then Cecilia moved closer to him and slid her hand into his. Pausing midstep, his fingers tightened on hers even as his eyes searched her face. "What are we doing, Cecilia?"

Letting her gaze roam over his now familiar features, she tried to keep her expression cheerful. "What do you mean? We're taking a walk on a lovely fall day. There's nothing so unusual about that."

He raised their clasped hands between them. "I mean, why are we suddenly acting as if we've made promises to each other?"

The confidence she'd been feeling started to drain with his words. Cecilia pulled her hand away and turned her back to him, looking out over the creek. "I don't know what's gotten into me, Simon. For once, I wanted to do something for myself, without worrying about what everyone had to say about it."

His hands grasped her shoulders as he moved close behind her. "I understand that. But when the time comes for me to return to New York, you're the one who'll be left here to face the gossip alone. I don't want that for you."

She twirled to face him again. "I don't care about gossip right now. That's the whole point. Just one time, I'd love to be able to do what I want, even if it isn't proper." The boldness swept through her again and she took a step closer to him, so close that she could almost feel his chest rising with each breath. "And what I want is to spend time with you."

Simon stared at Cecilia, wondering how much trouble he was getting himself into. Her words stirred that longing in him again, the one he'd always managed to force into a little corner of his heart. But now, with this beautiful woman standing in front of him, admitting she wanted to spend time with him, he couldn't keep lying to himself. He would never be able to completely deny that he wanted to fall in love, get married and have a family of his own. And after today, he wouldn't be able to forget that he wanted to do all that with Cecilia.

Unable to respond to her heartfelt words, he tucked her arm close to his side and started walking again. For several moments silence hung between them. He snuck a look at her from the corner of his eye and found that her gaze was glued to the creek. He cleared his throat against a rising tide of emotion. "I never realized how nice it is to have this kind of scenery around you all the time. It's one of the things I love the most about this place."

She turned to him, the peaceful expression on her face surprising him after her intense admission moments before. "Yes, it is beautiful out here. It's easy to take for granted, though. I tend to miss it most days."

He led her toward a stand of trees by the water, where the twins were poking around in the mud with sticks. "I'm going to have a hard time being cooped up on the trains on the way back to New York. And the city will seem stifling after all this open space and fresh air."

Her head tilted and her eyes took on a curious light. "It sounds like you're going to miss Spring Hill."

He nodded almost before she finished speaking. "I will. It's surprised even me, but I think I love it here."

Her voice turned quiet and she looked toward the creek again. He had to lean close to hear her words. "Do you ever think of staying?"

An ache cut through his heart. Talking about how much he liked the town was giving her hope that he wouldn't leave. He wished he could tell her what she wanted to hear, that he could say he wanted to stay. Part of him did want to stay, desperately.

But he still felt an irresistible pull to help the orphans. He could never go long before one of their hardened, world-weary faces crossed his mind. He shook his head. "It would be wonderful if I could choose a nice country town and settle down. But that's not my life, Cecilia. I have to help as many orphans as I can. That's where God's put me."

A sad smile turned her lips up slightly as she met his eyes. "I know. Please don't think I'm trying to get you to stay. You sounded so peaceful and happy talking about Spring Hill, I had to ask."

He could only nod, not sure he could speak around the lump in his throat.

The twins ran over to them with Cat trailing behind, breaking the emotion of the moment. Something the children said made Cecilia laugh, but Simon didn't hear it. Why did it always seem as if he had to take a harder road than everyone else? Why couldn't he have all the things he longed for?

While the twins grabbed Cecilia's hands and dragged her over to look at something by the creek, Cat moved closer to him, eyebrows raised in question. "That was an interesting scene earlier, you holding hands with my sister. Should I assume your plans are changing?"

Wishing she wouldn't talk so loud, Simon leaned closer and hissed his response. "No. And they aren't going to. That was a mistake."

Sending him an arched look, Cat pursed her lips as the twins started leading Cecilia back toward the picnic spot. "Well, I suggest you get your actions in line with your plans, then, Simon. I don't want to see Cecilia get hurt and I know Jake won't stand by and watch it happen, either. Don't think the rest of the family didn't all notice what was going on, too."

Up ahead, Cecilia had stopped the twins and was walking back to them. "Cat, Simon, are you coming?"

Simon swallowed hard again. Cat was right. No matter what Cecilia said, her heart was on the line just as much as his was. They couldn't continue this risky game.

Cat challenged the twins to a race and the three of them took off, leaving Simon alone with Cecilia again. But now he couldn't meet her eyes. What had he been thinking, kissing her and going off alone like a courting couple?

She reached for his hand as they moved to follow Cat and the twins, but he pretended not to notice and shifted farther away. He knew she caught the movement, but what else could he do? Either way, he was too deep into this to get out without hurting her. It was better to put a stop to it now rather than to let their connection get any stronger.

Tension rose between them as they joined Cecilia's family. Simon wondered how he could slip away without raising suspicions that something was wrong. But as he was about to stand and say whatever came to mind to get out of there, Jake spoke up from across the group.

"Simon, did you hear there was another robbery two nights ago? The sheriff said it was just like the others. He thinks either the man he arrested was a random theft he happened across at the right time, or that the thief was working with someone else that didn't get caught, yet."

Thinking back, a sick, sinking feeling hit Simon hard. Two nights ago would have been Thursday. He'd been trailing Patrick and Mr. Hartley all week, but that night he had ended up in a conversation with a fellow hotel guest at dinner and missed several hours. He'd assumed Hartley had been in the saloon like he was many nights, anyway. Could they have known Simon was watching them? Had they somehow planned a robbery for the one night he was occupied?

A discussion broke out among the adults about

who might be behind the robberies. From her spot on the other side of the twins, Cat caught Simon's eye. "Cecilia said you're keeping an eye on the orphans. Did you see anything suspicious? Do you think one of them could be involved, after all?"

Simon didn't want to admit how sure he was that Patrick was involved. He shook his head again. "I haven't seen anything yet. But I am watching. I can't believe I missed that."

Cat's expression remained troubled. "I enjoyed all the children so much when we worked on their program. It would be a tragedy for one of them to be involved with something so reprehensible."

Her words hit a sore spot in Simon's heart. A tragedy? The orphans' entire lives had revolved around tragedy. He tried to not hold the thoughtless comment against her, but the day was ruined for him. Rising, he mumbled something to the group that he hoped would suffice for an explanation and turned to go.

Unfortunately, Cat called his name before he got far, running to catch up with him when he paused.

"Simon, let me walk with you for a minute. I wanted to talk to you."

Holding back his irritation, he forced himself to agree and fall into step beside her. But he couldn't help wishing it was Cecilia who had run after him. She would know what to say to calm the burning in his heart that Cat's words had caused. "What do you need, Cat?"

Bouncing next to him, her words spilled over in a rush. "Since the children's recital went so well, I thought it could benefit children in other communities if the society knew about it. Maybe they would encourage other towns to do something similar. I'd like to write a letter to the director, detailing the event and how the town came together to make it happen. Do you think that might be a good idea? Could you help me write it? I want to make sure it sounds just right so your director will understand how valuable such an event can be."

With his mind racing to catch up, Simon found himself agreeing, although he wasn't certain what he'd agreed to. Cat squealed with her usual overly enthusiastic response. "Oh, thank you, Simon. How about tomorrow, after church? You can stay for lunch, too. One last time before you return to New York."

Simon's heart ached. He didn't want to spend Sunday afternoon writing a letter with Cat while Cecilia sat in the next room. He'd rather hunt down Patrick to try to find out once and for all if he was involved in the thefts. But, without thinking, he had committed to helping Cat. Maybe he would have time to follow Patrick again afterward. No matter what, he had to get his work wrapped up and leave Spring Hill before he lost his heart for good.

Chapter Eleven

It took every ounce of self-control for Cecilia to keep tears at bay while she watched Cat and Simon talking. Cat used her all her typical moves: batting her eyes, leaning in close, twirling a curled lock of hair she often left loose for that purpose. Simon nodded at something she said then Cat squealed loud enough to reach the other side of town. She even gave him a cheerful little wave as he turned to walk away.

Cecilia told herself there was no reason to ask Cat what she'd talked with Simon about. Or why it had made her so happy. Or what the determined expression on his face meant. Simon had already reminded her that they hadn't made any promises to each other. Cecilia had no right to demand to know what business Cat had with him. Even if she wanted to terribly.

But the entire walk home, she couldn't help sneaking glances at her sister. The way Simon had refused to touch her when Cat was looking at them—more than once—kept sticking in her mind. Was there something about Cat that made him feel guilty about the way they'd been acting? Did her presence make him regret kissing and holding hands with Cecilia?

By the time they reached the house and said good-bye to Jake, Coralee and the children, Cecilia had herself in a terrible mood. But as soon as they walked in the door, it was Cat who wasted no time in letting Cecilia know what she thought. "Cecilia, I couldn't help noticing your little moment with Simon by the creek. Growing rather fond of each other, aren't you?"

Removing her bonnet and smoothing her hair, Cecilia raised her eyebrows at her sister. "And what of it? We've done nothing wrong. It was a walk, that's all. In broad daylight with all of you sitting right there."

Cat propped one hand on her hip and smiled. "Ah, but that's not all, is it?"

A sliver of irritation cut through the calm she was trying so hard to maintain. "What do you mean by that?"

Turning to check her hair in the small mirror by the door, Cat shrugged. "I saw the way you threw yourself at him at the recital earlier. Not what I expected from you, I must admit."

Anger tightened her chest. "Of all the people who might accuse me of throwing myself at a man, Cat, you're the last one who gets to be critical."

Her sister spun to face her, eyes flashing. "And what does that mean?"

"It means that you throw yourself at any man who looks your way. Everyone knows it. That should hardly come as a surprise to you."

Stomping her foot, Cat threw up her hands. "Oh, that's it. I'm tired of everyone, even my own family, thinking I'm nothing but a flirt. I'll have you know, I do not throw myself at any man. They happen to gravitate to me and there's not a thing I can do about it."

Without waiting for a response, Cat pushed past her and stomped through the house. Cecilia heard a door slam a second later. She felt a little guilty for spewing such cruel words, but she was just as hurt by Cat's insinuations about her actions. And by the way Simon acted when Cat was around. And, maybe most of all, by how he'd apologized for kissing her as if he had a reason to feel guilt. Cecilia didn't harbor any delusions that her relationship with Simon was powerful enough to make him stay in Spring Hill. But she couldn't help worrying that his relationship with Cat could be. Maybe Cat was the reason he'd regretted their kiss.

The evening was tense in their house, but Cecilia couldn't find it in her heart to apologize to Cat. The guilt grew overnight, however, and by morning she wanted to clear the air with her sister. She looked for Cat before breakfast, but Aunt Lily told her Cat had left early for church. The apology would have to wait until later.

As if the tension of fighting with her sister wasn't enough, Mr. Collins met them outside the church, a smug gleam in his eyes. Aunt Lily greeted him tersely and hurried into the building to take her place leading the opening hymn. But Mr. Collins blocked Cecilia's path before she could get past him. "Miss Holbrook, I hope you're enjoying the fall term at school. Because it will be your last."

She was not at all in the mood to put up with his thinly veiled threats. "Mr. Collins, unless you have something pertinent to tell me, I'd like to get inside before the service starts."

His cheeks reddened and she started to regret her sharp tone. "Oh, you'll find this pertinent, all right. The board is almost ready to name your replacement for next term."

Narrowing her eyes, she crossed her arms. "And who do they intend to hire? I hadn't heard that any willing candidates were being interviewed."

His smile oozed insincerity. "We've kept it quiet, at Mr. McKay's request. He wanted time to think over the offer, you understand."

Her arms dropped to her sides and she searched the man's face for signs that he was lying. He had to be lying. "Mr. McKay? You can't be serious."

"Oh, I am. We've discussed the position at length and I expect his acceptance any day now."

Could it be true? Why would Simon agree to take her job? "I'm not sure I believe that. He hasn't said a word to me."

He shrugged. "Well, I can't speak for his motives, but it seems to me he might want everything in place before announcing that he's staying in town. You know, a man with his eye on a wife wouldn't want her to think less of him if the position didn't work out like he said it would."

Tilting her head, Cecilia fixed him with a hard

stare. "Now I know you're not being honest with me, Mr. Collins. Simon isn't looking for a wife. He's planning to return to New York quite soon."

That sly grin was back as if he was covering up details he knew she would want to hear. "Ah, that's where you're wrong, young lady. He told me all about how he's been wanting to settle down and how Spring Hill is growing on him."

Snippets of conversation with Simon floated through her mind. How he had been talking about Spring Hill as if he wished he could stay. The gleam of longing in his eyes when he'd watched her family yesterday at the picnic. Was it true? Was he just waiting for the details to work out so he could stay in Spring Hill to get married and start a family of his own?

Shaking her head, Cecilia's eyes darted over the horizon as she tried to piece together the truth.

Mr. Collins patted her shoulder with a rough chuckle. "You can see that I'm right if you think about it. And a bit ago, I saw him go into church with the young lady in question. You should take a peek. I'm sure you'll be interested to know who he has his eye on."

Her heart nearly stopped as the words sank in. Could it be true? Was that why he'd kept pulling away from her yesterday? The picture of Cat chasing after him and her squeal of joy flashed in Cecilia's mind.

Mr. Collins sauntered up the steps into the church building while she stood rooted to the spot. She couldn't decide if he was telling the truth or lying to get to her, but her heart trembled anyway. What if it was all true and Simon was getting his plans in order so he could ask Cat to marry him?

The first chords of the opening hymn were echoing from the building when she finally managed to move her feet up the steps. The only way to know was to ask Simon. After church, she would find a few minutes alone with him and learn the truth.

But as she sank into an empty seat in the back row, she couldn't resist looking around. There was one piece of Mr. Collins's story she could confirm right now. If Simon was with a woman, she would know Mr. Collins had at least woven some truth into his story.

Hoping she didn't look as tense as she felt, Cecilia scanned the room, her gaze coming to an abrupt halt when she saw Simon's broad shoulders sticking up above the crowd near the front. Her breath caught and pain sliced her heart as she watched his dark head lean close to whisper to a familiar, perfect face. He was sitting with Cat.

Simon leaned down to listen to Cat's tenth remark about Mrs. Meyer's oversize hat and wondered how so many men were captivated by her. Cat had her strong points, but he wasn't sure interesting conversation was one of them. His mind kept straying to his conversation with Cecilia while they'd walked along the creek the day before. Now, she was easy to talk to. And to listen to. And to look at.

Doing his best to keep his attention trained on

the sermon, Simon couldn't help wishing that he had plans to spend the afternoon with Cecilia. But he had agreed to help Cat write her letter and he would. No matter what his heart wanted, it was much better for both of them if he kept his distance from Cecilia, anyway.

Simon had known all along that opening himself up to her was like playing with fire. He still had to return to his life in New York, to his calling. But, at the same time, staying away was one of the hardest things he'd ever had to do. Every time he tried to put some space between them, he ended up right by her side again. The space was necessary but that knowledge didn't make it any easier.

The service ended and Simon realized he'd hardly heard a word. He rose and greeted those around him, all the while scanning the room for Cecilia. She was nowhere in sight. As Cat turned away from a couple she'd stopped to talk to, Simon leaned closer to her. "Did Cecilia come this morning?"

Huffing, she shrugged. "I suppose. Honestly, we had a bit of an argument last night and I left early this morning so I didn't have to see her."

He paused to shake the hand of a man who greeted him from the aisle. Following Cat's halting progress through the crowd, they finally emerged from the building into cool, damp air. Cat led the way again as they walked to the house, but Simon still didn't see Cecilia anywhere.

No one was at the house when they arrived. Cat assured him that Lily, Cecilia and the Hadley family would be there soon, but it still felt strange to be alone with her. Simon wondered why it was so different with Cat than with her sister. He'd never felt so out of place when he was alone with Cecilia.

They settled at the table in the dining room, Cat with several sheets of paper, ink and a pen laid out in front of her. She stared at the blank page as if envisioning what she'd write there. "I want this to emphasize the benefits to the children more than anything. That's the whole point, after all. What should I say to make the biggest impact on the director?"

Simon leaned back in his chair. "You'll want to talk about helping them fit into their new communities. That's an important issue when we place them out. As well as giving them a healthy outlet for creativity, one that keeps them from using their natural energy and imagination to get into trouble."

Leaning over the paper, Cat began to write while Simon read upside-down from across the table. Now and then, he would suggest a different wording, but most of her points sounded excellent. She articulated the benefits of her program for the children and the community better than he'd expected. She really might be on to something with this idea.

Cat finished the first draft of her letter then paused. Leaning back in her chair, she fixed an appraising gaze on him. "Simon, I can't thank you enough for helping me. I'm sure you would have been happier spending this time with Cecilia, wouldn't you?"

For a moment he started to protest. But her expression was so certain that he conceded with a grin.

"Yes, while I enjoy your company, I did wish I could have been with Cecilia."

All teasing disappeared from her face and she leaned across the table to put her hand over his. "Why are you both fighting your feelings? We can all see what's going on. But neither of you seems open to falling in love. I know I haven't been the most supportive of the idea in the past, out of worry for my sister. But, considering how deep your emotions really are, continuing to watch you two deny how you feel is silly."

Standing, Simon paced the length of the room. "It's not as simple as that for us, Cat. I have a job to do. There are children in New York who need someone to care about them. How can I abandon them to stay out here and pursue my own interests when they can hardly scrounge for enough food to stay alive?"

Cat joined him by the window, a soft smile lighting her face. "Why do you have to choose one or the other? Cecilia could travel with you. The two of you could work together and make a difference in the lives of even more orphans."

Shaking his head, Simon paced to the other side of the room then back to Cat. "What woman would want to travel back and forth across the country instead of having her own home and family?"

The laugh that rang out in response to his words caught Simon off guard. Cat laughed until she was gasping for breath. "Oh, Simon. Any woman in her right mind would want that if it meant being with the man she loves. People find ways to make their situations work with a family. You two can do the same. And believe me, Cecilia would be thrilled to travel. She'd never say no to the opportunity to see something new and help children in the process."

Unable to help himself, Simon grabbed Cat's arms. "What do you mean? I know she said she wouldn't travel. I asked her weeks ago."

Grinning up at him, Cat gave him a look that said he'd missed some vital information. "Are you sure she said she wouldn't? She's miserable here, but she always maintains that she couldn't travel alone. It isn't safe or prudent, she says. I know she would jump at the chance if she could. That must be what was behind her response."

Examining Cat's face, he wondered if she was teasing or if she could be right. Would Cecilia go with him, if he asked her to do it as his wife? He'd asked before without thinking about propriety or safety. But she was the sort of woman who would be concerned about that. Joy rose in his heart as the truth hit him. Cat was right. He could have it all.

Overcome by the realization, Simon impulsively leaned forward and enveloped her in a hug. "Thank you, Cat. You have no idea what this means to me."

As he pulled away, a shadow fell across the doorway. He glanced up, his heart doing a flip in his chest. Cecilia stood there, eyes blazing, but beautiful as could be. Her lips were pressed into a tight line that made him take an extra step away from Cat, a stab of guilt piercing his chest. "Hello, Cecilia. I'm glad to see you."

Eyebrows arched, she crossed her arms. "Oh, I'm sure. Do I get to be the first to hear your good news, then?"

Not sure what she meant, Simon took a step toward her. "I suppose it's good news. Cat and I are working on a letter for her to send to the director of the Children's Aid Society. Her idea for the children's recital worked so well, we thought he might want to use the program in other locations, as well."

Cecilia's face tightened even more. "Why would Cat need to send a letter? I'm sure he'll be interested in the idea when you return and tell him about it."

Simon's heart lifted. He glanced at Cat, thankful for her direct words that had helped him see that he might be able to have both his calling and a life with Cecilia. "Actually, I'm not sure I'll return right away. There's something else I need to take care of here, first."

She gasped and he looked back at her in time to see her face turn pale. "Indeed. Well, I'll leave you two to your…work."

Before Simon could stop her, she rushed from the room and he heard the front door slam. He turned to Cat. "I need to go after her."

Shaking her head, Cat sighed. "Haven't you learned by now? She needs to cool off for a bit. She'll come back and you can apologize."

Simon hesitated. Was she right? Did Cecilia need some space? His gut still screamed to go after her. But Cat had known her longer than he had. Maybe she did need time alone. Now that he'd realized it was possible he could pursue Cecilia, he didn't want to ruin things between them with the wrong response. Even though it seemed he'd already done something to upset her. But what? He went back over the conversation, trying in vain to figure out what had gone wrong to make her run away.

Before he made up his mind what to do, voices filled the house. Lily, Jake, Coralee and the children streamed in the front door, with Coralee explaining that they all had to stop and look for Philip's hat before returning home. Simon reluctantly joined in the chaos as they worked to put lunch on the table. He forced his mind to stop racing for long enough to eat. If she hadn't returned by the time the meal was over, he would go find her.

Cecilia ran, oblivious to any curious looks or whispered comments from neighbors on their way home from church. She ran all the way to the school and sank onto the front steps, ignoring the splinters cutting into her hands as she clutched the rough wood and gasped for air with heaving lungs.

Mr. Collins had been right. Walking into the house to see Simon with Cat in his arms had shattered the imaginary world she'd been creating for weeks. She had let her heart find hope in the illusion that Simon cared for her and that his feelings would be enough to make him stay. Well, he was staying, all right. But it wasn't due to any emotional attachment to her.

Trying to calm her racing heart, she leaned back and lifted her face to the gray sky, watching heavy clouds roll overhead. The weather reminded her of the night Simon and the orphans had first come to town. The night her whole world had changed.

Closing her eyes, she wondered if she could have avoided all this pain somehow. If she hadn't been the one to greet the orphans, if she hadn't agreed to help Simon, if she had minded her own business, would she still have let her heart run away with her? She longed for the chance to go back in time and find out.

Leaning forward again, she covered her face with both hands. Simon and Cat. She could hardly believe that Mr. Collins had been telling her the truth, after all. But finding them embracing was proof, made even worse by his sudden change of heart about staying in Spring Hill. It was no wonder he'd rejected her advances yesterday. His heart had already been given to her beautiful, perfect sister. And now he was staying in Spring Hill to court her.

She sucked in a sharp breath as the wave of pain hit her again. If Mr. Collins had been telling the truth about Simon's relationship with Cat, he must be right about Simon taking her position at the school, too. Once this term was over, she would have nothing left. No job, no independence. And she would have to live the rest of her life watching her sister and Simon marry, have children and build the life that she'd always longed for.

Every time she opened her heart to the possibility of love, she got hurt while someone else went on to find the happiness she wanted so much. And she couldn't deny it any longer. She wanted to fall in love and marry. She wanted children and a home. Without the possibility of those things, her life seemed cold and empty. Her quest for independence had only been an effort to forget the longings that would never be fulfilled. And now, even that was being taken away.

She wanted to pray, to seek help from the only One capable of comforting her now, but a vision of what she'd never have fractured her thoughts.

She could see the beautiful wedding where Simon awaited her at the end of the aisle, handsome and grinning in expectation. The darling children they would have—and maybe several adopted from the streets of New York. And the travel. Since the day he'd asked if she would ever consider working with the orphan train, she'd caught herself in daydreams. She saw the two of them riding across the country with groups of orphans, placing them out and visiting their homes together as a married couple. But that was only a silly delusion. Simon's heart had never longed for that as hers had. The whole time, he'd dreamed of Cat.

She stared at the familiar buildings and landscape of Spring Hill, the place that had been home since she was a tiny child. The place she loved, but that also seemed to hold her hostage, sometimes. As her eyes swept the town from her vantage point, one out-of-place movement caught her attention. A small boy, peeking into the windows of the bank. What could a child be looking for in the bank while it was closed on Sunday afternoon?

The temptation to sit and wallow in her pain was

strong but curiosity won out. She pushed to her feet and took a roundabout path toward the building, planning to sneak up behind the child. But as she got closer, her heart dropped. The small figure was Patrick.

Hiding the best she could behind a leafless tree, Cecilia peeked through the bare branches. Patrick had looked into every window at the back of the bank and had moved to the rear door. He tried the handle, shaking and pushing a little when it didn't open. Did he think someone would leave the bank unlocked on a day it was closed?

The boy reached into his pocket and pulled something out, but she couldn't quite see it. She crept around the tree to get a better look as he knelt in front of the door and started fidgeting with the knob. Her mind raced. He was breaking into the bank. Simon had been right. Patrick—and most likely Mr. Hartley—had been behind the string of robberies spreading through Spring Hill.

Thinking that she might be able to stop Patrick before he got into more trouble, Cecilia started to creep forward. But a sudden tug on the back of her dress hauled her backward, a short scream escaping her lips before a dirty hand covered her mouth.

She struggled but the arms holding her were too strong. It wasn't until his awful voice hissed in her ear that she realized her captor was none other than Mr. Hartley. "Well, what have we here? A pretty little sneak."

She tried to bite his fingers where they pressed

hard against her lips, but he laughed and squeezed her tighter. Something cold and hard pressed against her side. "You'll want to stop that fidgeting, my pretty. Or you'll get an unsightly hole in your dress."

A gun? She stilled, gritting her teeth when he laughed again. "Now, you and I are going to take a ride out to the farm while the boy finishes his work. I'll have to figure out what to do with you since you stumbled onto our scheme. I'm going to uncover your mouth, but I suggest you don't try to draw attention." He pushed the gun harder into her side and she nodded frantically.

He wrapped one arm around her waist and forced to her walk with him while the other hand, hidden by his coat, kept the gun barrel pressed against her. He marched her to the wagon he'd parked across the street from the bank. They were right in plain sight, but no one was around to see. She couldn't think of any way to save herself without getting shot.

He shoved her roughly up onto the wagon seat, then kept eye contact with her while he went to the other side, his expression warning her not to scream. Within moments, they were leaving the town and her hopes of rescue behind.

The drive to Mr. Hartley's farm seemed to take forever. While she was thankful the horrible man didn't try to talk to her, the silence gave her too much time to think and worry. How long would it take for someone to realize she was gone? After she'd run out in anger, would Simon or Cat even bother to worry about her?

Thinking of Simon brought a fresh wave of fear. She had no doubt Mr. Hartley would shoot anyone who tried to help her. What if someone she loved was injured? What if it was Simon? Panic rose in her chest but quickly subsided into a dull throb of fear. No one had seen them leaving town. It was unlikely that Simon or her family would be able to piece together what had happened. Cecilia would have to save herself.

Chapter Twelve

As soon as he could escape Cecilia's family, Simon checked all the places he thought she might run to. He started with the creek, walking along it the whole length of the town until he reached the spot she'd showed him that moonlit night. The spot where they'd kissed. But she wasn't there.

He returned to town and made his way up and down each street, stopping to ask the few people he passed if they'd seen the teacher that day. Finally, it hit him that she might have gone to the school. He made the trip in a fast walk, barely restraining his desire to run. But the building was locked up tight and she wasn't there.

After wandering back to the other side of town in the hope of seeing her, he stopped at the hotel. He'd change from his Sunday clothes, then rent a horse to search the countryside. Even if it took all day, he would find her and explain what she'd walked in on. He couldn't stand to leave her thinking he had romantic feelings for Cat. Cecilia was the only woman who had drawn his interest in a long time. He needed her to know that.

Deep in thought as he rushed up the stairs at the hotel, he almost tripped over the small body curled against the door of his room. "Patrick? What are you doing here?"

The boy turned his face up to Simon, showing the streaked marks of tears on his dirty cheeks. Simon crouched in front of the child, heaviness settling in the pit of his stomach. "What's wrong, Patrick? I need you to tell me what's going on."

The boy sobbed. Simon wrapped his arms around the child and let him cry, forcing himself to be patient even as every instinct screamed to know what had happened. Finally, Patrick sniffled and wiped his nose on his sleeve. Simon held the boy by his shoulders and tried one more time. "Now, can you tell me what has you so upset?"

Sniffling again, Patrick nodded. "It's bad, Mr. McKay. Mr. Hartley took Miss Holbrook. I wanted to stop him, but I didn't know how. He had a gun and everything."

Simon's heart raced. "Patrick, what do you mean he took her? Where? Why?"

Patrick winced and Simon released his hold on the boy's shoulders. The little head hung so low, Simon had to strain to hear him. "We're the ones who've been stealing things around town. At first, Mr. Hartley said it was like Robin Hood, taking from the rich to give to the poor. After a while, it made me feel bad, but he said if I quit on him, he'd tell people it was all me and I'd get in trouble."

So, Patrick and Hartley had been behind the thefts, after all. He hated that the little boy had gotten mixed up in such a terrible situation, but he'd have to deal with that later. Right now Simon had to know how Cecilia was involved in all this. "And what happened with Miss Holbrook?"

"Well, I was s'posed to get in the bank today, while folks were all relaxing at home. Mr. Hartley said if we got this one done, we'd stop robbing places because we'd get all we needed from there. So, I was picking the lock and I heard a scream. When I looked, Mr. Hartley was dragging Miss Holbrook to the wagon. He had his gun pointed at her and made her get in. I guess they went back to the farm. I was too scared to go see. So I came to find you. Didn't know what else to do."

His body slumped forward again once the story had been told. Simon rose and reached over him to unlock the door to his room. "Why don't you go lay down in my room and rest? Don't worry, I'll handle Mr. Hartley and Miss Holbrook. Then we'll figure out what to do about the thefts."

One corner of his heart relaxed when the boy plodded into the room and curled up on the bed. At least he would be safe for a bit. Simon pulled the door shut behind him and took the stairs at a run, racing to the livery stable. People stopped and stared as he passed, but he couldn't find it in him to care. He had to get to Cecilia before it was too late.

Swinging up onto the rented horse, he spurred the animal out of town as fast as it would go. He couldn't believe it had come to this. Cecilia's life was in danger, thanks to a greedy, foul, old man. Hartley had used a poor child to do his dirty work and now he was threatening the life of a beautiful, caring woman. Well, Simon was determined to stop it.

Panic rose in his chest but he forced it down. He had failed Michael and Patrick, but this time he wouldn't let harm come to a person who needed him. He would rescue Cecilia. He had to. And once it was all over, he would tell her what she meant to him.

The moment Patrick had told him she'd been taken by Hartley, Simon had realized the undeniable truth: he loved Cecilia. He'd found reason after reason to stay in Spring Hill. He claimed it was because of the orphans. But in reality, it was because he couldn't bear to leave her. And now, he was going to get her away from her captor and declare his feelings.

In spite of the uncharacteristic optimism he felt—more how Cecilia would usually respond than him—doubt snuck in. He still didn't know for sure if she would ever consider leaving Spring Hill. Cat had said her sister would leave in a minute, but Cecilia had only ever told him she wanted to stay and teach. Now that he knew he loved her, could he leave her behind and return to his lonely life if she didn't want to go?

But his heart told him it would all work out. Maybe this was God's way of changing Simon's direction, telling him it was time to settle down. Maybe there was a different purpose for him here in Spring Hill that he couldn't see yet. No matter where he ended up, he was confident it would be next to Cecilia.

He leaned forward, urging the horse to move even faster. Before anything else, he had to make sure she was safe. If he couldn't save her when she needed him most, he had no right to declare any feelings for her.

Scenes from the day Michael died flashed in his mind but Simon forced them away. Cecilia always had faith that things would be fine, in the end. He would try having a little of her confidence this time instead of letting the past come back to haunt him.

Still, tension built in his chest as Hartley's farm came into view. His eyes scanned the area, every corner and shadow, but nothing seemed out of place. Patrick said Hartley had a gun and Simon didn't doubt the man would shoot him on sight. He would have to sneak around to peek in the buildings and try to catch Hartley by surprise once he knew where the farmer and Cecilia were.

He left the horse some distance from the farm and covered the rest on foot, trying to keep out of sight as much as he could on the open prairie. The breeze had a cold edge to it that sent a chill through his body and he prayed it wouldn't start to rain. That would only make his task more difficult. He snuck up to the dilapidated cabin first and peeked through the windows. They were dirty, but he could see enough to decide no one was inside.

Moving to the shed near the cabin, he was relieved to hear muffled sounds. Two voices, one deep and one more feminine. At least Cecilia was still alive and able to speak. Crouching low, he snuck around the side of the shed, hoping one of the open windows cut into the walls would be bare so he could see in. But they were all covered tightly with greased paper to keep out the weather.

Sliding to the ground under the last window, he strained to hear what was going on inside and tried to formulate a plan. He didn't want to waste any time, but he couldn't run in without knowing what was going on and risk being shot. Getting injured wouldn't do Cecilia any good.

The voices grew louder as he sat figuring out what to do. He pressed one ear against the wall, holding his breath as Cecilia spoke.

"Mr. Hartley, I can't believe you stood by, making Patrick steal for you, using him to satisfy your greed. It's shameful."

If the situation hadn't been so serious, Simon might have laughed at her tone. She was a captive but still managed to sound like a teacher berating a misbehaving student. There was a bit of shuffling inside before Hartley responded. "Don't blame me. That boy was a pickpocket long before I met him. Those children learn it on the streets in big cities. I just helped him put his skills to use."

Simon's chest burned and his hands clenched. He wished he could barge in and land a solid punch on the man's jaw for using Patrick that way. Cecilia must have felt the same. He could hear the tension in her voice.

"But why? You have a solid farm here. If you put

in a little effort, it would provide all you need. So why go to the trouble of adopting a child, then using him to steal for you?"

The farmer responded in a low voice, leaving Simon straining to hear. Maybe it was due to his quiet tone, but Simon was surprised the man actually sounded sincere. "I never came by anything easily, Miss Holbrook. I've scrimped and worked my whole life to end up with this run-down farm and no one who cares enough to help me run it. My health's not good these days, you know. For once, I saw a short-cut and decided to take it."

Simon couldn't make out Cecilia's reply. He decided he had to make a move sooner or later, and it might as well be now. Sneaking around the front of the shed, he found a crack in the door, not wide enough to see through but enough to slide his fingers in and slowly pull the door open. The scene that greeted him froze him in place.

He'd expected to see Cecilia sprawled on the floor with Hartley pointing his weapon at her. Instead she was leaning against a post across the shed from the old farmer, who was standing with both hands tied to another post. The gun was in her hand but pointed at the ground. Her other hand held a bloody rag against her side. His heart stuttered and a wave of dizziness made him hesitate. Without waiting for it to clear, Simon pushed the door fully open and rushed headlong into the shed as both occupants looked up.

"Simon!" Cecilia ran and greeted him with a long hug.

Frantic to know why she was bleeding, he pushed her back and tried to move her hand away from her side. "Cecilia, what's happened? You're hurt."

She gestured toward Hartley with the gun, causing the man to duck his head and yell. Simon pried the weapon from her fingers with care and set it outside on the ground as she explained. "I saw Patrick trying to break into the bank, but before I could talk to him, Mr. Hartley abducted me at gunpoint." She scowled at the man then turned back to Simon. "I had no idea how to get help. I was hoping Patrick would come here and I could send him to find you."

Desperate to make sure her wound wasn't serious, he grabbed her shoulders. "You're bleeding. We should go find Jake and get that looked at. You can tell me about it later."

To his surprise, she shook her head and moved her hand to let him see the injury. "It's minor. The gun went off when I hit him, but the bullet just scratched me. At first I thought I was going to die out here before anyone even realized I was missing. But how did you find me so fast?"

Simon's head was pounding from trying to piece together what had happened and to determine how badly she was hurt. He slumped against the rough wall, rubbing his temples as he let his eyes roam the inside of the little building. Most of the space was empty, but piles of what he thought might be stolen items filled the corners. "Patrick found me and told me what happened. I rushed out here to save you, but I guess you don't need me for that."

She didn't seem to hear his frustration. In fact, she was so full of excited energy, she was practically bouncing on her toes. "Oh, I didn't even know he saw what happened. My plan was to stall Mr. Hartley, keep him from figuring out what to do with me until someone came. But he was careless. Can you believe that I hit him on the head with a big piece of wood I found in the corner while he was outside? Then I was able to tie him up before he came to."

He wanted to feel relief that the situation had turned out all right. Relief would be a more reasonable response to finding out she'd rescued herself. Of course, he was thankful she wasn't seriously injured. But alongside that thread of joy, heaviness filled Simon.

Once again, he had been too late to save someone who'd needed him. He'd failed her, left her to fend for herself. She shouldn't have had to hit a man on the head and tie him up. Simon should have been there to keep her from getting shot, even if she claimed it was minor. Every muscle in his body tensed. She had been shot. He could have lost her.

His intention had been to tell her how much he cared, but now that didn't seem like a good idea. She didn't need him to rescue her, and he wouldn't have been able to if she had. He wasn't the man she needed. No matter what Cat thought, it would be better for Cecilia if he returned to New York and let her take care of herself like she wanted.

* * *

Cecilia's joy at the sight of Simon in the shed doorway was short-lived. As soon as she showed him that the wound on her side was hardly more than a scratch, his brow furrowed and he tensed. The grumpy look hadn't left his face since. Was she such a burden on him that finding out she wasn't dying put him in a bad mood?

While Cecilia hitched Simon's horse to Mr. Hartley's battered wagon, Simon all but pushed the man into the back. With his hands bound and a strip of cloth tied over his mouth, Mr. Hartley didn't have much choice except to comply. They would take him straight to the sheriff and pray that justice would be swift. Cecilia was just relieved that Patrick would be free from the horrible man's influence once and for all.

The wagon ride back to town was strained and Cecilia couldn't put her finger on why. Shouldn't Simon be happy that she was safe? But he sat there with a frown pulling his lips tight. It didn't help her mood that Mr. Hartley moaned pitifully from the back every time they hit a tiny bump. The man acted as if he was the one who'd been shot. But Simon's behavior was the worst part. His rescue attempt was not what she'd expected. Or, more honestly, it wasn't what she'd hoped for.

Everything in Cecilia's world had shifted while she'd been held captive. For a few moments in that dark shed she'd thought that, if she survived the ordeal, she would find the courage to ask Simon outright if Mr. Collins's claims were true. To learn if Simon had a romantic interest in Cat and if he was going to take the teaching position from her.

At the worst moments, she'd imagined that Simon would burst into the shed and knock Mr. Hartley right onto his back. Then Simon would kiss her and explain what had been going on when she'd found Cat in his arms. In her mind, there would be an innocent reason for the embrace and they would laugh about it. And Simon would profess that he had feelings for Cecilia alone.

But now, with him brooding beside her, Cecilia's daydream crashed around her. She wasn't sure she was up to the challenge of demanding the truth. All the joyful courage she'd felt after freeing herself from Mr. Hartley's control ebbed away, leaving her drained and ready to get home. But at the same time, it left her longing to lean on Simon and soak in some of his constant strength. Her heart ached. If only he didn't look so angry.

As soon as they drove into town, people paused along the street to watch them pass. She couldn't blame them. It was far from normal to drive around with a man tied up in the back of a wagon, especially with her sitting there looking a mess from the ordeal. By the time Simon stopped the wagon at Jake's clinic, the news must have spread through Spring Hill. Her family members were already running up from all directions.

Coralee and Cat helped her climb out of the wagon, which she had to admit was more painful than she'd expected. One on each side, they walked her into the clinic. Simon was pulling away in the wagon to take Mr. Hartley to the sheriff when Jake arrived and got to work examining her injury.

After Jake announced that she would, indeed, survive the minor wound, her family insisted she go straight home.

Aunt Lily and her sisters wouldn't let her out of their sight. All Cecilia wanted was to make sure Patrick was all right and to talk to Simon. But they kept blocking her efforts to leave the house, claiming that she needed rest and the sheriff would have to come by and get her statement of what happened.

Sitting alone in her room, Cecilia stared out the window as she retraced the events of the long day. It seemed like far more than a few hours ago that she had walked in on Simon and Cat embracing in the dining room. The intense heartbreak had washed away in the midst of being kidnapped and rescued. All that was left was a painful longing to be with Simon.

A quiet knock sounded at the door and Coralee cautiously stuck her head in the room. Cecilia waved her in. "I'm sorry I was so obstinate about leaving right away. You're right that I need rest. It feels good to sit down."

Coralee perched on the edge of the bed near Cecilia's chair. "I'm glad you're finally seeing reason. We want you to recover without complications, that's all."

Cecilia's smile felt forced as she glanced back outside. The clouds weren't as ominous now as they had been a few hours ago, but it was still gloomy. Her mood was starting to resemble the overcast weather more and more with each passing minute.

Coralee grasped her hand, drawing her attention. "Are you sure there's nothing wrong besides the bullet wound? You seem bothered."

Pushing to her feet while fighting to ignore the stab of pain in her side, Cecilia paced the length of her small room. "I don't know, Coralee. So much has happened today. I suppose I need time to process it all."

Her sister nodded but didn't look convinced. "Sure, you've been through a lot. But it seems there might be something deeper going on."

Spinning to face Coralee, Cecilia threw up her arms. "Of course, there's something deeper. When Mr. Hartley forced me into that wagon, I realized that if those were to be my last moments, the only person I wanted to see was Simon. He's the one I thought about. Not you and Cat, or Aunt Lily, or any of the children. I didn't even think about Papa. I wanted Simon."

Coralee stood and took her by the shoulders, her eyes soft and understanding. "And what do you think that means?"

Hoping that her sister could understand, she whispered, "I think I love him."

She didn't expect the crushing embrace, but Cecilia relaxed into her sister's arms, letting the comfort wash over her bruised soul. "Oh, my dear Cecilia. I've watched your infatuations over the years and I wondered if you would learn what real love feels like.

It isn't as easy as the word 'falling' makes it seem. Sometimes there are ups and downs. Crazy twists and turns. But it's real and solid and worth all the effort."

Staring at Coralee, Cecilia tried to keep her mouth from hanging open. "But this is like those other times. He's not in love with me. I saw Patrick trying to break into the bank because I walked in on Simon and Cat sharing an intimate moment and I ran away."

Pulling her to sit on the bed, Coralee took Cecilia's hand again. "Sometimes, things aren't exactly how they appear. Did you ask Simon to explain what you saw?"

Cecilia had to shake her head no. Coralee patted Cecilia's knee, her eyes shining with certainty. "I've seen the way he looks at you. And the way he goes to you for everything. He's not in love with Cat, I can promise you that. Give him a chance. No jumping to conclusions. Just trust him. And trust God. We all see that the feelings you have now are deeper than any you've had for another man. Trust that God allowed that for a reason."

Cecilia's gaze darted around the room as she thought through all her sister's words. She hardly even noticed when Coralee rose and left. Could this time be different? And did that mean it was wise to give Simon a chance? Laying her heart out with the possibility that he could break it into bits was such a risk. Could she trust God enough to do what He was urging her to?

Chapter Thirteen

Outside the Holbrook house, Simon paced the board-walk with his hands jammed into his pockets to keep from fidgeting. It was growing dark and Jake had already told him twice that Cecilia needed rest, but Simon couldn't to go back to the hotel. She was in that house in pain and it was his fault. How could he sleep without seeing for himself that she was all right?

He took three steps toward the house to knock again when the door cracked open and Jake stuck his head out, stepping outside when he caught sight of Simon. "I had a feeling you'd still be here. Come in. She's up and wants some company."

Relief and fear started throwing punches in his chest as they walked through the house. When they reached the parlor, Jake paused. "Please try not to upset her. You have ten minutes, then I'm coming to make sure she goes to bed."

In any other circumstance Simon might have laughed at Jake's obvious overprotectiveness. But the sight of Cecilia wrapped in layers of blankets and sitting in a rocking chair in the dim room made any thoughts of humor flee. He approached her with measured steps, wishing he was better with words. What did a man say to the woman he'd failed and nearly let die?

The silence stretched, broken now and then by quiet voices from the kitchen, where her family must be gathered. Finally she cleared her throat and spoke, her voice rough. "Simon, thank you for coming to my aid today."

He barely managed to bite back a harsh laugh. "You certainly had it under control without me bumbling in."

Her eyes widened and he realized the words had come out harder than he'd intended. "Are you angry with me? You were so tense on the ride back to town, but I thought it was concern for Patrick."

Staring at her beautiful face, tense with confusion because of him, a cold sweat washed over Simon. Soon, there would be nothing holding him in Spring Hill. Nothing except Cecilia. A vision of his old life in New York crossed his mind. Meals eaten in silence. Nights filled with tossing and turning as he worried about the orphans alone. Hours traveling on trains with strangers and other people's children.

It felt as if the walls would close in on him. How could he turn his back and leave her here? Cat had said Cecilia would go with him. But what if she was wrong? He focused on Cecilia's face again and saw anew the pain he'd caused. He knelt in front of her, taking her soft hand in his. "No. I'm not angry with you, Cecilia. I feel terrible that you got hurt, that I didn't get there in time. Again."

She squeezed his hand and he realized he'd actually muttered that last word aloud, though he hadn't meant to. "Simon, you must know you're not to blame for this. Or for Michael, if that's what you're thinking."

He stood and paced again, unable to stay still. "But if I'd been there a little sooner, it would have been different. How can I live with that knowledge?"

When she didn't answer right away, he turned to make sure she was all right. Her eyes were brimming with tears. "Maybe that's not the right question. Maybe you should think about how you live because of that knowledge. Because you lost Michael, you've dedicated your life to helping others. And that's the most fitting tribute possible."

Something hard released in Simon's chest as he considered her words, opening a part of him he'd thought long gone. Gentle peace smothered the guilt he'd lived with for much of his life. She was right. It didn't do Michael any justice to dwell on the tragedy of his death. Simon had to live in a way that showed he was changed.

And standing there in front of Cecilia, he realized that leaving Spring Hill without making an effort to win her hand would be another life-long regret. That wasn't the way he wanted to live. He opened his mouth to tell her so, but one glance at her face showed drooping eyelids and tired lines creasing her forehead. Declarations could wait. He whispered goodbye, but she didn't even raise her head.

* * *

Cecilia opened her eyes to bright sunlight streaming through the window of her room. She hadn't expected to sleep well after napping most of the evening, but she'd hardly lasted a moment after Aunt Lily helped her into bed. Sitting up, she found the pain in her side was worse but still tolerable.

Moving with care, she left her room and found her family gathered in the dining room, talking and laughing over a big breakfast. Even Aunt Lily and Jake were there, which was unusual for a Monday morning. Silence spread as, one by one, they noticed her standing in the doorway.

Jake jumped up and hurried to help her into a chair. "How do you feel this morning? How's the pain?"

Clutching the table, she found sitting was harder than getting up. "It hurts. But I imagine that's normal for a person who was shot yesterday."

Once she'd assured them all that she was fine, Jake took his seat and her family returned to eating their meal. Coralee handed her a plate that was piled far too high with hotcakes, sausage and eggs. They must think she'd been starved while Mr. Hartley held her hostage for two hours.

The conversation revolved around everyday topics, but Cecilia happened to hear several quiet words between Jake and Aunt Lily that caught her attention.

"What did you say about Simon?"

All the adults turned to look at her. A heaviness

settled in her chest, making it hard to draw a full breath. "Jake, please tell me. Did you say Simon's leaving?"

Her brother-in-law's lips tightened. "It looks that way. On the way here this morning, we saw him at the stagecoach ticket window. I don't know any more than that."

The twins started squabbling over the last hot-cake, distracting the other adults. But Cecilia was already lost in a swirl of pain. Simon was leaving, without even saying goodbye to her? Just when Cecilia thought she could take a chance on her feelings, Simon was running away.

She couldn't do more than pick at her food while the others ate. The family members left one at a time to start their day. Aunt Lily planted a kiss on her head before going next door to the café. Jake's parents came to get the children so he and Coralee could open their clinic and apothecary shop for the day. Soon, only Cat and Cecilia remained at the table.

Cat's fork scraped across her plate as she pushed food around. It looked like she was trying to hold something back. Before long, she dropped the fork with a clatter and words burst out of her. "Cecilia, what you saw yesterday wasn't what you thought."

Leaning back in her chair, Cecilia was surprised that she wanted to listen to what her sister had to say. Yesterday that sentence would have made her angrier. But now she needed to know the truth, even if it hurt.

"That's the same thing Coralee said. So, what did I see? Why were you in Simon's arms?"

Tapping her fingers on the table, Cat spoke in a rush. "It wasn't intentional. We were talking about you, actually. Would you believe that all this time, he thought you would never leave Spring Hill? I was trying to explain to him how much you want to do something different with your life, but you didn't feel like you could. Of course, a man wouldn't understand that. He can go wherever he wants, right? I don't see why he likes this place so much he'd be willing to stay when he could go anywhere."

Seeing that her sister was getting off track in her nervousness, Cecilia cleared her throat. "Cat. Finish the story."

Pulling herself together, Cat nodded once. "Right. So, I had to explain to him that he was wrong and you'd be thrilled travel with the orphan train if you could do it in a safe and respectable way. It took some convincing, but he finally believed me. He was so excited by that revelation that he hugged me and that's the moment you walked in on."

Cat leaned forward, hands pressed against the table-top. "Cecilia, I promise you, Simon's not romantically interested in me. Since the moment he arrived, he's only had eyes for you. I know enough about men to see that."

Examining the still full plate in front of her, Cecilia licked her dry lips. "I'm trying to believe that, but I have trouble trusting that he could actually choose me. No man's ever chosen me over you."

Cat's wide, beautiful eyes misted over. "Oh, Cecilia. I'm sorry for the pain I've caused you for so long. Honestly, I never meant to hurt you. I like the attention. It took me far too long to realize that consequences come with it."

Cecilia smiled at her sister. "I know that now. And I don't hold any of it against you. But it is hard to believe that Simon could be different from every other man I've known. What if you and Coralee are wrong? I don't know if I can bear that kind of pain again. Not this time. And now, Jake said Simon's leaving. Without even telling me."

Standing, Cat stacked the last few plates that had been left on the table. She paused next to Cecilia before heading into the kitchen. "Only you can decide if it's worth the risk. But if it was me, I wouldn't let a man like that go so easily. Maybe it's time for you to fight for your happiness."

Alone in the dining room, the realization hit Cecilia with an almost physical force. Cat was right. Coralee was right. Cecilia had never fought for what she wanted before. Sure, she'd tried half-heartedly to fight for her job. But that wasn't even something she truly wanted. Every time a man had overlooked her for Cat, she'd sat back and let it happen.

Pushing through the pain in her side to stand, she knew what she had to do next. She couldn't let Simon slip out of her life without trying. It was time to trust God and trust the man she loved. She was going to declare her feelings to Simon and believe that good would come of it.

* * *

Sitting on a bench outside the stagecoach station, Simon watched Patrick drag a stick through the dirt. His heart ached for the boy. He'd been through so much, both as an orphan in New York and as Mr. Hartley's lackey. And it wasn't over yet. The sheriff had advised them to go to the county seat and meet with the judge there. He said the man was often compassionate where young people were concerned and might give Patrick a light punishment if they explained the situation.

Simon stretched his legs out in front of him and crossed his ankles. Making this trip wasn't what he wanted to be doing right now. He wanted to run to Cecilia's side. Every instinct in him screamed that he needed to be with her. But he had a plan and he would stick to it.

It had taken him all night to come to a realization of what he needed to do. Once Patrick's future was settled, Simon would be finished with his work in Spring Hill and free to clear up the situation with Cecilia. A tremor of fear mixed with excitement raced through him.

The thought of returning to New York without her was enough to knock the breath right out of his lungs. He couldn't stand it. And he knew now that he couldn't leave Spring Hill without trying his best to convince her to go with him. Cat had been certain Cecilia would love to leave. But if she was wrong and it came down to it, he would stay, just for her.

In his sleeplessness, Simon had prayed all night

and his path had never been clearer. God would give him the opportunity to help children wherever he ended up. But the chance to love a woman like Cecilia? Well, that required him to act. He was ready to settle down in this frontier town and work for years to win her heart if it came to that.

A cloud of dust on the horizon signaled the approaching stagecoach. Simon called Patrick over and they waited for the vehicle to arrive. But before they could even make out the shape of the horses, Simon heard his name and turned.

Cecilia was rushing toward him, absolutely beautiful in a dark red dress with a matching jacket, her hair coming loose as she hurried. But his attention shifted from her stunning looks to the hand she had pressed to her injured side. Fear froze his heart and he broke into a run toward her, stopping her with one hand on her shoulder. He pulled at her hand, desperate to see if her wound was worse.

His heart started working again with hard, thumping beats when he realized that her injury didn't seem to be the problem. "What are you doing? You need to be at home resting or you'll never heal. Is something wrong?"

She gasped for air in between words. "I didn't want to be too late."

Urging her chin up with his fingers, Simon searched her face. "Too late for what?"

"To catch you."

Was that emotion in her face what he hoped it was? Her eyes were shining with unshed tears but she looked radiant. Unable to help himself, Simon pulled her to him, trying not to press on her wound but needing her close. Against her hair, he whispered, "You're not too late. I'm not going anywhere, my love."

She pulled back to look up at him. "But you are. Jake said he saw you getting tickets for the stage earlier. And now you're here waiting for it."

Had she missed the endearment that slipped out or was she ignoring it? He tried to pull her close again but she stood her ground. "Fine, you're right that I'm leaving at the moment. But only to take Patrick to the county judge. We have to settle matters before I can place him out with his new family."

Leaning over to look past him to the boy sitting on the bench, she caught one full lip between her teeth. "Will a family want him now? Have you found someone that's willing to take in a child the whole town knows is a thief?"

His heart lifted as he told her the good news. "Yes. In fact, his sister Jane's family has welcomed him with open arms. As soon as the legal issues are taken care of, he'll be joining their family."

Cecilia's hand rose to cover her mouth as a happy gasp escaped her. "That's wonderful. Do you think he'll be held accountable for the robberies?"

Simon's throat thickened with emotion. He loved her genuine concern for the orphans. "The sheriff thinks this judge will be lenient, due to Patrick's young age and the situation with his guardian being behind the entire thing."

Her shoulders sagged in relief. But then she

straightened again and turned to face him. "Simon, I owe you an apology."

"For what? You haven't—"

She cut him off with a wave of her hand. "Let me finish before you say anything."

He fell silent and nodded, noticing the way her hands shook when she clasped them together in front of her. "I thought terrible things about you and Cat. I was certain you were leading me on while pursuing her. And I was jealous. I'm so sorry."

Simon's hands clenched in an effort to keep from crushing her against him, saddened that she'd gone through all that without him knowing. "Cecilia, no. None of that is true. But you don't need to apologize. The fault is all mine for acting in a way that made you think such things."

The peace on her face knocked him speechless for a moment. "I know that now. I spoke with Cat and I prayed about it. And I realized that I let my fear make me see things that weren't real."

He couldn't resist grabbing one of her hands, cradling it in his. "So, I guess I can admit that it was more than Patrick's situation that kept me in Spring Hill all this time."

Pink spread across her cheeks and she ducked her head, only to look up again with worry in her eyes. "What will you do once he's settled with Jane?"

Reaching out to run his fingers over her cheek, Simon stepped closer. "Well, that depends on you."

He almost lost himself in the depth of emotion

shimmering in her eyes when she looked at him. "It does?"

"Yes, it does." Simon took both of her hands in his. "You see, I've come to the conclusion that I need to be where you are. If you want me by your side, that is."

The tears that had been pooling spilled over onto her soft skin. "Oh, Simon. I do. I never want to be without you."

He drew her close, his lips finding hers in a desperate attempt to brand the feel of her kiss in his mind forever. It was several long moments before either of them pulled away. Simon's eyes searched her face, reveling in the love that reflected from her eyes. "Does that mean you'll marry me, Cecilia?"

Slight hesitation made his heart thump hard. "What about your work with the orphans? Will you give all that up?"

"Well, I had something else in mind. It would be a dream come true to work with the orphan train with my wife by my side. If you'll go with me."

She laughed, light and joyful in a way that he'd never seen from her before. "I will, Simon. Of course, I will. I love you."

He held her tight again. "And I love you. Forever."

She gasped and he suddenly remembered her injury. Letting go, he examined her side again for signs of bleeding. "Did I hurt you?"

A giggle escaped her, surprising him. "Only a little. But that kiss was worth it."

The crunch of hooves and wheels on dirt reminded Simon that they were standing in the middle of the street. In the middle of the day. He led her to the bench outside the stagecoach station and slid his arm around her waist again, careful to avoid her injured side. "You'll be all right while I go take care of Patrick?"

She nodded and smoothed the collar of his shirt with one hand. "I'll be fine. But I'll miss you terribly."

Leaning down, he planted another long kiss on her soft lips. "So will I."

Pulling away, Cecilia planted one fist on her hip and raised her eyebrows. "There's one thing I need to hear from you."

Glancing over to make sure Patrick was still waiting by the station, Simon saw the stagecoach had pulled up by the building and the driver was unloading baggage. They didn't have long. "Just ask. I'll answer anything."

She licked her lips and swallowed hard before speaking. "I… I need to know if you were planning to take my job."

Simon's mind must not be working quite right. "Why would you ask that? Of course, I'd never do that."

Her eyes shifted to the street and she twisted a button on her coat until he thought it might pop off. "Well, Mr. Collins said—"

The memory hit Simon. In all the confusion of yesterday, he'd completely forgotten Mr. Collins's offer. He couldn't help chuckling, even though her eyes shot up to meet his in shock. He held her shoulders again, running his thumbs over the velvet trim on her dress. "Mr. Collins did offer me the position and I told him I'd think about it. But only because I thought it would keep the school board from looking for another candidate who would actually try to get the job. I would never have taken it."

She blinked a few times then a giggle escaped her lips. "And to think he told me you'd all but accepted. I suppose he thought I might quit if he convinced me I didn't have a chance. I can't wait to see his face when he finds out that his ruse didn't work."

The tension drained out of Simon. She wasn't upset about his slight deception. Behind them, the stage-coach driver finished loading the vehicle and called for passengers. His heart sank at the thought of leaving her. "I guess we have to go. We should be gone a week or two at the most."

Her eyes held his as he released her, but he couldn't move away. Out of the corner of his eye, he saw Patrick climb into the stagecoach. The driver yelled to him. "Hey, if you're coming, better get in now."

Against his will, Simon waved at the driver and took several steps toward the stagecoach. Giving in to his heart's urging, he spun back to her, wrapped an arm around her waist, and kissed her again, just because he could. "I love you."

She laughed and pushed him toward the stage. "I love you, too. Now go, so you can get back sooner."

It took every ounce of his self-control to leave her and get in the stagecoach, but he had one more duty to complete. He watched her from the window as they rode away, reminding himself that this was the only time he'd have to leave her behind. After this, no matter where God led them, they would go together.

Simon fought to quell his impatience and focus on the joy he'd found. As an orphan, he'd searched his whole life for a place that felt like home. And now he'd found that place in Cecilia's heart. The stage had hardly even traveled past the edge of town, but Simon couldn't get back to Spring Hill fast enough.

Epilogue

Simon stepped out of the stagecoach in Spring Hill with Patrick at his heels. That trip might have been the longest ten days of his life, but it was finally over. Patrick was free to go to his new home and Mr. Hartley would be held accountable for the entire situation. The young orphan was getting another chance to start over and Simon knew that, this time, Patrick was well aware of how precious that opportunity was.

Jane and the rest of the Stolt family waited on the boardwalk. The little girl raced over and gave her brother a long, happy hug. Simon smiled to himself when Patrick ruffled his sister's hair then ambled over to the family and greeted his new siblings shyly, his hands stuck deep in his pockets. The family had impressed Simon and he had no doubt that soon enough, Patrick would be wrestling and teasing right alongside the other two boys.

Patrick and his new family headed off toward their home while Simon looked around. He'd sent word that they would return that day, so he was a bit disappointed that Cecilia wasn't there to greet him. For a brief moment he worried that she had changed her mind while he'd been away. Had she decided she didn't want to commit herself to a man who wandered the country, who had nothing permanent to offer her?

He immediately shook off that thought. With all the things in his life that had been uncertain, one thing he was sure of was her love. Even before either of them had recognized the feeling, he'd felt her love for him in her actions. Like she'd once said about little Edwin, God had brought Simon and Cecilia together on purpose. He had absolute faith in that, now.

The sound of voices and music floated on the cold wind, coming from the direction of the church. He headed that way, wondering if he'd missed the announcement of some community-wide celebration. From the amount of noise, it sounded like the entire town could be gathered there. And he didn't pass a single person going about their business. Curious, he walked a little faster.

The sight that greeted him when the church came into view took his breath away. The whole town really was gathered outside the building, all dressed in their Sunday best, even though it was Wednesday. Several musicians had set up near the church and the strains of a cheerful tune filled the air. To his surprise, a shout went up when the first few people saw him approaching and many turned to wave at him.

Jake broke free from the crowd and bounded over

to greet him with an unexpected hug. "Simon, welcome back."

Glancing around again at the surreal scene, Simon shook his head. "What's this all about, Jake? Did I miss something?"

The doctor laughed and clapped him on the shoulder. "I'll say you did. Your fiancée decided she couldn't wait one more day to marry you and took a chance that you would agree. Welcome to your wedding."

Blinking rapidly, Simon tried to absorb the words. "Cecilia did this? And…we're getting married? Now?"

Jake laughed again. "Are you ready?"

Looking around at the people of Spring Hill, all gathered to celebrate the love he and Cecilia had found so unexpectedly, Simon knew there was only one right answer. "Absolutely. But I'm hardly presentable for my wedding. I just got off the stage."

Leading the way to the church, Jake winked. "She's got that covered. There's a suit for you in the minister's office at the back here. And a basin to wash up in. Take your time, the ceremony won't start until you're ready."

Once the door to the small room closed behind him, reality hit Simon. He was getting married. Right now. To the most amazing woman he had ever met. He chuckled to himself. She'd put this whole thing together while he was gone. In only ten days. What other woman would have done that?

Beyond a doubt, he knew now that his moment of

worry about her backing out was nowhere near the truth. She'd been so anxious to join her life with his that she had planned their entire wedding in a few days, while he wasn't even in town. Simon found that the knowledge put a smile on his face he couldn't suppress, even if he wanted to.

Despite Jake's assurance that he could take his time, Simon raced through cleaning up and getting ready. If his bride was that anxious to marry him, he didn't want to keep her waiting a second longer. He left the office and found Jake leaning against the white boards that lined the outside of the church. When he saw Simon, Jake straightened. "Ready to go?"

Simon grinned. "I sure am."

Jake led him around the side of the church. All the guests had gathered in two groups with a path between them. Jake and Simon took that path and joined the minister, then turned to wait, watching the front of the church where Jake said the women would come out.

It seemed like an eternity, but finally the church door opened. Coralee and Cat came out first, both grinning ear-to-ear. They walked the path through the crowd to stand at the minister's other side. Finally the band started a formal tune and the church door opened again. And there was Cecilia.

The air left Simon's lungs in a rush. How could she be more beautiful than he remembered? Her white, ruffled gown was lovely and he briefly wondered how she'd gotten one so fast. But as she walked closer, his mind emptied of any thought except how happy he was to be by her side again.

When she stood before him, he could see nervousness hiding in her eyes. He took her hands and pulled her close, speaking for her ears alone.

"I can't believe you did all this."

She bit her lip, eyes wide. "I hope you don't mind. The idea came to me while I watched the stagecoach drive away and I went with it."

Leaning close to her, he chuckled near her ear, thrilled when she shivered. "Mind? Oh, no, my love. I don't mind marrying you one bit."

* * * * *

*If you enjoyed this book by Mollie Campbell,
be sure to read Coralee and Jake's story:*

TAKING ON TWINS

Available now from Love Inspired Historical!

Find more great reads at www.LoveInspired.com

Dear Reader,

I hope you enjoyed Cecilia's story. Of all the Holbrook sisters, her struggles are closest to my own, so writing about her journey was a challenge! I pray that the things she and Simon learned are an encouragement to you like they have been to me.

I've had a fascination with the orphan train for a long time, so getting to write this story was a thrill for me. Starting in 1854, thousands of children were "placed out" to foster families through the orphan train. It wasn't a perfect system, but it offered a solution for many children who were alone on the streets. It was fun to take real accounts of children who rode the orphan train and work them into Cecilia and Simon's story.

Thank you for reading! You can find me on Facebook as Mollie Campbell and on Twitter as @MollieACampbell.

Mollie Campbell

We hope you enjoyed this story from
Love Inspired® Historical.

Love Inspired® Historical is coming to
an end but be sure to discover more
inspirational stories to warm your heart
from **Love Inspired®** and
Love Inspired® Suspense!

Love Inspired stories show that
faith, forgiveness and hope have the power
to lift spirits and change lives—always.

Look for six new romances every month
from **Love Inspired®** and
Love Inspired® Suspense!

Get 4 FREE REWARDS!

We'll send you 2 FREE Books plus 2 FREE Mystery Gifts.

Love Inspired® books feature contemporary inspirational romances with Christian characters facing the challenges of life and love.

FREE
Value Over
$20

SPECIAL EXCERPT FROM

*Her family's future in the balance, can Clara Fisher find
a way to save her home?*

Read on for a sneak preview of
HIS NEW AMISH FAMILY *by* Patricia Davids,
the next book in **THE AMISH BACHELORS** *miniseries,*
available in July 2018 from Love Inspired.

Paul Bowman leaned forward in his seat to get a good look
at the farm as they drove up. Both the barn and the house
were painted white and appeared in good condition. He
made a quick mental appraisal of the equipment he saw,
then jotted down numbers in a small notebook he kept in
his pocket.

"What is she doing here?" The anger in his client
Ralph's voice shocked Paul.

He followed Ralph's line of sight and spied an Amish
woman sitting on a suitcase on the front porch of the
house. She wore a simple pale blue dress with an apron of
matching material and a black cape thrown back over her
shoulders. Her wide-brimmed black traveling bonnet hid
her hair. She looked hot, dusty and tired. She held a girl
of about three or four on her lap. The child clung tightly
to her mother. A boy a few years older leaned against the
door behind her holding a large calico cat.

"Who is she?" Paul asked.

"That is my annoying cousin, Clara Fisher." Ralph
opened his car door and got out. Paul did the same.

The woman glared at both men. "Why are there padlocks on the doors, Ralph? Eli never locked his home."

"They are there to keep unwanted visitors out. What are you doing here?" Ralph demanded.

"I live here. May I have the keys, please? My children and I are weary."

Ralph's eyebrows snapped together in a fierce frown. "What do you mean you live here?"

"What part did you fail to understand, Ralph? I… live…here," she said slowly.

Ralph's face darkened with anger. Paul had to turn away to keep from laughing.

She might look small, but she was clearly a woman to be reckoned with. She reminded him of an angry mama cat all fluffed up and spitting-mad. He rubbed a hand across his mouth to hide a grin. His movement caught her attention, and she pinned her deep blue gaze on him. "Who are you?"

He stopped smiling. "My name is Paul Bowman. I'm an auctioneer. Mr. Hobson has hired me to get this property ready for sale."

Don't miss
HIS NEW AMISH FAMILY by Patricia Davids,
available July 2018 wherever
Love Inspired® books and ebooks are sold.

www.LoveInspired.com